ENDGAME

"So," Barbara Price asked after Katz broke the connection, "what's this rescue plan?"

"The President is working on it, but the Iranians are screaming in the UN about a raid by Russian and American air and ground forces. The President is denying that U.S. troops took part in any such action, and Moscow is backing his play."

"But is he doing anything positive to try to get the team out of there before the guys are overrun?"

Brognola paused. "He's not going to leave them there."

Price gave him a hard look. "You don't sound sure of that, Hal, and I don't like it."

"Barb, the Man's in a difficult situation on this."

"The clock is running," she said bluntly. "And, since there's no overtime in these playoffs, he'd better get a move on it."

ther titles available in this series:

DON PENDLETON'S
MACK BOLAN®
STONY MAN™

BIRD OF PREY

A GOLD EAGLE BOOK FROM
WORLDWIDE®

TORONTO • NEW YORK • LONDON
AMSTERDAM • PARIS • SYDNEY • HAMBURG
STOCKHOLM • ATHENS • TOKYO • MILAN
MADRID • WARSAW • BUDAPEST • AUCKLAND

First edition September 1996

ISBN 0-373-61908-1

Special thanks and acknowledgment to
Michael Kasner for his contribution to this work.

BIRD OF PREY

CHAPTER ONE

Tabriz, Iran

Abrim Bengali had devoted his life to defending his adopted country, but this time it looked as if he were going to give his life for it. Although he'd been born in a small village northeast of Baghdad, he was a Jew. When he was eight years old, the expulsion of the Jews from the Arabic states in the late 1940s had driven his family to seek refuge in the newly created state of Israel. In his last year of high school in his adopted land, he had been contacted by the government and informed that his services were wanted by the Mossad, Israel's famed secret service.

Bengali's value to the spy agency lay in the fact that his native tongue was Arabic, not Hebrew, and his persona—an Iraqi with international business connections who lived in Lebanon—was a perfect cover.

But he seemed to have run out of luck, and what had been advantages before didn't mean a thing. He was only a little more than a hundred miles from safety across the border in Turkey, but it might as well have been ten thousand miles for all the good it was going to do. The hounds were hard on his trail, and there was no way that he was going to make those last hundred miles in the hour or so he had left before they caught up with him.

There was still a faint chance that he could go underground in Tabriz and wait until the pursuit died down before trying to make his escape, but it was only a faint chance. If only his old but reliable Land Rover hadn't taken a rock through the radiator, he would be out of Iran and in Turkey by now. He had managed to limp the four-wheel-drive into the city, but it would go no farther until the radiator was repaired.

Buying or renting another car wasn't an option in Tabriz. He was too well-known in the city, and the word was certain to have been sent ahead for him to be arrested on sight. The Iranian Internal Security Force had honed its skills with ten thousand deaths of both spies and dissenters alike, and there was no way someone like him would be allowed to slip through the net.

His cover had been blown big time, and his only hope was to avoid anyone who knew him as his cover persona. Fortunately he had been able to stow his vehicle in the dilapidated garage on the southern approaches to the city without being seen. Bengali figured that he had an hour, though, to do what he had to do before he needed to find a place to hole up and ride this out.

He'd had a bad feeling about this mission from the start and wasn't too surprised that it had gone sour. Staying at his villa on Cyprus, he had been contacted about supplying some special fittings for industrial plastic-molding machines to an Iranian buyer. He was covering as an Iraqi, but this wasn't an unusual request for him. Even though Iran and Iraq had fought a bloody eight-year-long war, Tehran had no qualms about going through an Iraqi businessman to get what was needed.

Although Iran wasn't under a formal UN interdiction on certain high-tech goods—as was Iraq—most Western nations had taken a realistic view of selling to the radical mullahs of Tehran. The lure of Iranian petrodollars was strong, but not strong enough to flirt with selling weapons to people who made no pretenses as to what they would do with them. National suicide wasn't usually in a businessman's best interests.

This wasn't to say that no one was willing to sell to the Iranians. North Korea and Red China had supplied them with billions of dollars' worth of modern weapons. The Chinese sent Silkworm antishipping missiles, and the North Koreans had been happy to provide them with long-range Rodong-1 versions of the Russian Scud missiles. There was also the deal the Iranians had cooked up with the Russians to build four nuclear power plants at Bushehr, which had been only narrowly averted. How many other secret deals had gone through was another matter.

A bigger problem was that since the breakup of the old Soviet Bloc, thousands of top-notch scientists were out of work, and hundreds of them were weapons specialists. These men were being hired by Iran and put to work at their trade, and Bengali had proof now that they were helping the Iranians manufacture some kind of radioactive cobalt weapons. Some of the machinery he had seen at the research facility at Shabaz in northeastern Iran could be used to create radioactive isotopes that could be used in weapons production. And he had also seen the stocks of metallic cobalt that was waiting to be radiated.

That he had somehow been discovered after he had left Shabaz was one of the risks a man in his business took. He'd had to leave immediately so he could get his information out, and the risk had been worth it. Now it was time for him to pass on that information.

Taking his laptop computer out of the back of his Land Rover, Bengali attached the disguised satcomlink antenna and turned on the machine. Inserting the minifloppy disk in the port, he booted the system and keyed in the sequence to align the antenna with the Israeli satellite that was due to be over the horizon for at least another hour. When the screen told him that the antenna was locked on, he hit the transmit code to send the fifteen-second burst transmission.

When the message on the screen indicated that his burst transmission had been received, he switched back over to the normal computing mode. Knowing the dangers of leaving the laptop intact to be captured, he entered a coded sequence that erased the hard-drive disk. A last command sent a surge of electricity to an incendiary charge that lined the back of the case. In seconds the computer was smoking as the charge set the plastic case on fire.

Leaving the laptop to burn, Bengali grabbed his rucksack and folding-stock AK-47, then left the garage.

It was all in the hands of God now.

The Israeli agent hadn't gone more than a few hundred yards from the garage when he heard a low-flying helicopter and saw several vehicles racing toward him. The Iranian security team that had been tracking him had closed in on Tabriz even faster than he had thought that they would.

Ducking into a nearby alley, he checked the magazine in his AK and prepared to take as many of the bastards with him as he could before he died.

AFTER CIRCLING the collection of hovels and back alleys for fifteen minutes, the sand-and-brown-camouflaged Russian-made Mi-8 Hip helicopter settled down on an empty lot. The man who stepped out of the chopper wore an Iraqi army uniform with major's-rank badges in the epaulets and a bloodred beret emblazoned with the gold crescent-and-daggers badge of the feared Internal Security Force, or ISF.

Major Karim Nazar was an imposing man. In a land where a real man submitted to no one but God and the words of his Prophet, even strong men feared to find the major's gaze resting upon them. There was something in his light green eyes and mocking smile that turned even the strongest man's bowels to water. Some said that he got his eyes from his English concubine mother; others said that they were a gift from Satan that let him see into men's souls.

The major's eyes were flashing now, and his face didn't wear its accustomed smile. Instead, he was enraged. "Show me his body," he snapped when he was told that the Israeli spy he had been tracking for the past two days had been killed in a firefight.

The man known to Tehran as a respected Iraqi businessman, but who had been exposed as an agent of the Mossad, lay dead with three bullet holes in his upper body. It was good shooting but bad timing. And in the major's business, timing was everything.

"Who killed him?" Nazar asked, his green eyes moving from one man of his handpicked counterintelligence squad to the next. "Speak up!"

"I did." A man stepped forward, his eyes meeting his superior's squarely. He knew that he was going to die and wanted to do it with some dignity. He had been on the major's squad long enough to know that those who begged didn't receive a clean death at his hands.

Nazar looked him straight in the eyes. "You know what awaits you, don't you?"

The man wore a smile. "The ineffable glory of a merciful God."

Reaching for the holster at his belt, Nazar drew the 9 mm Makarov pistol and slipped off the safety. "As God wills it."

The man in front of him stood tall as a man should who was going to meet his God. "As God wills it."

The 9 mm round took the man in the center of his forehead and mushroomed in his brain. He was dead before he crumpled to the ground.

The major watched the rich red blood pump from the man's brain before holstering the pistol. "See that he is buried properly," he ordered. If a man met his death with dignity, he should be accorded the honor of a burial. "And the Jew, bury him beside him."

"We found the Jew's Land Rover," the team leader reported.

"Take me to it."

The only thing of interest in the vehicle lay smoldering beside it. The laptop computer was a mass of melted plastic, and even though Nazar wasn't a computer expert, he knew that none of the information it had once contained would be recovered from the smoking mess. The Israelis were too clever to allow something like that to happen. Nonetheless, at least the spy had been killed before he had been able to pass on his information.

Since Bengali's satcom-link antenna looked like a small, metal-bladed clip on a car fan, the major paid no attention to it. Many vehicles in the Middle East used the small fans to stir the hot air inside of non-air-conditioned vehicles. Not many of them, though, could stir the air as far away as this one could.

Turning away from the vehicle, Nazar sought out his team leader. "Bring in anyone who had contact with the Jew, anyone at all."

"The women, too?"

"Particularly the women. This man was clever and used women to hide his treachery."

Nazar didn't expect that he would get anything useful from anyone his men brought in. But he also knew that a properly conducted interrogation would result in at least some confessions. And since a confession meant a public execution, they were useful in themselves. The people always needed to be reminded what awaited anyone who tried to thwart the will of God's government on earth.

Anyone who thought about spying for the Israelis and their decadent Western allies needed to see what lay in store for those who betrayed God and his spokesmen on Earth, the Iranian Imams.

Soon, though, the Israelis, the Russians and even the Americans would no longer be a threat to Iran. God had been good to his chosen people and had shown them the way to take their proper place in the world. It wouldn't be long before the enhanced warheads would be ready at the Shabaz Facility. The only question that remained was who the weapons would be used on first.

There was an element in Tehran that insisted the first target had to be the outlaw Jewish state. Another faction insisted that they had to be used to wipe the Great Satan of America from the face of the earth. But these weren't matters that concerned Nazar. His job was merely to see that the team of foreign scientists at Shabaz was able to do its work in peace and security. Killing the Jew went a long way to ensuring that goal.

Abrim Bengali hadn't been the first spy to be found sneaking around the research facility. But he had been the only one who had escaped. And had it not been for the damage to his vehicle that had slowed his flight, he would have gotten away clean. That had been a near-disaster, and it couldn't be allowed to happen again. As soon as he got back to Shabaz, Nazar vowed that he would tighten up the facility's security.

WHEN THE RETRANSMISSION satellite came up over Israel again, the antenna automatically aligned itself with the tracking-and-receiving station in the Negev Desert. When the retrieval signal was sent from the ground station, the satellite dumped its electronic storage bank in a series of compressed, coded bursts. Bengali's last transmission had been coded with an urgent flag and the computer automatically separated it from the rest of the messages for immediate attention.

When the crypto officer logged on to the satcom computer that night, he saw the blinking message indicating an urgent transmission waiting to be retrieved. Punching in the access code, he was surprised to see that the message was in plain language instead of being encoded. Then he read the word "Masada" and realized that he was viewing the last transmission of a Mossad agent.

After running the lengthy message through the decrypt program to make sure that nothing else lay buried under the plain text, he encrypted it for transmission to his headquarters. The skip-phase encryption system he used changed every ninety minutes to keep the hackers from reading the Mossad's e-mail and was considered to be fail-safe. At least for now.

After affixing the data-block entries at the front and rear of the text, he e-mailed a copy to the Mossad office that handled Masada messages. When he received the acceptance signal, he stored the agent's report on the mainframe and turned to dealing with the more routine messages from the Israeli consulates and attachés around the world.

The crypto officer thought that he had the dullest job in the Mossad. He was little more than a telephone operator who made sure that everyone's calls went through, and it was only things like the Masada message that made his job even bearable. As he forwarded a request for approval of a holiday leave for the military attaché in New Delhi, he wondered what had happened to the agent who had sent the Masada message. He would never know, though. He was just a high-tech telephone operator who sometimes passed on a 911 call. Someone else always handled the emergencies.

CHAPTER TWO

Stony Man Farm, Virginia

As Aaron "The Bear" Kurtzman made his way along the specially prepared track that ran through the Farm's apple orchard, he reflected on the notion of how nice it would be if he could take more time to enjoy the wonders of nature. Wheeling his chair through the orchard was a favorite pastime, but lately he'd had little time to indulge himself.

Only eighty air miles from Washington, D.C., the small farm carved into the foothills of the Blue Ridge Mountains didn't look much different from the other farms in the fertile valley, but it was the command center for the elite antiterrorist and anti-organized-crime operation. It's innocent-looking buildings concealed the equipment and personnel needed to track data, gather intelligence and make war on the nation's most elusive enemies, both foreign and domestic.

Video cameras, motion and heat detectors and emergency spotlights were hidden in the trees and fences of the outer perimeter. Even the rusty barbed wire surrounding the property was loaded with sensors as part of the first line of defense. But the Farm's security wasn't left solely to the wonders of modern technology. For real security there was nothing like having well-trained men with sharp eyes and weapons ready in their hands.

The men who saw to the Farm's day-to-day operations were more than your run-of-the-mill agricultural workers. Though they were clandestinely armed during the day, at night they traded their work-worn blue jeans and faded shirts for combat blacksuits, combat cosmetics, night-vision goggles and high-tech firepower. Patrolling the grounds during the hours of darkness, they added their trained eyes to the mechanical and electronic security systems.

With coverage like that, Kurtzman's every move would be followed and recorded if he decided to go outside for a stroll in his wheelchair. But he would have gone ballistic had that not been the case. Even when he was out enjoying himself, he was on call in case he was needed immediately.

Kurtzman hadn't always been confined to a wheelchair. He was a big, bulky man, built like an old-time blacksmith. A terrorist bullet in the spine had taken away the use of his legs, but it in no way diminished his importance to the Stony Man Sensitive Operations Group.

He ran the state-of-the-art intelligence data bank center in the main farmhouse. While the rest of the nation was just learning about the so-called information superhighway, it was old news to Kurtzman and his Computer Room staff. In an age when everything imaginable was stored in a computer somewhere, there was nothing they couldn't ferret out if they kept at it long enough.

Now, though, he had someone to sit in for him when he wanted to take a break, someone he trusted almost as much as he trusted himself. Having Yakov Katzenelenbogen working in the Farm's ops center was a pure blessing. Kurtzman hadn't known how much he had needed someone to help until Katz decided to come in out of the field. And as far as Kurtzman was concerned, it was about time that the old Israeli warrior hung up his war suit and left the front line. The man deserved a rest. He'd done his part. Now it was up to younger men to carry the torch.

Not that Katz was going to get much leisure time around the Farm. The fall of the Soviet empire and the end of the cold war had done little to make the world a safer place to live. In fact, with the Russians out of the business of policing what had been their half of the world, things were even more perilous than they had been at the height of the American-Soviet standoff.

Without the Red Army to keep peace along the borders of what had been the fragile Soviet empire, many nations had decided to go back to killing their neighbors as they had done before the Soviets had put an end to that practice. The post-cold war "peace" that the liberals had trumpeted was proving to be far more dangerous than the cold war with its threats of nuclear annihilation had ever been.

Stony Man Farm's primary mission was to watch over the world's trouble spots to ensure that things didn't get too far out of hand and threaten the survival of Western civilization. When a threat loomed too large and looked as if it would engulf the world, Stony Man would be ordered to send in an action team to take care of the situation. But that was only the end result of the main job at the Farm, watching and evaluating was the day-in, day-out mission.

THE TALL BLOND WOMAN who walked out of the main house and headed for the orchard looked right at home on a farm. Her long legs were tightly sheathed in well-worn blue jeans and cowboy boots, and a pearl-button Western shirt worn with the tails out completed her ensemble. Her long, honey-blond hair was pulled back in a simple ponytail, and she wore only the barest trace of makeup. She looked the part of a young farmer's wife, but Barbara Price didn't spend her days pitching hay or baking pies for the hands. Far from it. She was a part of the Stony Man Farm crew, all right, but she was the boss.

In a day when more and more women talked about reaching for the reins of power, Price had had them in her hands for a long time now. She was the mission controller for the Stony Man teams and supervised the operations at the Farm. On the surface, this would seem to be an unusual job for a woman who looked like a fashion model, but Barbara Price was an unusual woman. She was where she was because she was good at what she did.

"Aaron," she called out as she walked up behind the man in the wheelchair, "Hal called and he's on his way in."

Kurtzman wheeled his chair around to face her. "What's up?"

Price knew that Kurtzman was fully aware that Hal Brognola never gave out any information about a pending mission before he arrived at the Farm. Even though Brognola's office in the Justice Department building was every bit as secure as the President's Oval Office, the big Fed didn't trust even his own secure phones. He always delivered the news in person.

"You know how he is, Aaron," she answered. "He likes to lay it all out when he gets here."

"Yeah, well, a little advance warning can go a long way."

"I'll push you back," she offered, taking hold of the handles on the back of his wheelchair.

Though Kurtzman's powerful arms were more than able to propel himself faster than she could push him, he sat back and acquiesced because he knew that her offer meant she wanted to talk.

"How's Katz working out as your tactical adviser?" Price asked, getting right to the point.

"Real good. It's nice to have someone to take some of the operational-planning chores off my back. Plus, even though I hate to admit it, I think he's better at it than I am."

Price laughed good-naturedly. "Why are you surprised at that? Yakov is probably one of the best tactical strategists in the world today. He could get a job on any nation's top military staff just by asking."

"There is that."

"One last thing," Price said as they approached the main house. "Hal asked me to call Mack and see if he was available to get in on this."

"It's serious, then."

She nodded. "It must be."

Mack Bolan—the Executioner—wasn't a part of the Stony Man team as far as any of the organizational charts went. It was true that he had been in on the creation of the organization from the very beginning and took part in most of the operations, but he was still a free man, as he liked to say. He had an arm's-length association with the Farm, but was able to turn down a mission if he so chose.

"You got hold of him, I assume?"

"Yeah. He'll be in as soon as he can."

AN HOUR LATER Barbara Price was waiting at the helicopter landing pad when the unmarked Bell Jet-Ranger appeared from the north. "He's inbound," she said into her hand-held radio.

"Roger," the communications center sent back. "He's squawking green and is cleared to land."

The dirt landing strip that cut through the farm looked like any well-to-do valley farmer's landing strip. But like everything else at Stony Man, its looks were deceiving. Under the dirt, grass and camouflage was a concrete runway long enough to accommodate jet fighters. Any aircraft that attempted to land at the Farm without landing clearance, however, could expect to be blasted to flaming wreckage before its wheels touched down on the camouflaged runway.

A full air-defense system with radar-directed weapons protected the skies over the Farm. Anything that survived that onslaught faced a last-ditch, rooftop gauntlet of two dozen FIM-92A Stinger missiles. If they were good enough to be used in that role for the White House, they were good enough for Stony Man.

The man who stepped out of the chopper had a briefcase handcuffed to his wrist and an unlit cigar clamped between his teeth. On the government's books, Hal Brognola was listed as a high-ranking official in the Justice Department and was assigned as a liaison officer to the White House. In the shadow world of covert operations, however, he was the director of the Sensitive Operations Group and Price's boss.

Price noticed that Brognola looked weary, which didn't bode well. Since it was only midafternoon, his appearance meant that he had been up all night chasing a crisis. Since he was the man who passed the President's orders down to the people who would carry them out, his visit could only mean another mission for the Farm's action teams.

Even though the Farm wasn't under an alert, a Jeep full of "hands" met the chopper anyway. As soon as the pilot and the passenger disembarked, they quickly went over it to make sure that it wasn't carrying any unwanted packages: particularly explosive or tracer beacon packages. When the chopper was cleared, the aircraft was towed to the fuel tanks to be readied for the return flight to Washington, D.C.

"I don't have a mission for you as yet," Brognola stated as they walked toward the main house, "but I want to discuss a problem. I need input on how to handle it."

Price frowned. Usually by the time Brognola arrived at Stony Man, a situation had developed, and a decision had been made to commit one of the action teams to sort it out. His coming only to ask advice could be either good news or bad.

CHAPTER THREE

At the main door to the farmhouse, Price quickly entered her pass code into the security lock and opened the door to let Hal Brognola inside. "They're waiting in the War Room," she said.

The big Fed kept silent as he walked to the elevator and rode down to the basement level with her. Walking into the large room where the Stony Man missions were planned and conducted, he stepped up to Yakov Katzenelenbogen and offered his left hand to the one-armed man. "I'm glad to see you here, Katz," he said. "I need a lot of Middle Eastern expertise on this one."

"Glad to be here," the Israeli said as he shook with his left hand. Grave doubts regarding his ability to continue to perform at full capacity in the field had helped Katz decide to accept the offer of a desk job at the Farm. During his last mission, it had crossed his mind more than once that soldiering was a young man's game. And Katz knew that if the situation warranted it, and if he was needed, he'd join his teammates of Phoenix Force for an occasional foray into the field—but only if his special skills were called for.

Kurtzman was at his accustomed spot at the table talking to a tall, distinguished-looking black man. Huntington ''Hunt'' Wethers had been a professor of advanced cybernetics at Berkeley before Kurtzman contacted him about joining the Stony Man team. Wethers had jumped at the chance to work with one of the nation's most advanced artificial-intelligence systems, and he added balance to the team by bringing a touch of dignity to what sometimes seemed little more than a vulgar brawl.

''First off,'' Brognola started, ''I want to say that this isn't a mission briefing. This is more of an FYI in case this situation has to be dealt with later.''

Kurtzman smelled a rat and frowned. It wasn't like Hal Brognola to make a courtesy call and offer information about a situation they weren't being tasked to deal with. The big Fed was far too busy to fly ninety miles out of his way just to chat with old friends. Whatever this involved, it had to be up to the armpits in politics.

''Here's the site in Iran we're interested in.'' Brognola flashed the slide of a Keyhole satellite photo on the screen. ''Right now we're calling it Shabaz Site A.''

''It looks like a hydroelectric power plant,'' Price said, correctly interpreting the aerial view of a dammed river with several buildings clustered around it and a large electric-power transmission station.

"That's what it is," Brognola said. "And they want us to think that's all there is to it. But..."

He moved his light pencil to point out a long, low building set well away from the others. "We have information that this building has little to do with the dam except for taking power from it to run the equipment and machinery we believe to be inside."

"You have to admit that it's a good cover for whatever's going on," Kurtzman stated.

"The dam does give them a legitimate cover for what they're doing, yes," Brognola agreed. "If we take any action against the site, the Iranians can say that we wantonly destroyed a harmless electrical plant needed for regional agricultural development."

"That sounds a lot like a rerun of Khaddafi's infamous fertilizer-plant scam back in the eighties," Katzenelenbogen commented.

The Libyan fertilizer plant in a remote desert location had actually been an East German–run nerve-gas manufacturing facility that was about to go into production when it was mysteriously destroyed one night. While no one ever got the official credit for it, it was widely believed that the plant had been taken out by SEAL Team 6, the U.S. Navy's elite commando team.

"It's the same cover story," Brognola agreed. "But it isn't working for the mullahs in Tehran any better than it did for Moammar."

"It didn't work for Saddam either when he tried to use the 'Baby Milk Factory' cover story during the Gulf War," Kurtzman added.

The CNN videos of the Baghdad command post after it had been gutted by two-thousand-pound "smart" bombs had been impressive to say the least. The English-language sign calling the building a Baby Milk Factory had been too obvious to merit comment except by hysterical antiwar liberals.

"It's a little different this time, though," Brognola said. "This place was actually built with UN agricultural-development funding, so it's listed as a legitimate facility. There's no wet paint on the English sign this time. With the exception of that one building, this actually is what it looks like—a hydroelectric power plant."

"So," Price said, "what's the story on that building?"

"That's the problem," Brognola admitted. "We aren't sure yet, but the Company thinks that—"

"They think that the Iranians are making some kind of radioactive cobalt-based warhead," Kurtzman interrupted.

"How did you know that? This has been kept real close."

Even as Brognola said the words, he knew the explanation. To say that Aaron Kurtzman was good at what he did was a serious understatement. The up side was that time after time he delivered the goods when no one else could have even understood the problem. He could pull obscure data out of its cyberspace hiding place and make instinctive connections where no one else could even see a relationship. The downside was that it was impossible to hide anything from him.

Kurtzman shrugged his massive shoulders and grinned. "I've been keeping an eye on that situation for a long time now. The Israelis got the first lead on it over a year ago, and they just lost one of their top agents investigating it. He was able to get out a Masada message before he was killed, which confirmed their suspicions. They're convinced Tehran is up to no good and have been talking to Washington about launching a preemptive strike like they did on Osirik."

The Israeli Pearl Harbor–style air raid that took out the Iraqi nuclear reactor at Osirik in the eighties had taken Washington completely by surprise. Since then, the Israelis had been forced to promise not to conduct any more raids like that or they wouldn't be permitted to buy American warplanes and military supplies.

"If the Israelis have the goods on this place, why doesn't the President simply give them the word to go in and do what they do so well?"

"I don't know," Brognola admitted. "This time he wants to have proof positive of what's going on before he does something about it. I think that the Europeans are giving him a hard time because they want to open up more oil-business ties with Iran, particularly the Germans and the Italians. Something like this will impact on several multimillion-dollar deals that are in the works, and that will bring a lot of heat down on the President.''

He shook his head. ''He's having so much trouble with the Europeans on so many fronts as it is right now, he doesn't want to create another one.''

''The Israeli information isn't good enough for him to act on?'' Katzenelenbogen asked. ''It was a Masada message, and those are taken seriously.''

Brognola shook his head. ''The Man has to have the Intel wrapped in the red, white and blue before he's willing to take it seriously, and that's where you come in. I want you people to study this place. Find out as much as you can about the facility itself, what's in it as far as machinery, who they're buying it from and who might be working with them on this project.

''And while you're doing that, the President is sending in a recon mission to try to get the goods on this place once and for all. Depending on what we get out of it, the President wants to have several options in hand before he makes any decision. As always, the Joint Chiefs will be working up the purely military options, and the Company will be doing their regular spook stuff, but I want to have a Stony Man option ready in case we need it.''

None of the people at the table had to be reminded how many times the Stony Man option had had to be used when more-conventional methods had either failed or weren't politically viable. If the Man was having as much trouble on the political front as Brognola said he was, the chances were good that the Stony Man option would be the one chosen again.

"So, for now you don't want me to alert the action teams?" Price asked.

"Let's hold off on that."

"Okay," she replied, "you're the boss."

WHILE THE BRIEFING was going on in the War Room in the main house, the newest member of the Stony Man family was getting the ten-dollar tour of the armory in Outbuilding One. And for once John "Cowboy" Kissinger, the Farm's resident armorer and weapons expert, didn't have to hold anything back as he conducted the tour. The man he was showing around was almost as knowledgeable about small arms and other implements of destruction as he was.

Kissinger's main job was to see to the personal-weapons needs of the Farm's action teams, Phoenix Force and Able Team. But when he wasn't working on their small arms and equipment, his mission was to ensure that the Farm's defensive arsenal was fully operational at all times. If the Farm was ever hit again, there would be no excuse for not being prepared to withstand anything less than an assault by an armored battalion.

"As you can see," Kissinger concluded, "if it shoots or goes boom, we either have it on hand or can get it on short notice."

"I'm impressed," Thomas Jackson Hawkins said honestly. "I've seen Army arsenals that don't have the facilities you guys have here."

"That's because I need to be able to do just about anything to customize or fabricate hardware for the missions we run here."

Hawkins had come to Stony Man by a twisted path. He had been born in the Army hospital at Fort Benning, Georgia, the middle of three sons of a career infantry NCO. His father had been an adviser to an ARVN Ranger battalion when he was killed during the Tet Offensive. Hawkins was five when his widowed mother resettled with her children outside Fort Hood in El Paso, Texas, to continue her life.

When Hawkins graduated from high school in 1980, he enlisted in the Army to follow in his father's footsteps. After completing basic training, he volunteered for Airborne training and, after getting his para wings, had been accepted for Ranger training. While with the 75th Rangers, he took part in the Grenada and Panama operations as part of a first-in-last-out recon team.

After several years in the Rangers, he was accepted into Delta Force, the Army's elite counterterrorist unit. During the Gulf War, he led one of the deep-penetration recon teams that was spotting Iraqi Scud missile launchers for the Air Force to bomb. He received a Silver Star when he led his team to safety after their Blackhawk chopper went down right outside Baghdad.

It was during the UN operation in Somalia that Hawkins's military career ran aground. He and a dozen of his men escorted a UN team to try to secure a remote village that was being threatened by a petty warlord with two dozen gunmen. When the Swedish officer leading the mission backed off from the gunmen's threats and was ready to stand by while the thugs killed the villagers, Hawkins refused to stand down. When the warlord threatened him with a pistol, Hawkins simply shot him dead. His fellow Rangers easily ran off the rest of the gunmen and saved the village.

Back at the UN headquarters in Mogadishu, the Swedish major threatened to bring Hawkins up on murder charges. Hawkins countered by threatening to go to the press with the story of the major backing down and being willing to watch while the villagers were slaughtered. Due to the explosive political nature of the incident, Hawkins was allowed to resign from the Army, was given an honorable discharge and returned to his home in Texas.

When he was initially contacted to be interviewed for a job with Phoenix Force, he turned down the offer cold. It was only after his old Delta Force commander called him that he agreed to meet with Katz and Bolan. But even then, it wasn't an easy sell to get him on board.

If Hawkins had learned anything from the Gulf War and the UN debacle in Somalia, it was that politicians screwed up military operations and he had been afraid that Phoenix Force had too many political connections. It was only when Katz and Bolan let him in on some of their after-action reports that he was convinced that Phoenix Force wasn't just another political hand job.

Now that he was meeting the Stony Man personnel, that impression was being reinforced. So far, everyone he had met was far from being a political hack. If anything, they were almost anarchists and he loved it. He wasn't completely sold yet, but it was looking better all the time.

WHEN BROGNOLA LEFT to fly back to Washington, Kurtzman and Katzenelenbogen went back upstairs to the computer center to start their search for information, while Price returned to her office. Even with a new mission shaping up—and she knew that a mission would come out of Brognola's "recon" for information—she still had to keep track of the more routine affairs of the Farm.

One thing she needed to check on was how the tour was going for Thomas Hawkins, the new Phoenix Force recruit. A glance at her schedule revealed that he was supposed to be wrapping it up with Kissinger right about now, and she wanted him to report to the Computer Room for a briefing by Kurtzman and Wethers.

She knew better than to make snap judgments, especially about people, but Hawkins seemed to be a promising addition to the Stony Man team. What she had seen of him so far looked good. His service record was impressive, and the so-called misadventure in Somalia that had ended his Army career was actually to his credit. He had been faced with a situation where many more-experienced men might have backed down. But even though only a young sergeant, he had thought fast and had prevented another UN-sanctioned tragedy.

The men of Phoenix Force always had to think fast in many situations, so he should fit right in. If, that was, the team members would accept him into the closed circle of their dangerous profession.

She knew how tight the Phoenix Force warriors were. They had worked together for a long time under circumstances that had bonded the men in a way nothing else could. Blood was the strongest of all bonds, and the men of Phoenix Force had bled for one another many times. Hawkins's acceptance wasn't something that she could influence, nor would she even if she could. Since the commandos were the ones who would be putting their lives on the line, they had the sole right to chose whom they would trust with their future. Nonetheless, she hoped that young T. J. Hawkins made the cut.

According to his personal files, compiled from his Army records and what Kurtzman had been able to dig up on him, Hawkins was the rarest of Americans. He was of almost pure Anglo-Saxon stock and could trace his ancestry on both sides back to before the American Revolution. He was Southern born, as had been almost all of his ancestors, and had been named after the famous Confederate general, Thomas "Stonewall" Jackson.

Southern families like his had been the backbone of the U.S. Army throughout its long history, and his ancestors had fought in almost every conflict the United States had engaged in. Like most Southern families, the Hawkins clan was quietly proud of its history and military service.

Many of the nation's greatest warriors had come from the South, and from what she had seen so far, he looked as if he was going to be another one.

CHAPTER FOUR

Diego Garcia Island

Situated in the middle of the Indian Ocean, the island of Diego Garcia was no stranger to American warplanes. For a long time it had been used as a stopover point for U.S. aircraft deploying to the Middle East or the Pacific. Since the island was roughly two thousand miles from the nearest land, it was like having a stationary aircraft carrier able to handle even the largest aircraft. During the Gulf War, the B-52 bombers that had carpet bombed Saddam Hussein's Republican Guard units in Kuwait had been staged out of Diego.

Now, however, the single jet bomber that was being prepared for a mission in a closely guarded hangar wasn't carrying iron bombs. The weapons-deployment systems in her bomb bays had been removed. One bay had been reconfigured to carry a fuel cell, while the others were filled with ECM—electronic countermeasures—dispensers, sensors and recon cameras. The B-1B Lancer bomber hadn't been designed as a spy plane, but since the United States didn't have anything else available to do the job, this makeshift recon aircraft was being readied for the mission the nation's deep-space satellites couldn't handle.

It wasn't the ideal aircraft to perform this particular mission, but it was the best that could be put to the task immediately. The Keyhole satellites weren't getting the information, and the last of the high-flying Mach 3 SR-71 spy planes had long been out of service. The Lancer had had a checkered career, but this operation would write a completely new chapter in the bomber's troubled history.

Originally designed as a Mach 2-plus nuclear-weapons carrier, the B-1A had barely started its flight testing when newly elected President Jimmy Carter personally halted its development in 1977. His rationale for killing the program was that he believed the world would be a safer place if the United States didn't have a modern nuclear bomber. Making sure that he didn't frighten the Soviets was the keynote of his liberal administration. But strength through weakness wasn't the best way to deal with the Evil Empire. Four years later one of Ronald Reagan's first actions to rebuild America's military might from the ruins of Carter's policies was to resurrect the B-1 Lancer program.

However, this new incarnation of the bomber, designated the B-1B, was a different aircraft than the original. For one thing its mission had been changed from high-speed nuclear-weapons carrier to a barely supersonic, standoff cruise-missile carrier. It was also given the ability to drop iron bombs in conventional war missions as a replacement for the overaged B-52 fleet. This downgrading made the swing-wing bomber cheaper to build and maintain, but it also seriously affected its survivability in a high-tech combat environment.

For one thing, the B-1B wasn't a very fast aircraft. Even with the four thirty-thousand-pound thrust F-101-GE-102 turbojets at full throttle and the variable geometry wings swept all the way back to 67.5 degrees, the B-1B was only capable of flying at Mach 1.2. By comparison, almost any decent jet fighter could do Mach 2 without straining.

To help offset the lower speed, the B-1B was outfitted with a full ECM suite, a terrain-following-radar navigation system and was "stealthed" as much as possible. Radar-absorbing materials—RAM—were used in much of the bomber's construction, and the jet-engine intakes were modified to limit returns from the spinning fans. All this was topped off with a coat of magnetic RAM-type polyurethane paint. This resulted in the B-1B having only one-hundredth the radar signature of a B-52.

And this was what the four-man crew of this particular B-1B was counting on to carry it through this mission. They might be flying relatively slowly, but if no one could see them, no one could shoot them down.

THE DESERT-CAMOUFLAGED B-1B lifted off the runway at Diego and headed northeast. The coast of Iran was more than two thousand miles away, and even at their top cruising speed, they were in for a long flight. A little over halfway to the target, the B-1B met the KC-10 aerial tanker that had been sent ahead earlier to wait for her at twenty-eight thousand feet. The refueling hookup went without a hitch, and the book operator in the KC hit the switches to transfer several tons of JP-4 jet fuel to the bomber.

After topping off, and while she was still roughly seven hundred miles from the Iranian coast, the Lancer dropped low to start her recon run. Though the aircraft was stealthed, if she was down under the radar, there was even less chance of her being spotted.

To keep the Iranians from being tipped off, the Lancer was completely on her own. There was no airborne command-and-control bird aloft to keep an eye over her, there was no fighter escort and there was no one to call upon if something went wrong. There were only four men and a multimillion-dollar airplane counting on surprise and stealth to get them through.

Stealth, though, was more than mere advanced technology. In this case it was a matter of everything working properly. To aid in meeting up with aerial tankers, the B-1B was fitted with a small transponder that sent a signal easily picked up on airborne radar. This allowed the bulky tanker to make her rendezvous with the faster bomber on the first try. Once the hookup was completed and the fuel had been transferred, the transponder was switched off.

This time, however, when the copilot looked at his panel, he saw that the transponder light was out. Thinking that he had already hit the switch, he didn't double-check. What was off, though, was only the warning light; it had burned out right as the tanker boom locked into the refueling receptacle on the top of the Lancer's nose.

As the bomber raced north across the waves at Mach 1.2, the transponder continued sending its electronic "Here I am!" message.

WITH ALL of the advanced Russian weapons systems on the market after the breakup of the Soviet Union, the Iranians hadn't hesitated to upgrade their air-defense capabilities. In particular, they had invested millions of their petrodollars in three Il-76 Mainstay AWACS command-and-control aircraft to guard their aerial frontiers. To upgrade their interceptor force, they had also bought a dozen missile-armed MiG-25 Foxbat fighters.

Designed as a high-flying Mach 3 bomber interceptor, the MiG-25 Foxbat had been considered to be the major Soviet threat to SAC bombers of the seventies and eighties. Even after a Russian defector delivered a Foxbat to the West and its shortcomings were discovered, it still wasn't discounted. But when they had first been met in combat over the skies of the Middle East, they had proved to be poor dogfighters and had been easy meat for American and Israeli pilots.

Even so, the Foxbat was still a potent air-to-air-missile-armed interceptor of larger aircraft. With the upgraded look-down-shoot-down Doppler-pulse radar systems and the improved AA-7 Apex missiles that had been fitted to the MiGs before their sale, they were as capable in that role as almost any fighter in the world, and they were faster than most.

The Iranian ground radar station on the island of Greater Tumb in the Gulf of Hormuz picked up the B-1B when it hit its refueling point and tracked it as it dropped low for its recon run. Because of the curvature of the earth, they lost their blip when the aircraft got too low. But since the blip had been heading directly for Iran, they alerted the air-defense headquarters, which sent one of its Russian-built Mainstay AWACS planes aloft to see if it could reacquire the target.

As soon as the Mainstay reached eighteen thousand feet, its radars picked up the American bomber.

Since it was still headed directly for Iran, two Russian built MiG-25 Foxbat interceptors were scrambled to investigate this aerial intruder.

IN THE COCKPIT of the B-1B, LTC Skip Beaverton kept his eyes on the terrain-following Navstar radar navigation system as they crossed the Iranian coastline. Behind him and the copilot, the bomber's two system operators—SOs—sat at their stations. One of them handled the aircraft's defensive systems and the other the offensive. For this mission the recon and sensor pods were all computer driven, so the offensive operator had little to do but watch the lights on his panel.

The defensive operator, however, had his hands full. The Eaton AN/ALQ-161A Defensive Electronics System was troublesome and required full-time hands-on treatment. Even before they reached the coast, the DSO had activated his passive systems. When the radar-warning scope lit up, he punched his intercom mike button.

"Skip," he said tensely, "I've got someone painting us. I think it's a Russian AWACS."

Since activating their own radars to take a look at the AWACS plane would cause them to show up on the enemy's scopes, the DSO couldn't confirm his hunch. But the radar bands and frequencies that were painting them matched those of a Russian Il-76 Mainstay.

"Keep an eye on him," the pilot ordered.

"He's got a lock on us," the DSO replied trying hard to keep his voice under control. "I'm activating ECM now."

In the cockpit Skip Beaverton wished that he had a Quail or two in the forward bomb bay as he would have had on a normal bombing mission. The Quails were jet-powered decoys that transmitted signals that showed up on an enemy's scopes as if they were jet bombers themselves. The bulky recon and sensor packages, however, had taken up all of the room, and he would have to rely on the DSO's electronic countermeasures suite to decoy for them.

Though the B-1B's ECM defensive systems were state-of-the-art, they did absolutely no good this time. The Iranian AWACS had locked on to the refueling transponder signal and was ignoring everything else that the ECM system was sending out.

"Skip! It's not working!" The DSO was now in a barely controlled panic. "He's still on us. We've got to abort!"

Beaverton was an old-school SAC pilot. He had cut his teeth in aerial combat as a young captain in a B-52 bomber in the skies over Hanoi during Operation Rolling Thunder back when the mission meant something important. He had flown his eight-engined "Buff" through flak, SAM missiles and MiG fighters to drop his bombs on North Vietnam. That had been a real situation back then, and he had made it through, so no bunch of second-rate sky jockeys in cast-off Russian fighters was going to make him turn back now.

"I'm taking her down in the dirt," he announced calmly. Sweeping his wings forward slightly to take greater advantage of the Lancer's fighterlike maneuverability, he nosed the bomber even closer to the ground. Even if the AWACS was on him, it would have a difficult time picking him out of the ground clutter at that altitude.

Beaverton put on a masterful display of high-speed, low-level flying. No one in the history of the B-1B program had ever flown so fast, so low to the ground. But with the refueling transponder on, it didn't matter.

"I have a targeting radar lock-on!" the DSO shouted. "The computer reads out Foxbat!"

The NATO code name of the MiG-25 alone was enough to send chills through even the most experienced SAC pilot. Even though Beaverton knew the interceptor's limitations, he also knew that it still had plenty of bite. Since he was flying a B-1B instead of the B-1A, the Foxbat was twice as fast as the Lancer, and there was no way he could outrun it.

He wasn't carrying Quails, but Beaverton still had his decoy-flare launchers. If the Foxbats could pick him out from the ground clutter, he could deploy his decoy flares along with a little fancy flying to break the lock-on. If there was anyone who could get away with it, he could.

"Launch!" the DSO screamed. "I have multiple launches!"

Reaching out, Beaverton hit the decoy-flare launcher. It was programed to fire the flares from alternate sides of the bomber, and since the heat of their burning was much hotter than the B-1B's jet exhausts, the incoming missiles should lock on to them and explode harmlessly.

The problem was that the flares only worked on heat-seeking missiles, and the AA-7 Apexs fired by the Foxbats were beam riders. With the MiG's look-down-shoot-down fire control locked on to him, there was no escaping the inevitable.

BECAUSE OF THE SECRECY of the mission, all of the Lancer's sensors, cameras and black boxes were hooked up to a real-time satellite retransmissions link. Everything that the bomber did or saw was instantly transmitted to the secret National Reconnaissance Office—NRO—in Washington, D.C. The four-man crew's intercom chatter was also being sent to the NRO.

The last thing that was recorded was the sound of one of the crew members muttering the *F* word as the B-1B impacted the ground. The voiceprint analysis indicated that it was Beaverton.

IF ANYTHING, the political fallout of an American aircraft being shot down over Iran was worse than it had been back in the early sixties when Francis Gary Powers's U-2 spy plane was shot down over the Soviet Union. The liberal press exploded with lurid headlines implicating the administration and the CIA in a plot to threaten the post-cold war world peace. Others accused the government of racism for always making the Islamic states out to be terrorists. Liberal congressmen called for an independent prosecutor to investigate whether any wrongdoing was involved. Others called for a top-to-bottom cleaning of ''renegade'' elements in the CIA.

On the floor of the UN, the Iranian delegate made an impassioned speech damning the United States as the Great Satan bent on world domination and accused the President of provoking a war with his country. He went on to say that any further violations of Iran's airspace would be met with the same response.

At the end of his tirade, the United States delegate countered by saying that the recon flight had been ordered to ensure that Iran was in compliance with the various UN resolutions regarding the nonproliferation of weapons of mass destruction. His speech wasn't very effective, as all of the Islamic delegates walked out in protest.

Regardless of the urgent need to have concrete information about what was being done in the secret

Iranian facility, congressional reaction to the incident effectively tied the President's hands. It prevented him from ordering any more recon flights by either the Air Force or the CIA. But the military and the Company weren't the only arrows in America's quiver. There was always Stony Man Farm.

CHAPTER FIVE

Hal Brognola looked a little less rumpled than he had when he had flown to the Farm the day before yesterday. But Barbara Price knew that didn't mean the Iranian situation was any less critical. All it meant was that he'd found the time to clean up and change his clothes.

As soon as everyone was gathered in the War Room, Brognola launched right into it. "First I want to bring you up to date. We lost a B-1B bomber over Iran last night with the entire crew."

"What was one of our bombers doing over Iran?" Yakov Katzenelenbogen's question was directly to the point.

Brognola shrugged. "Like I said, the President was in a hurry to get a closer look at that suspected weapons site and an Air Force recon mission was the fastest way the Joint Chiefs could think of to do it."

"What's wrong with the NRO satellites?"

"Nothing's wrong with them," Brognola replied. "They're on-line, but they aren't showing us anything. Those guys know the orbital schedules as well as we do and every time a Keyhole bird comes over, they duck under cover and show up as clean as rain. Plus we wanted to get sensor readings to try to confirm the presence of nuclear materials.''

''So what's the next move? Send in Phoenix Force to take it out?''

Brognola shook his head. ''The President's almost ready for a Stony Man option, but he doesn't want to go that far just yet. He still wants to get the goods on that place so he can placate Congress and the Europeans before he orders it taken out.''

''You mean that he wants me to send in Phoenix Force to do a ground recon?'' Price couldn't believe what she was hearing. That would be as good as signing their death warrants.

Brognola paused as if trying to find a way to break the bad news to her.

''How about using an SR-71 Blackbird to take a look when they aren't expecting it?'' Katzenelenbogen broke in to keep that particular line of thought from going any further. He had grave reservations about his former comrades-in-arms walking into that particular kind of situation, especially since the Iranians would be alerted and ready for something like that to happen. Risking Phoenix Force was one thing—that was in their job descriptions—but throwing their lives away was entirely another.

"I understand that NASA still has three of them in the air. It shouldn't take much to stage one out of Diego Garcia and make a Mach 3 run over the site."

"That has already been suggested," Brognola said. "But we have a big problem with that solution. The SR-71s are a big stumbling block in our current round of negotiations with the Red Chinese. They're worried that we're going to use them to keep track of their defense buildup, and they want rock-hard assurances that we aren't going to violate their airspace with them."

He shrugged. "They have long memories and they haven't forgotten the Blackbird recon runs we made over China during the Vietnam War. The Chinese have a spy satellite that comes over every two days and checks to make sure that all three of the remaining Blackbirds are where they're supposed to be, namely Edwards Air Force Base. Their satellites aren't as good as our Keyhole birds, of course, but they can take a picture and pick out the shape of an SR-71."

Brognola looked as if he was going to smile, but didn't. "Those things are rather hard to miss, you know. And the Chinese are so damned paranoid that if they find one of the Blackbirds missing, they'll automatically assume that we're cruising over the Great Wall at eighty thousand feet."

Katz thought for a moment. "How about pulling a shell game on them?"

"What do you mean?"

"We can play a game of three-card monte with the Blackbirds. How many of those planes are sitting in museums somewhere?"

"I don't know," Brognola said, "but I can find out."

"There are some seven or eight Blackbirds parked in museums," Kurtzman said, looking up from his computer screen. "And there are another dozen or so in storage at various places, such as the Lockheed Skunk Works at Palmdale, California."

"What's the closest museum exhibit to Edwards Air Force Base?" Katz asked.

"There's one parked in the outdoor display area at the Pima Air Museum in Tucson."

"That's next to another Air Force base, right?"

Kurtzman nodded. "Davis-Monthan."

"Perfect." Katzenelenbogen grinned. "That's the one we'll use. It should be easy enough to snatch it and transport it."

"What in the hell are you two talking about?" Brognola frowned.

Katz was in his element now. Tactical dirty tricks were one of his specialties, and the art of the ruse was one he had perfected. "As long as the Chinese can see that there are three Blackbirds sitting on the tarmac at Edwards, they'll stay cool, right?"

Brognola nodded.

"It's simple, then," he said. "We're going to free up an operational Blackbird by playing a shell game on the Chinese. We'll give them their three SRs to look at, and we'll still have one to use for the mission."

Katz quickly ran through his plan. Beyond freeing up the one Blackbird it wasn't a simple solution, but it was better than sending men in on the ground to look at the Iranian site. If it worked, it would give the President the proof positive he wanted before taking more-violent action.

Brognola thought it over for a moment. "This isn't our usual solution," he said, "but since this thing has been turned into a full-fledged rat screw, I think the President might like your idea. With the fallout from the downing of that B-1B, it's the only way we can get the goods on those guys without risking Phoenix Force on a ground recon."

He smiled. "So, while I risk my health with a cup of Kurtzman's coffee, whip me up a white paper I can take back and try to get his stamp on it ASAP."

As soon as Hal Brognola was airborne back to Washington with the Blackbird plan in his briefcase, Barbara Price held her own meeting on the Iranian situation. Stony Man didn't have the presidential go-ahead as yet, but she wasn't going to waste any time waiting for him to get off the dime. Experience had taught her that the more lead time they had to prepare for a mission, the better off they were.

It would probably take days for the Man to make up his mind about implementing Katz's idea, but when he did, he would want results immediately if not sooner. This mission wasn't going to be a kick-down-the-door-and-kill-the-bad-guy operation that lent itself to an immediate solution. There was too much hardware involved, and hardware always meant lead time. Therefore, the time they spent planning now would give him the results he wanted all the faster.

"What's Able Team doing?" she asked Kurtzman.

He didn't have to consult his notebook to know what Carl Lyons and his two partners were doing at the moment. He'd taken a phone report from them just the night before. "They're still running that surveillance operation on those guys we think are followers of the fundamentalist Sheikh Abaid."

"Why don't I give them the mission of stealing the Blackbird?"

"Good idea. I know Ironman has been going crazy following these guys around. We can turn what we have so far over to the FBI and let them waste their time on that project."

"If you'll remember," Price said dryly, "Hal gave us that assignment because the FBI violated someone's civil rights when they were working that case, and the ACLU forced them to back off."

''Maybe the agents who were responsible have attended a couple of sensitivity lectures and are more aware of the nuances of multicultural diversity now.''

Price smiled. ''I doubt that, but Hal should be able to get them to spell our guys while they grab the Blackbird.''

''We sure as hell can't ask the FBI to get the plane for us. Can you imagine J. Edgar's boys sneaking around an air museum? The old bastard would roll over in his grave.

''By the way,'' Kurtzman added, turning to Katzenelenbogen. ''While I was doing the background work on the site, I came across a piece of information that should make your day.''

''What's that?''

''The Mossad seems to think that Wilhelm Kessler and his team are involved with this Iranian weapons project.''

''The Red Baron,'' Katz said.

''Exactly.''

The renegade East German scientist came from an old baronial family in what had once been eastern Prussia, more recently East Germany. Even though he was a dedicated Communist, he had been given the nickname by Western Intelligence services because of his imperious attitude. A brilliant scientist, he had been in charge of East Germany's secret chemical- and nuclear-weapons programs.

When the Berlin Wall fell, Kessler had fled his homeland to avoid facing charges of crimes against humanity for using political prisoners to test the effectiveness of chemical weapons. With the Soviet Union also in turmoil at that time, he hadn't been welcome there and had been forced to seek refuge with the outlaw Islamic states of the Middle East. Since then, he had made his living as a high-tech mercenary offering his services to any and all who could meet his price.

Wilhelm Kessler was someone Stony Man was interested in, and if he was involved with the Iranian project, taking him out would become a top priority. Closing his file would make the world a much safer place for everyone.

"That gives this operation an entire new twist," Katz said. "If we can terminate him, we'll be saving ourselves a lot of trouble later."

"That's the way I look at it," Kurtzman agreed.

BROGNOLA SURPRISED everyone by calling Price the next day and telling her that he was inbound again. She didn't even have to ask why he was coming down this time. He could only be bringing them the President's approval for the mission.

"You have a go on the Blackbird option," the big Fed said. "The people you'll need to coordinate with on the Air Force side have all been informed and will cooperate to the fullest. Regardless, the Man wants to keep the participation in this as tight as he can. And in that light, he wants to know if Jack Grimaldi can be used to operate the sensors and cameras from the backseat of the plane so we can keep it down to just the pilot being in on the actual mission."

"I'll ask him," Price said. "But I don't seen why not. I'm sure that he'd love to get the chance to fly in a Blackbird."

Jack Grimaldi was Stony Man's resident pilot and had flown everything from Huey gunships to F-14 Tomcats.

"Where will we be staging out of, Mildenhall or Diego?"

"Neither," Brognola said. "We'll be staging out of a yet-to-be-disclosed Russian air base."

For a long moment there was stunned silence in the room. "You're joking," Kurtzman said. "The President wants to give the Russians an SR-71?"

"We won't be giving it to them," the big Fed replied. "We'll just be using one of their runways and a hangar to park it in while we prepare it for the mission. After all, that's an old plane. It's not like we were going to give them a guided tour of the Aurora or anything like that."

"If Aurora was on-line, we wouldn't have to go through with this in the first place."

Brognola rolled the stub of his chewed cigar to the other side of his mouth. "Tell that to the boys in Washington who cut the Aurora's funding in the name of post-cold war peace, love and brotherhood. Getting that aircraft in service as soon as possible is one of the most important things we can possibly do right now to make sure that the world stays a nice, safe place for all of us."

"You obviously haven't been listening to the six o'clock news lately," Kurtzman chided. "The cold war is over, and we don't have a reason to spy on our neighbors anymore."

"Tell that to the French. Even after that blowup in the press a few months ago about French spies in the U.S. Embassy staff, they're still at it."

"They'll be at it a hundred years from now."

"Let's get back to the topic, gentlemen," Price said. "If we're going to be staging this mission out of Russia, we have a lot of logistical details to work out."

"The Air Force will be handling most of that," Brognola explained. "They will provide the C-5A transports to carry the Blackbird's ground crew, the support equipment and an air-traffic-control team. All you will need to provide will be a security team from Phoenix Force."

"McCarter is not going to like baby-sitting an airplane," Katz commented, grinning.

"He'll learn to love it."

"I doubt it."

"The Russians will also be providing a company of Spetsnaz commandos for security, but I'm pressing for an agreement to have them placed under our control."

"He doesn't trust them?"

"He trusts them, but we'll be staging out of a remote airfield, and with all the trouble the Russians have been having with the locals lately, he wants to ensure the safety of the aircraft and ground crew."

"I'll get Striker to handle that end of it. He's better with the Russians than McCarter."

"Good."

Brognola turned to Price. "How soon can you get everyone assembled?"

"Phoenix Force has been alerted," she answered, "and I can get Able Team en route to Arizona as soon as the FBI can take over for them."

"That'll take place this afternoon."

"The last thing, then, is Grimaldi. When and where do you want him to report for training?"

"Tell him to report to Travis Air Force Base for transport to an undisclosed location and to pack light."

"Will do."

Brognola glanced at his watch, then swept his eyes around the table. "I want the first progress report tonight and then every twelve hours until the Blackbird is airborne for Russia. Any questions?''

There were no questions, and he'd expected none. This was going to be a little more complicated than the usual SOG mission, but the Stony Man Farm team had been down this road before and knew what had to be done.

CHAPTER SIX

Shabaz, Iran

The hydroelectric dam across the Qezel Owzan River in northeastern Iran wasn't one of the world's major electric-power dams. It was, however, tall enough to back the river up for almost thirty miles upstream and create a sizable artificial lake behind it. What had once been thousands of acres of fertile farmland along the river's valley was now under the backed-up water of the dam.

The farmers who had worked their small plots along the banks of the river before the dam had been built hadn't been happy about moving to the barren, rocky hills overlooking the now flooded valley. But they'd had little choice. Islamic Revolutionary Guards with sharp bayonets had made sure of that by killing the first two men who had protested the eviction. After that, the rest of the farmers quickly backed down, packed their meager belongings and got on the trucks waiting to relocate them. The fact that most of them died the next winter was of no concern to Tehran.

Those who survived moved again to more-fertile lands as soon as they could.

The dam wasn't that impressive, but the security surrounding it was worthy of a major military installation. Not only was there an electrified fence enclosing the entire complex, but a series of manned concrete bunkers, trenches and fighting positions also backed up the fence.

On the hills overlooking both sides of the dam were four Russian-built SAM-6 antiaircraft-missile batteries capable of reaching more than twenty miles to strike down aerial intruders. From the high ground their powerful radars could reach out to control the skies over the entire region.

The huge, low, concrete-block structure to the north of the power-transmission station was located well away from the rest of the complex, but it was also within the security fence. In fact, there was a second electrified fence and bunker line isolating it from the rest of the complex. And while this building, known only as the Shabaz Facility, was isolated from the power-generating plant, it was connected to it by a five-hundred-kilovolt umbilical cord.

The continuous electrical power generated by the dam was the sole reason that the Shabaz Facility was situated in this out-of-the-way location, more than a hundred miles from the nearest town. The facility soaked up electrical power as if it were a sponge. In fact, most of the power lines leaving the generating plant's substations were dummies. They carried no power because there was little to waste. Most of the electricity generated by the dam was taken by the facility to run its machinery, particularly the French-made linear accelerator that had been smuggled into Iran in violation of the nuclear-nonproliferation pact.

This accelerator was capable of generating enough radiation to make even dirt radioactive for a hundred years. What it did to metallic cobalt was nothing short of miraculous.

IN HIS OFFICE in the isolated Shabaz Facility, Internal Security Force Major Karim Nazar was going over the background reports on the new set of businessmen who had been contracted to supply the facility. The infiltration of the facility by the Israeli spy Abrim Bengali had almost been a disaster. Fortunately he had been killed before he could get his stolen information back to the Mossad.

Nazar was reviewing all of the facility's contacts with the outside world to make sure that there would be no more slipups. Every man, woman or child who came into the secret installation had to be checked out and placed on the new access list before being allowed entry. Anyone found inside without the proper clearance would die during interrogation.

Even so, Nazar wasn't content with the state of the overall security of the complex he was tasked to secure. And the news he had just received from Tehran made him even more uneasy. He had been informed about the Yankee B-1B bomber that had been destroyed. Even though the spy plane had been shot down almost as soon as it had crossed into Iranian airspace, its flight path had been aimed at the Shabaz Facility. If the Americans were concerned enough about what was going on at Shabaz that they had risked losing an aircraft on a recon flight, they might take other actions. He had to be ready for them.

This meant that extra precautions had to be taken to make the site even more impregnable. The top-secret enhanced-warhead project was about to go into the manufacturing phase and it had to be protected at all costs. Particularly from air attack.

As soon as Nazar had heard about the Yankee aerial intruder, he requested that at least three batteries of HAWK antiaircraft missiles be sent to him immediately. The Russian SAM missiles that were already in place were designed to be used against high-flying aircraft. As the Yankee air pirates had learned in Vietnam, they were good in that role. But they were of little use against low-flying targets or helicopters. The HAWK missiles, however, were sudden death to low-flying aircraft of all types. They were beam riders with an internal radar and couldn't be turned aside once they had locked on to their targets.

Nazar enjoyed the fact that the HAWKs had been manufactured in the United States and had been supplied to Tehran during the so-called Iran-Contra affair. It was fitting that the Great Satan's weapons were being used to defend the Islamic republic against Yankee aerial intruders.

But even with the measures he'd taken, Nazar still wasn't satisfied with the security of the installation. He understood that as long as the Americans were concerned about Shabaz, they would continue to probe its secrets. The best way he knew to get the security he wanted was to divert attention away from the facility he guarded.

If the fears of the American public could be focused on something else, the President would have no option but to take action to calm those fears. Fortunately there was no need to create an operation that would strike fear into the hearts of the American people—there was an operation already in place that would do just that.

While the Internal Security Force was designed to combat internal subversion of the glorious Islamic revolution, it had other missions, as well. One of them was to finance, train, equip and control the so-called terrorist groups sent to the West and to the faltering Arab nations who were resisting the Islamic revolution. The Islamic action groups in Algeria and the New York Trade Center bombers were just two of the many revolutionary operations that had been sponsored by the Iranian ISF.

Most of the action groups that had been sent to the West were dormant in their target countries, living normal lives while waiting to be activated. Also none of them consisted of Iranian nationals. Iranians who traveled outside of Iran were closely watched, but Iranians weren't the only followers of the Prophet who had committed their lives to the success of the glorious revolution. Sudanese, Algerians and Shiite Pakistanis made up most of the Islamic action groups, and they weren't watched the way Iranians were.

Since the enhanced-warhead project had the highest priority, Nazar was certain that the Islamic council would approve his request to activate some of the action groups in the United States. And once they were mobilized, it would be only days before Americans started dying in their own towns and cities.

KEEPING TRACK of the team of foreign scientists working in the Shabaz Facility took up much of Nazar's precious time, far too much in his estimation. Even having to be in the same room with unbelievers was more than he liked to put up with. But here he had to cater to their every whim, from supplying forbidden alcohol to seeing that their women came every

Saturday. He didn't know why Westerners wanted to party on the night before their holy day, but it was a custom with them and they demanded it. The French and Italians were the worst. They called themselves Communists but they lived like decadent Americans in their home countries and expected to do the same when they were in Iran.

The leader of the foreigners, though, the former East German scientist Wilhelm Kessler, was easy to work with. As a dedicated Communist, he wasn't as contaminated with Western heresy as the others were. Kessler was well-known in the Middle East for his expertise as a weapons designer. He was equally well-known for his determination to do anything in his power to see that the outlaw Jewish state ceased to exist and the Jews driven into the sea. His nuclear-weapons project for Moammar Khaddafi had been well organized and would have been successful had it not been for the American raid that had destroyed his desert facility.

That action was one of the reasons that the Shabaz Facility had been chosen as the site for the Iranian weapons project. The Libyan plant had been isolated in the desert and hadn't had adequate security. Khaddafi had depended upon its remote location to protect it, but its isolation wasn't enough to prevent its destruction.

Not only was Shabaz better protected, since it was situated with the electric plant that had been constructed with United Nations agricultural-development funds, but it also had the added protection of UN recognition. Any attack on it would draw international outrage, and the Americans were deathly afraid of international condemnation. That the most powerful nation on earth should be afraid of what some tenth-rate nation barely a dozen years old thought of them was a complete mystery to Nazar. All he could think of was the old saying that whom the gods would destroy, they first made mad.

That the United States was fated to be destroyed, Nazar had no doubt. The work that was being done at Shabaz would see to that. Even spread by conventional explosives, radioactive cobalt would render thousands of square miles of America desolate and uninhabitable for centuries.

WILHELM KESSLER WAS in a good mood when he walked out of his office in the Shabaz Facility at the end of the day. Unlike his last experience working in the Middle East, the disastrous episode in Libya, things were going his way this time. Working with the Iranians wasn't at all like working in Libya. He should have known better than to get involved with Moammar Khaddafi in the first place. The man was an obvious mental case, but the pay had been right and the target even righter.

Though he was a mercenary and would ply his trade as a weapons designer for anyone who would meet his price, he was more inclined to accept a project if it targeted Israel or the United States. The Libyan contract had fulfilled both of his requirements, but the loss of the hijacked metallic cobalt he needed and the destruction of the manufacturing facility had ended the Libyan adventure. Now, though, he had a chance to put his enhanced-warhead program back on track.

After the Libyan debacle, he had vowed that he would never work for undependable and volatile Arabs again. But as always, they were the ones with the money, and now that the European Communist world was no more, money was one of the few things that Kessler had any use for.

He also knew that the Iranians weren't Arabs. They were Persians, an Aryan people, members of the master race, and not Semites like the Arabs. Their language, Farsi, was an Indo-European language, a distant cousin of German, Latin and Greek, rather than a Semitic language like Hebrew or Arabic. He had always found it amusing that the Jews and the Arabs were really the same people and their languages were related.

It was true that the Iranians had an overlay of Arabic culture—it came with the religion. But they thought and acted like Indo-Europeans, which made his work here not only possible but enjoyable. The conditions at the Shabaz Facility were everything he had asked for. He would be able to produce the weapons he had contracted to make without facing the difficulties he'd fought to overcome in Libya.

He was proud of the warheads he had designed and was anxious to see them put into use. Anyone could make a nuclear bomb; it could be done in an outhouse with a hardware-store lathe if you could get the material. He had come up with a weapon of mass destruction that didn't need difficult-to-obtain nuclear material. All he needed to make his warheads was a simple high explosive—plastique worked well— sheathed with powdered metallic cobalt set in a special plastic matrix.

The secret, of course, was to render the cobalt radioactive so that it became one of the most dangerous substances known to man. The French-made accelerator did a nice job of transforming the metallic cobalt dust into its most radioactive isotope. This isotope was so poisonous that a single breath of the dust was enough to kill a man in less than twenty-four hours.

The problem was that in that isotopic state, the cobalt released heat, as well as radioactivity. The heat was great enough to set off many explosives and had to be contained. Kessler had developed a method of mixing the cobalt dust into a plastic resin matrix that resisted heat well, then casting it in a shell that fit over the explosive warhead. When the warhead detonated, this special plastic vaporized and released the cobalt to be dispersed by the shock wave of the explosive gases.

The system had worked well in tests. A hundred-kilo bomb had contaminated well over a square mile. When the thousand-kilo warheads of the Iranian advanced Scud rockets were fitted with their cobalt sheaths, a single hit would contaminate a city as large as Tel Aviv. They were dirty weapons in that they would render their targets uninhabitable for centuries, but that wasn't a concern. The land would lay empty as a warning to others who thought to threaten the march of Islam.

Not that Kessler really gave a damn about Islam or any other religion, for that matter. All he cared about was that the Americans and their Jewish allies would be removed from the face of the earth. They were responsible for the death of his homeland, Germany, and the deaths of the best of his people. Those they hadn't killed in the two world wars, they had turned into capitalistic, decadent swine who could hardly even be called Germans anymore.

Once the world had trembled at the sound of German boots and it would yet again as soon as the Americans were destroyed and Germany resumed its rightful place as the leader of nations.

CHAPTER SEVEN

With the mission go-ahead in hand, the men who would make it happen started arriving at Stony Man Farm. The first two Phoenix Force warriors to arrive were Calvin James and Gary Manning, who had been mountain climbing in Canada.

James was originally from the mean streets of Chicago. Navy SEAL training had given the lanky black top-level proficiency in knife fighting, parachuting and scuba diving. He was also an expert in martial arts and small arms. His secondary training as a Navy hospital corpsman was put to good use, as he was the team's medic.

Manning, on the other hand, was a mild-natured Canadian with the build and dress of a northern woodsman. After a tour of duty as an officer in the Canadian army, he became a well-known explosives and demolition consultant for business. When his cool, professional, single-handed settlement of a terrorist incident attracted international attention, he was tapped to be Phoenix Force's explosives and demolition expert.

James and Manning were closely followed by Rafael Encizo, who drove up from his home on the coast of Florida. Encizo was a Cuban patriot who had been captured at the ill-fated Bay of Pigs invasion of Castro's Cuba. When he was repatriated from the infamous Isle of Pines prison camp to the United States, his experiences left him with a deep-seated distrust of authority. When Mack Bolan originally contacted him about joining the team, he'd had a difficult time convincing the skeptical Cuban. It was only when Encizo realized that he could use Phoenix Force as a vehicle to see justice done that he had agreed to join.

The last Phoenix Force commando to arrive was David McCarter. He was a British national whose easygoing, casual manner concealed a short-fused temper and a love for danger. His personal philosophy was that a life untested by constant brushes with death was hardly worth living. Military duty with Britain's Special Air Service—SAS—hadn't been able to satisfy his love of danger, so he had jumped at the chance when Bolan offered him a slot on the team.

Now that Katzenelenbogen had retired from the field, the command of Phoenix Force had passed on to McCarter, but he wasn't sure that he wanted what went with that job. He had been Katz's unofficial second-in-command for years, but that was different than being the actual man in charge. For one thing it meant that he would have to be even more involved in mission planning than he had been before.

Under Katz's leadership, he'd had his say, as did all the team members, but in the end he had more or less done what he had been told. Now he would have to sit in on meetings, argue about logistical details, get involved with all the other details that Katz had so excelled in. McCarter liked to just be aimed at a mission and turned loose to get the job done. Planning and briefings bored him to death. That wasn't to say that he didn't think that he was up to the job; he could do it in his sleep. But the question was whether he wanted to put up with the extra hassle that went along with being the man in charge.

Also, now that Katz had retired, there was the new man on the team to deal with, T. J. Hawkins. It had been a long time since he'd had to break in a new man to the way Phoenix Force did business. Bolan and Katz had vetted Hawkins and said that he would make a great addition to Phoenix Force, and McCarter knew that it was difficult to argue with their judgment.

Even so, a new man always brought changes to a unit as small as Phoenix Force and he wasn't sure that he was ready to trust his life to a man he didn't know.

As soon as McCarter checked in, he went right to the War Room with Price, Kurtzman, Katzenelenbogen and Wethers to start hammering out the details of the mission.

"This is going to be a little different than anything we've ever done before," Price started out. "Hunt will give you the background."

With a nod to Price, Hunt Wethers took the podium. He had spent years behind a lectern and still looked and sounded like a college professor as he quickly briefed them on the suspected Iranian weapons-manufacturing facility, the information that had been obtained from the Mossad spy and the ill-fated B-1B recon mission.

"So," he concluded, "with Congress up in arms over this fiasco and the UN following suit, we had to come up with a way to check out this place without having to send you people over there on foot to look at it."

"Thank God for small favors," McCarter muttered.

"Instead, you're going to escort an SR-71 Blackbird spy plane to a Russian airfield and it will fly the recon missions."

"Why Russia?" McCarter asked. "Don't we have a base we can use in the Middle East or Europe?"

"It's a problem of secrecy. If word of another American flight over Iran gets out, the President will have trouble staying in office. Plus the Russians also have a big stake in the outcome of this, and they've offered to help. If you'll remember the map, they're a lot closer to Iran, and they're on the target list as much as we are. The Iranians want to expand their influence into the Muslim regions of Russia, and this would be a good way to accomplish that.''

''Then what?'' McCarter asked.

''That's what we don't know yet,'' Price said. ''Hal has to present the President with the recon results before that part of it is settled.''

That wasn't what McCarter wanted to hear, but he knew how situations like this developed. With this much potential political fallout at stake, like it or not, the President would only allow a ''measured response.'' But it was this kind of measured response that had given the nation the debacle in Vietnam, to say nothing of every UN peacekeeping mission since Korea.

''Since we're going to Russia,'' McCarter said, ''I want to take Katz with me to run the ops center we'll have to set up there. He speaks the language, and that will clear Phoenix Force to do whatever Hal decides without leaving a man behind.''

''Damn,'' Kurtzman grumbled. ''I was just getting used to having someone around to give me a hand.''

''You handled the job without him for a long time, Bear,'' McCarter reminded him. ''And I'll give him back to you when we're done.''

''You'd better.''

"I agree with David," Price said. "If Phoenix has to make a ground insertion on the site, they'll need the full team. And, since we're depending on the Russians for backup this time, we'll need to have someone coordinating it who knows their operational situation cold like Katz does. We can't have a breakdown in the support end because somebody uses a slang word or expects something to happen over there because it works that way here."

"Also," McCarter said, "I want to have full mission packs with us for this operation. I don't want to have to depend solely on the bloody Russians to guard us while we are there. If we're fully equipped and the President gives us the go-ahead on the target, we won't have to wait to be outfitted. We'll be able to go right on in and do our job."

"I don't see a problem with that," Price said. "But Hal may not want to use the extra aircraft cargo space that will entail. He's trying to keep this operation as small as possible."

"Hal will just have to lump it, then, won't he?" McCarter said bluntly. "There's hardly any point in sending us over there if we're not going to be ready to fight."

Price could see that having McCarter in charge of Phoenix Force was going to be interesting. If things went as she thought they would, Brognola would be ordering his antacid by the case before too long.

"I'll pass that on to him."

T. J. HAWKINS SAT at the table in the dining room and watched the Phoenix Force warriors talk with the easy confidence of men who had worked together for years. They were discussing what they had been doing since the last mission and speculating about what they would be doing on this new one. From his days with the Rangers, though, he knew that this was more than just another bull session. It had been a while since they had been together and, as they talked, they were going through the process that would weld them into a fighting team again.

He still wasn't sure that he had done the right thing by signing up with them. So far, he had been very impressed with the facilities he had seen at the Farm and with most of the Stony Man crew. The only concerns he had were about the men of Phoenix Force.

Although Phoenix Force was an arm of the United States government, he was surprised to find that he was only the second native-born American on the team. James was from Chicago, but Encizo was a naturalized Cuban, Manning was a Canadian and the team leader was a Briton. He could only assume that these men had been chosen solely for their skills rather than for their birthplace. And from their record, he knew that they worked well as a team.

Even more important, though, he still had to get a feel for how well he would fit in with them. He had worked with elite units long enough to know that there was always a problem when a new man signed on with a well established team. It would take a while for him to become a real member of the team.

All he could do was sit, listen, evaluate and see how it turned out. One thing he knew right now, though, was that this was unlikely to be a boring way to live.

IT WAS NIGHT when Mack Bolan saw the lights of Stony Man Farm through the windshield of his Land Rover. The Farm couldn't really be called home, but it was the closest thing to home that he had. This was where he could get a home-cooked meal, have his laundry done and go to sleep without needing to wear a weapon in his shoulder holster. In his line of work, that meant a great deal.

He was late for the mission briefing, but Hal Brognola had called and brought him up to speed on the situation and he had opted in on the mission. Until the threat of weapons of mass destruction could be taken out of the complicated Middle Eastern equation, there was never going to be a peace in the area.

Bolan wasn't given to wishful thinking, but he had chosen to try one more time. He was always willing to do anything he could to stop the madness from getting out of hand.

CHAPTER EIGHT

Pima Air Museum,
Tucson, Arizona

Hermann "Gadgets" Schwarz pulled the rented Pontiac Grand Am four-door sedan into the gravel parking lot in front of the Pima Air Museum on the outskirts of Tucson, Arizona, and cut the engine. "Here we are," he said. "Let's take a look at this airplane we're supposed to grab."

Skilled with anything mechanical or electronic, Gadgets had picked up his nickname in Vietnam because of his work with booby traps and surveillance devices. Now he took care of the technical side of the Able Team operations. Stealing a Blackbird was a challenge he was looking forward to.

"I still think that this is one of the dumbest things I've ever heard come out of the Farm," Carl "Ironman" Lyons growled. "If they want the damned thing back in service, why don't they simply send the Air Force in here to take it and fix it? This cloak-and-dagger crap is stupid."

Lyons was an ex-LAPD detective sergeant whose path had crossed that of the Executioner's several times during the Mafia Wars, as they had come to be known. Now that America's need to combat international terrorism and drug cartels had given birth to the Stony Man action teams, he headed Able Team, which was targeted against domestic terrorism and violence in the United States. His nickname, "Ironman," reflected his mental attributes more than his physical. But he also had the physical prowess to go along with his mental style of dealing with the obstacles life threw in his path.

"You heard what Barbara said," the third man in the Pontiac reminded him. "The Chinese are keeping a close eye on the three Blackbirds we still have in service, and we need to steal this one to replace the one they want to use so we won't come up one short the next time their satellite comes over Edwards Air Force Base."

The third man of Able Team was Rosario Blancanales, a man known as "the Politician" because of his unique ability to work people and situations to his decided advantage. While Schwarz was the brains of the team and Lyons the brawn, Blancanales liked to think of himself as the voice.

"I still think it's a stupid plan," Lyons growled. "We ought to just tell the Chinese to stuff it."

"'Ours not to reason why,'" Schwarz quoted.

"Think of it as a college prank," Blancanales said. "We've never stolen a spy plane before."

"If you're ready, guys," Schwarz said, reaching for the door handle. "let's go. I want to get a look at this Blackbird."

"MAN, WILL YOU LOOK at that thing." Schwarz's voice was as awe-filled as if he were talking about a European Gothic cathedral instead of a flying machine. "That is some kind of airplane."

The Lockheed SR-71 sitting in the sand of the museum's outside exhibit area was 180 feet long and as black as a crow's wing. At one time it had been the fastest air-breathing vehicle that had ever flown. Now it was one of the biggest attractions at one of the nation's largest air museums. But not for long. The Blackbird had just been enlisted for another tour of duty.

"If this thing is such a hot rod," Lyons said, "why did they take it out of service?"

The ex-LAPD cop should never have asked that question. Now he was in for a lecture. Not only did Schwarz like electronics, but he was crazy about anything high-tech, and the SR was about as high-tech, as aviation went.

"When the last of the SR-71s were taken out of military service in the late eighties," Schwarz started out, "they weren't grounded because they were no longer needed for recon missions, because they were. They were grounded because they were getting old and were too expensive to maintain in flying condition. The plan was that when the Blackbirds were retired, the newly launched Keyhole spy satellites would take over their strategic recon mission, and another one of the famous Skunk Works projects would soon replace them to do the tactical recon work.''

''What happened, then? Why do they want it back now?''

''Like I said, the plan was to replace them with the recon satellites, but it just didn't quite work out the way they wanted it to. The problem came during the Gulf War. The Keyhole birds did their job, but since deep-space satellites move in orbits that can be easily tracked, all anyone needed to do to escape being seen by a spy satellite was to hide while it was overhead. Much of what we needed to know to be able to target Saddam's forces simply couldn't be seen from space.''

''What about the replacement spy plane?''

''That was the second thing that went wrong,'' Schwarz said. ''The SR-71's replacement was supposed to be a real-life science-fiction machine code-named Aurora. It's a space plane even more sophisticated than the space shuttle and, since its development hadn't gone as smoothly as planned, there was nothing to use to fly tactical recon missions in the Gulf. The Pentagon panicked and ordered two of the remaining airworthy Blackbirds flown by NASA to be made ready for military missions again. But the Gulf War ended before the work could begin, so the order was cancelled.''

''So, what's the story now?''

Schwarz shrugged. ''The Aurora still isn't in service, so the Keyhole satellites are the only way we have to keep an eye on the bad guys. But, as we found during the Gulf War, the view from space isn't always enough. If the Bear needs to take a closer look at whatever's going down in Iran, this is going to do it for him.''

''I still think it's a crazy idea.''

''So do I,'' Schwarz said, his gaze glued to the sleek black aircraft. ''Real crazy, man.''

''Just don't get too hypnotized by that sleek body,'' Lyons said to Gadgets. ''Remember, we see the museum's director at 14:00 hours. He got the call from Washington, but we're here to remind him that it's not a joke—he'd better not screw up.''

THE NEXT EVENING Carl Lyons felt completely out of place in the security guard's uniform. After having served in the LAPD for years, the last thing he had ever pictured himself as was a rent-a-cop. But the security guard getup was part of the plan. He, Schwarz and Blancanales were replacing the museum's regular guards for the weekend.

Along with that simple ploy, a detour routed the traffic on the U.S. interstate that ran past the Pima Air Museum onto a temporary blacktop road to the south of the elevated freeway. That put the cars down at a lower level so their drivers couldn't look to the north and see the outdoor exhibit areas from the raised roadway.

Toward midnight, what would be reported as a lightning strike at an electrical substation killed the power to a large portion of southwestern Tucson, including the Pima Air Museum and all the streetlights in its vicinity. With the traffic diverted and the security lights killed, Able Team was ready to go to work.

Blancanales drove the borrowed yellow Air Force towing tractor up to the access gate in the museum's fence, where he was met by Schwarz and Lyons. They unlocked the gate, let the tractor through and closed the gate behind it. It was a short drive to the Blackbird's location in the middle of the museum's open-air exhibit area.

"Hand me that tow bar," Schwarz said after Blancanales backed the tractor up to the long nose of the SR.

"Those tires don't look too good to me," Lyons commented as he knelt to give Schwarz the tow bar.

"They'll do to get her out of here. When we get her across the fence, the Air Force can put some air in them."

It took but a few minutes to hook the tow bar to the Blackbird's nose gear. What was more difficult was finding a path through the maze of parked aircraft to get out to the access road. Fortunately, though, the Blackbird had been parked next to the main access road that ran through the display area. Blancanales had to be careful not to scrape her wings as he towed the plane through the exhibits of smaller fighters that surrounded her, but with Lyons and Schwarz guiding him, he made it without mishap.

Once on the museum's internal access road, he towed the Blackbird past the rows of parked aircraft to the far southern end of the seventy-five-acre complex. There a small Air Force work crew had been busy dismantling sixty feet of the chain-link perimeter fence. As soon as the chain link was rolled to the side, he guided the SR through the tight gap and out onto the paved road. From there, he towed it back past the museum to the paved access road that led to the air base's southern perimeter.

At another temporary gap in the base's outer-perimeter security fence, he handed over the tractor to an Air Force sergeant. Making sure that the plane's wings cleared the fence, the sergeant drove the SR back inside an Air Force base for the first time in several years.

Once the SR was inside the fence, the work crew that had just reerected the museum's fence restored the air base's perimeter, as well. When that was done, Lyons and Schwarz went back to the museum to finish their tour as security guards, and Blancanales went to take down the detour and tell the power company to turn the lights back on again.

There was little cleanup to be done inside the museum itself, but Schwarz did put up a professionally painted sign saying that the SR-71 Blackbird exhibit had been moved to the restoration hangar for touch-up work and would be back on display soon.

When the power was restored to southwest Tucson an hour later, no one noticed that one of the Pima Air Museum exhibits was missing. Since the museum was out of the way, no one would notice until it opened the next morning, and the cover story should serve to explain its absence.

ONCE THE SR-71 was safely inside the security hangar at Davis-Monthan, its wings and vertical tails were quickly taken off and the airframe prepared for shipment. As soon as everything was ready, the spy plane was loaded into the gaping maw of a waiting C-5A Galaxy transport that had been towed nose first into the hangar. When the transport's cargo doors were closed behind it, armed Air Police guards were placed on the plane.

Early the next morning, the C-5A carrying the Blackbird lifted off and set course northwest for Edwards Air Force base, home of the Right Stuff, the nation's flight-test center in the Nevada desert.

WHEN THE C-5A ARRIVED at Edwards, the first thing that was done was to taxi it into a hangar safely out of the way of prying eyes. Inside the cavernous building, the SR-71 was quickly off-loaded and prepared for repainting. The U.S. star insignias on the wings and fuselage, the U.S. Air Force logo and the red serial number 951 on the twin tails were painted over with a special matt black paint known officially as FS 35402 Indigo Blue. As soon as the black was dry, a white band bearing a cursive, red NASA logo was added to the tails. And under that band, a white serial number 971 was painted.

As soon as the paint was dry, the wings were attached to the fuselage and the "new" NASA SR-71 was towed outside to a parking spot on the tarmac in front of the Blackbird maintenance hangar. A team of technicians soon swarmed over the machine, tools in their hands. Two hours later the SR had all of her maintenance bays open, and one of the J-58 engines had been halfway removed. Once that was done, the technicians returned to their regular work and left the Blackbird sitting by herself on the tarmac.

Now, whenever the Chinese satellite flew over Edwards, it would see that SR-71, tail number 971, assigned to the NASA high-speed flight-test program, was undergoing an overhaul or refitting. There would be a great deal of speculation in foreign capitals as to what was being done to the spy plane, but as long as all three of the last flying SRs were accounted for, everyone would be able to breathe easier. No foreign countries would have to worry that a Blackbird was cruising at eighty thousand feet overhead watching what they were doing.

"WE'RE ON TRACK," Aaron Kurtzman reported to Barbara Price. "The first step has been completed. The decoy Blackbird is sitting on the ground at Edwards, and the real SR has been flown to Groom Lake to be prepped for the mission."

"When's Grimaldi due to arrive?"

"He gets in tomorrow morning."

"And he'll be there for five days, right?"

"Right. They figured that was the minimum time that he could learn to run the cameras and sensors."

"So far so good," she said. That they were on schedule so far didn't surprise her, as they were still in the mission-prep phase. To stay on schedule after the team deployed to Russia would be the trick. But with Mack Bolan leading the ground element, the only hang-ups would be due to enemy action.

CHAPTER NINE

Groom Lake, Nevada

Jack Grimaldi watched with great interest as the unmarked Bell JetRanger chopper turned on its final leg of the landing pattern to the sprawling air base on the empty desert below. The most prominent feature of the base was the eight-thousand-foot runway, long enough to handle even a space-shuttle landing.

To the U.S. Air Force, this air base was commonly known as the Groom Lake Test Facility, or simply Area 51. In popular thrillers and TV shows about secret air bases and UFOs, it was called Dreamland. By whatever name it was known, the remote, totally isolated installation was home to America's best-kept secrets in aviation hardware. Some even said that captured alien spacecraft were being tested there and that their technology was finding its way into the latest Skunk Works projects.

The chopper flared out and touched down on the big white *H* painted on the tarmac in front of the main control tower. As Grimaldi grabbed his kit bag and stepped out of the aircraft, he saw an Air Force officer waiting for him.

"So this is Dreamland," Grimaldi said as the young captain approached him.

"You'd better not let the base commander hear you saying that, sir," the officer replied, smiling thinly. "The general goes ballistic every time someone uses that name. He says that we're not filming 'Unsolved Mysteries' here."

"I guess that asking for the tour of Hangar 49, where you keep the UFOs, is out of the question, then?"

"Please, sir," the captain said. "I'd appreciate it if you didn't even make jokes about that. That isn't considered to be a funny joke around here."

Grimaldi had sense enough not to ask why this was such a sensitive topic to the Air Force. He hadn't made up his mind about all the flying-saucer stories he'd heard over the years, particularly the one known as the Roswell UFO. But he knew that if alien flying machines had been captured, this was where they would be tested.

"Okay," he said, extending his hand. "Let's go back to square one. I'm Jack Grimaldi. You can drop the 'sirs' and just call me Jack."

The captain took his hand. "I'm Jim Blevins and I've been assigned to be your aide while you're here."

"My keeper, you mean?"

Blevins grinned sheepishly and said, "Let me show you to your quarters."

"Can I see the Blackbird first?"

Blevins hesitated for an instant. "Sure, why not. That's what you're here for." Not that the Air Force officer knew exactly why an unknown civilian was being checked out in the world's fastest airplane, and he wasn't sure that he wanted to know. If you wanted to work at Dreamland, you soon learned to check your curiosity at the gate.

Getting into an Air Force blue sedan, Blevins drove to an isolated hangar at the edge of the base complex. An armed sentry met the car and examined their passes before allowing them to proceed.

"Your security's tight," Grimaldi commented.

"Even though it takes an act of Congress to get in here," Blevins replied, "it still doesn't mean that you can just wander around once you're inside. And if a sentry ever tells you to halt, stop abruptly or he'll shoot you dead. There'll be no second warning."

"I'll remember that."

The forest of lights dangling from the girders of the hangar's roof made the inside of the building almost as light as the desert sun outside. Sitting in the middle of the building was the long black shape of a Lockheed SR-71. This wasn't the first time that Grimaldi had seen a Blackbird up close. Nonetheless, it was still a thrilling sight that was made even more thrilling by the knowledge that he would actually get to fly in this magnificent machine.

For an airplane that had been designed in 1957 during the Eisenhower administration, it still looked like something straight out of a science fiction movie. It said a lot about the state of American technology that the world's most advanced airplane was American and had been built almost forty years earlier. When its replacement arrived, it would be even more advanced and a harbinger of the coming millennium.

"This was one of the NASA birds based out of Edwards, right?"

"Right, this is 971, the first of the NASA ships to go through the FY 95 refit. She's been completely gone over and is ready for military missions again."

Not taking his eyes off the sleek aircraft, Grimaldi started to walk around it. "You guys must have solved the fuel-leak problems. I don't see a pool of JP-7 spreading out under her."

Because of the heat generated by air friction, when the SR flew at Mach 3 the entire airframe expanded some several inches. In the earlier SRs, the fuel tanks, which also expanded with the heat, were difficult to seal when they were cool. In fact, one early SR had been lost on a short, low-speed test flight when all the fuel had leaked out because the tanks had not expanded enough to seal properly.

"They did that several years ago," Blevins explained. "Lockheed came up with a tank-sealing compound that could take the heat and the expansion and the Blackbirds don't have to wear diapers anymore."

"I'm glad to hear that," Grimaldi said. "I'm going where I can't call a KC-10 tanker if I need a quick fill-up."

Blevins was dying to know what in the hell was going on, but he knew enough not to ask. The only time a civilian not on the government payroll got into Dreamland was when a high-ranking congressman on the Defense Appropriations Committee came for a look around. For a non-blue-suiter to get checked out in an SR, even in the backseat, was unheard of. He didn't know who this Grimaldi guy was—in fact, the base commander didn't even know—but the word had come down that he was to be treated as if he was God.

"If you'd like," Blevins broke in on Grimaldi's reverie. "I can show you to your quarters now."

Grimaldi took one last look at the SR and reluctantly turned away. He'd be seeing more of this fantastic aircraft over the next few weeks, and he did need a shower. "Sure," he said. "When do I get to meet my pilot and get this program on the road?"

"You can meet Major Hoffsteader this afternoon if you'd like, and the first briefing is scheduled for 2000 hours tonight."

"Good. Let me get cleaned up, and then I'd like to meet the major."

THE BLACKBIRD'S PILOT looked as though he was right off a fifties Air Force recruiting poster. He was tall, blue eyed and had a blond crew cut. He wore a flight suit with the normal name tapes and rank badges, and a Habu patch was over the left breast pocket. Back when the SRs had been staged out of Okinawa during the Vietnam War, the natives had called the spy plane "Habu" after a particularly nasty snake found on the island. Though the war and the snakes were long gone, the name had remained as an in-group nickname for the aircraft, and the patch indicated that the pilot was one of the elite of the aerial elite.

"Pete Hoffsteader," the pilot said as he stepped up, his hand extended. "You must be my new backseat."

"Jack Grimaldi, and I'm your man."

"I'm not supposed to ask you too much about your background," the pilot said, his eyes serious as he looked Grimaldi up and down. "So all I have is one question. Are you up for this?"

Grimaldi smiled. "I understand your concern," he said seriously. "I've got a lot of stick-and-rudder time, and most of it has been in military aircraft, including fast movers. And while I fly myself, I also know how to take orders when I'm in the backseat."

Hoffsteader visibly relaxed. The last thing he wanted to hear was that he had been given a novice to work with in the world's most sophisticated flying machine.

"And on the topic of being my backseater," the pilot said, "there's something you need to know. While the SRs that flew over China and Vietnam during the war were unarmed, the birds do have an internal missile bay that can hold four AIM-54 Phoenix air-to-air missiles. And for whatever reason, this particular Blackbird will fly with a full set of claws."

The pilot grinned. "I know that's only four shots, but when you're shooting Phoenixes, that's four targets destroyed. Those things are good."

Grimaldi grinned back. "I know. I've fired them hot from F-14 Tomcats."

The pilot looked impressed, but he knew better than to ask where and when this civilian had managed to snag a ride in a Navy Tomcat fighter, much less the chance of a lifetime to fly one in combat. But if he was being put into the backseat of a Blackbird, he had to be real good. There were hundreds of hot-rock Air Force combat pilots who would kill for even a checkout ride in an SR, to say nothing of flying a supersecret mission over enemy territory. But as he had been told, he was not to ask his new RSO anything that wasn't directly related to the mission at hand.

"Okay, then, since you know the fire-control system, the first thing I'll do is to start checking you out on the sensors and cameras. Since that's what they're paying you to do, you need to know those systems cold."

"When do we start?"

Hoffsteader glanced at his watch. "How about right now? Unless you have a hot date waiting for you at the O club."

Grimaldi shook his head. "I haven't been here long enough to even know where the officers' club is."

"You haven't missed much," the pilot said. "But they do keep the beer cold."

"Why don't we try a couple later on tonight?"

"That's a deal. I like to get to know who I'm flying with. You know, I like to see if they can hold their own on a bar stool without a shoulder harness."

Grimaldi grinned. "That's a plan."

BARBARA PRICE WAS in her office taking a break from the Iranian situation to clear her desk of the routine paperwork that had built up since Brognola's first visit. Ongoing mission or not, there was always her other job to be done. She had just checked the fuel expenditures for the past month when Aaron Kurtzman's voice came over her intercom.

"Barbara, I think you'd better come down here."

"What is it?" she asked.

"We just had a terrorist attack in California," he said curtly. "Eight dead, a dozen wounded."

She closed her eyes briefly. "On the way."

When she walked into the cluttered Computer Room, Kurtzman was wearing the rumpled white lab coat that was his war suit when he ran the electronic intelligence-gathering center for the Farm.

She wasn't surprised to see Yakov Katzenelenbogen there, as well. Having spent much of his life in the intelligence business, he knew that the success of field operations depended upon the amount and quality of information that could be amassed, analyzed and passed on to the men in the field. With his new role as tactical adviser, he would be spending most of his time with the computers. The tight confines of the room left only a twisted path for Kurtzman to wheel his chair from one keyboard to the next, but Katz was following him around and looking over his shoulder.

"What happened?" she asked.

"It's still coming in." Kurtzman pointed to the small TV set that was always tuned to CNN's "Headline News." "But it looks like a Tel Aviv-style car bombing in San Francisco. It took out a fast-food restaurant, and they're still looking for bodies."

This wasn't good. Carl Lyons and Able Team had been working that surveillance mission in California before they had been pulled off to do the Blackbird snatch. She hoped that there wasn't a connection between the two events. Brognola would go ballistic, and that was the last thing she needed right now.

"Has anyone claimed responsibility yet?"

Katz nodded. "They are calling themselves the Islamic Action Group. They say that they are fighting American imperialism in the Third World. You know, the usual self-serving rationalizations for killing people who have nothing to do with whatever they think their problem is."

She continued to watch the CNN broadcast when the scrambled phone rang. "Price," she answered.

"Brognola," the voice on the other end said. "I want you to get on top of this right away. The President wants results immediately."

"How about the Blackbird mission?"

"Keep that on track, as well, but peel off Able Team to get on this bombing incident."

"Will do."

As Price put down the phone, she saw that the CNN newscast was showing shots of another bombing at a different location in California. The first thing she had to do was to get hold of Carl Lyons and get him back on the job. They should be back in California by now and able to focus on this new crisis immediately.

CHAPTER TEN

Oakland, California

"You did what?" Carl Lyons's face was a study in complete disbelief as he faced the FBI agent. Barbara Price's call had caught them right after they had arrived back in Oakland and were on their way to the FBI surveillance team's location. The news that the Feds greeted them with, however, wasn't what he had wanted to hear.

FBI Agent John Thrope looked out the motel room's window. "We lost them," he said flatly. "On Thursday night they had a prayer meeting, or whatever they call it, and about a dozen people came. We logged the visitors in and out and counted them. But when Agent Chavez went to clean the room the next morning, the four people who were there weren't the same ones we had been watching."

Schwarz grinned. "The old bait-and-switch trick. It works every time."

"Could I talk to Agent Chavez?" Blancanales asked gently. "There's a chance she saw something that might help us."

"I debriefed her myself," Thrope said defensively, "and she didn't have anything."

"Not that I'm doubting your thoroughness," the Politician said smoothly, "but can I talk to her anyway? She might have seen some little thing that we can tie in to what we already have on those guys."

"Sure." Thrope sighed. "I was told to cooperate with you guys any way I could. And I guess that since we screwed up big time, we have no other choice."

The FBI agent shook his head. "I'll be tracking cigarette bootleggers on Indian reservations for the next ten years for this."

"This could have happened to anyone." Blancanales tried to sound as reassuring as he could. "It was just your bad luck to be sitting in for us when it happened. I can promise that you won't get any complaints from us."

"We appreciate that." Thrope sounded relieved as he reached for the phone. "Let me call Chavez and get her over here."

FBI Agent Maria Chavez looked like a real motel maid in her uniform as she walked into the room the surveillance team had taken. Although she had done nothing wrong, she looked defensive.

"Agent Chavez." Blancanales stepped forward before Lyons could start talking. "My name is Rosario Blancanales, and I'd like to talk to you about what you saw in the target room."

She glanced over to Thrope. "I already gave my report to Agent Thrope, sir."

"If you don't mind, I'd like to go over it with you myself." Blancanales motioned toward the coffee service in the suite. "Can I get you a cup of coffee?"

When Thrope nodded his consent, Chavez relaxed. "Sure, black."

Blancanales poured and handed her the coffee. "Now," he said, "have a seat and run me through your contact this morning. Tell me everything you saw or didn't see. Everything is important."

She took a seat on the couch and took a sip of the coffee. "Well, I showed up at the usual time to clean the room, and four men were in there as usual, but it wasn't the same four men. They could pass for the others at a distance, but they were all younger, and only one of them spoke much English."

"How were they dressed?"

"Well, they were dressed in typical California clothing, but it didn't quite match up, if you know what I mean."

"Like they had not been wearing it for very long?"

"Yes, kind of like that."

"Did you talk to them?"

"Yes, I asked them . . ."

WHEN THE TWO FBI AGENTS left an hour later, Blancanales flopped down on the couch. "Man," he said, shaking his head slowly, "they really humped the pooch on that one."

"I can't believe it," Lyons added. "We had those guys cold, and they blew it. We spent over a month keeping track of them, and they couldn't hang on to them for a couple of days."

"But Chavez said that the stand-ins are still there," Blancanales continued. "What do you say we snatch a couple of those guys and see if they know anything?"

"Why not?" Lyons asked.

The Able Team leader drew the .357 Colt Python from his shoulder holster, swung out the cylinder and checked the load. "Let's do it," he growled.

"Guys," Schwarz said, "hadn't we better at least wait till it gets dark? I mean we're going to be a little obvious busting a door down in broad daylight. Particularly at Howard Johnson's."

"I want to be obvious," Lyons said. "I want those bastards to know that we're serious about this."

"It'll be serious enough if the local police bust us for busting them."

"We've got our get-out-of-jail-free cards if we need to use them."

Schwarz shrugged. There was no talking to the Ironman when he got in that state of mind. All you could do was hold on and go along for the ride. "Sure," he said brightly, "why not? As Mr. Rogers says, 'It's a beautiful day in the neighborhood.' Let's go bust down a door and shoot somebody.''

"Smart ass."

"I do think that we'd better do this in our civvies, though," Blancanales cautioned. "Going out in our blacksuits would be a bit much."

"I don't care if we do it in our Jockey shorts," Lyons said. "As long as we do it now."

"Okay, okay. We're going."

TARIQ AL-HAUK WAS proud to have been selected to stand in for one of the four Islamic freedom fighters who were risking their lives in the name of the Prophet. His Pakistani passport had an expired student visa in it, but he knew that there was almost no chance that the Immigration and Naturalization Service would ever catch up with him. There were estimated to be over three million illegals in the Los Angeles area alone, and with that many people to chose from, the chances were good that he wouldn't be caught.

The big-screen TV in the motel suite the action group had taken was blaring as it always did when "Wheel of Fortune" was on. For some reason he couldn't fathom, Akhmed was completely infatuated with the woman who turned the letters for the game. Al-Hauk had to admit that she was attractive.

His gaze was focused on the woman on the television show when the door of their room flew open and crashed against the wall. Three men with ski masks on their faces and weapons in their hands rushed in.

"On the floor!" one of the men shouted.

Akhmed didn't speak English and leapt for the AK-47 that lay by the couch. One of the masked men spun and triggered his submachine gun. Though the weapon made no sound, the bullets ripped through Akhmed's chest, slamming him to the floor. The gunman then turned and fired a single round into the TV set, shattering the glass.

Al-Hauk held his hands high in the air and went down to his knees. "Do not shoot," he said, his voice wavering. "We will give you our money."

"On the floor!" the biggest man snapped.

The two other men raced past him for the bedroom, where Ali, the third man of the cell, was sleeping. The shots had awakened him, and he appeared in the door with a pistol in his hand. For some reason, though, he hesitated, and both men fired short bursts into him at point-blank range. The bullets slammed him against the wall, and he was dead before he slumped to the floor.

"One of them's missing," the shortest of the men said when he came back out of the bedroom.

The big man placed the barrel of his pistol against Al-Hauk's nose. "Where's the other one?"

"There's no time for that," the third man said. "Get his ass out of here."

The small man knelt and slapped a piece of tape over his prisoner's mouth before handcuffing the man's wrists behind his back. Once his hands were secure, he put a blindfold over his eyes and small plugs in his ears.

Gagged, bound and blindfolded, the Pakistani had no choice but to let himself be carried down the back stairs to the parking lot. There, he was shoved into a van that quickly drove away.

SCHWARZ HELD THE DOOR to their motel room open while Lyons and Blancanales quickly hustled their prisoner inside.

"How do you want to handle this one?" Blancanales asked. "The old Mutt-and-Jeff routine?"

Otherwise known as good-cop, bad-cop, this tactic involved one interrogator threatening the subject while the other one pretended to befriend him. Though it was the oldest trick in the world, it was known to work time after time.

"That won't work," Lyons said. "This guy's a fanatic. He's ready to die for the cause, and he won't buy into it. We need to come up with something that will break down the barriers real fast."

"How about the lie-detector scam?" Schwarz asked. "The chances are good he's never seen a polygraph, so I can whip something up and he won't know the difference. We won't need a readout to tell us when he's lying.''

"That's not a bad idea, Gadgets." Lyons smiled thinly. "And can you rig up some kind of electric chair, as well?"

"You mean fifty thousand volts?"

"No, just something that looks like it would kill."

A smile spread over Gadgets's face. "That's the best idea you've had all day. I have just the thing."

WHEN THE BLINDFOLD was removed, Al-Hauk saw that he was in another motel room with the three men, and they still wore their masks.

"Before I get started," Lyons told his prisoner, "I want you to understand something. We aren't from the police or the FBI. We have no connection with the government at all."

"Who are you?"

"We are men who don't like to see foreigners come to this country and kill our people."

Lyons stepped back and let Schwarz fasten several fake electrodes to Al-Hauk's head and bound hands. The Pakistani tried to wiggle away from them, but he was tied too tightly.

As soon as they were in place, Lyons leaned over his prisoner. "I'm going to ask you a few questions," he said. "And if you lie to me, my partner will know it.

His machine will tell him. When he tells me that you have lied about something, electricity will shoot through you. The first time, it'll hurt, but it won't kill you. Each time you lie, he will increase the power. If you tell me too many lies, you'll die. Do you understand what I am saying?"

Al-Hauk nodded.

"Let me make sure," Lyons said, and reached for the set of battery-charging cables Schwarz had connected to a battery and capacitor. The cables had large, spring-loaded alligator clamps on the ends and looked like something found in a Frankenstein movie.

Holding the clamps in front of the Pakistani's face, he leered at him. "Let me tell you what will happen when I clamp these things on you and let the electricity flow. First you will piss your pants. Then you will bite your tongue, and I will have to be very careful that you don't bite it off. It might choke you, and you would die. Also too much electricity will blind you. It'll cook your eyes like boiling an egg.

"If you live through all of this, you'll no longer be a man as you are now. You'll be like a man who has been shot in the head but doesn't die. You'll be blind, your tongue will be gone, bitten off, so you won't be able to speak. You'll have no control over your bladder or bowel movements."

Al-Hauk shuddered. Strict rules of personal hygiene were important to his people.

"Okay, let's get started. What is your name and where are you from?"

"My name is Tariq Al-Hauk, and I am from Peshawar, Pakistan."

"Why are you in the United States?"

Al-Hauk hesitated. He had memorized a phone number of an Arabic-American lawyer who would help him if he was arrested. Then he would be safe because the American government always followed the laws even if they did little to protect the country. But if these men weren't from the government, he wasn't in safe hands. Maybe if he told the truth, these men would turn him over to the police or the FBI and he would live.

"I am an Islamic freedom fighter," he said proudly.

"Whose freedom are you fighting for?"

"I fight for all the people of the world who are oppressed by the Great Satan of the United States."

"And to do that you kill women and children, right?"

"I have not been chosen yet to make an attack," Al-Hauk stated honestly. "All I have been called to do is to support the other fighters."

"But they are killing people, right?"

"That is not for me to know."

"He's lying," Schwarz said.

Lyons leaned over his captive and touched the two electrodes together. A fat blue spark snapped between them and left an ozone smell hanging in the air.

"I thought I warned you not to lie to me," he said, his voice low. "Do you want me to kill you with these?"

Al-Hauk tried to pull himself as far away from the electrodes as he could. "Please."

"Tell me the truth," Lyons ordered.

"I will," he promised. "I swear it."

"Tell me about the other freedom fighters. Where are they and what are they planning to do?"

Al-Hauk took a deep breath. He had sworn to die if his life was required by the Islamic revolution and its leaders, but no one had said anything about dying in agony while a Western demon tortured him with electricity. Surely merciful God hadn't intended for him to die a shameful death contaminated with his own waste.

Looking Lyons straight in the eyes, he blurted out everything he knew about the action groups and their plans.

When he was finished, Lyons laid the clamps back on the table. "Since you have cooperated with us," he said, "we are going to turn you over to the FBI. But to be protected under the law, you must tell them everything that you have told me. I made a tape recording of everything you said, so I will know if you leave anything out. And if you do, I'll take you back from the FBI and electrocute you myself.''

''I will tell them everything I have told you,'' Al-Hauk promised. ''I swear by God.''

''You'd better, because He won't protect you if I ever get my hands on you again.''

CHAPTER ELEVEN

"We've got what we need," Carl Lyons told Barbara Price over the scrambled phone link to Stony Man Farm. "Our boy gave it up and spilled the whole plan for his so-called action group."

He could hear Price sigh with relief. Having to split the Farm's resources to handle two crises at the same time wasn't an easy task, and she really needed the good news. "What's their program?"

"We really don't know exactly what's going down yet, but this guy's leader got the word to hit several targets in California—a theirs-is-not-to-reason-why kind of thing, just get out there and kill some people."

"He didn't give a reason?"

"Nope. This isn't like the Trade Center bombers. The target wasn't as important as the fact that they could rack up a body count."

"What's the story on your prisoner?"

"He's a Pakistani on an expired student visa, and apparently he's a newcomer to the group. He was planted and told to go dormant until he was activated, and this is the first call he's had. The leader is an Algerian named Ali Ben Abi, whose been in the States for at least two years now. This Ben Abi acts as paymaster for the group, as well as the sole contact with whoever's behind this.''

''Can you nab him?''

''We're going to try. But if we're going to take these guys out, we may not have the time to pick and choose who goes down.''

''I understand.'' If they were going to eradicate the threat before more people were killed, they would have to move and shoot fast and couldn't take too much time to worry about prisoners.

''I want to turn our guy over to the FBI so they can continue to work on him. Can you set that up with Hal?''

''I'll let the Bear handle that,'' she said. ''All I want to know is if you can take care of the people you got a lead on ASAP?''

''No problem.''

''How soon can you start?''

''We'll need at least a day to check out the target locations and make sure that they are the right targets. I'd hate to take out someone who isn't involved.''

''Of course,'' she answered. One of the biggest problems in their line of work was making sure that civilians stayed out of the line of fire.

"A bigger problem," Lyons said, "is that this California activity might be part of a larger program. Our man said that he overheard Ben Abi make a phone call to another Islamic Action Group cell in Florida."

Brognola wouldn't like hearing that. Even though there hadn't been terrorist attacks in Florida yet, it was a prime target. Since the state was a popular vacation and retirement spot for the East Coast power structure, terrorist attacks in Florida would set Washington on its ear.

"I'll pass that on so Hal can alert the FBI."

WHILE JACK GRIMALDI WAS learning how to operate the sensors and cameras that would be carried in the SR-71's recon bays, a Blackbird ground-support team was getting its equipment together for the deployment to the Russian air base. They hadn't been told that they would be going to Russia, only that they would be operating from foreign soil with limited support.

Working on foreign soil wasn't as much a problem as the limited-support part of it was. The Blackbird wasn't a run-of-the-mill airplane, and it had very specific needs that other aircraft didn't. For one thing its J-58 engines burned a JP-7 jet fuel, which required special handling equipment. Also the oils and lubricants were all special high-temperature mixtures that were shared only with the space shuttle. Even the SR's tires were made of a unique plasticized rubber compound and were filled with pressurized nitrogen, not compressed air. Because of that, everything that the Blackbird might need on the mission would have to be taken with them.

As soon as the equipment and supplies had all been checked over, they were loaded into C-5A cargo pallets, covered and placed under guard. The crew then packed its gear and stood by.

HERMANN SCHWARZ PULLED the V-10 Dodge Ram pickup into the parking lot behind a second-rate motel and killed the engine and lights. The dilapidated building was home to one of the action-group cells Tariq Al-Hauk had given up.

The corner of the building masked the nearest street lamp, so they were in deep shadow. After checking the vicinity, the three men stepped out of the truck's cab without a word, their weapons in their hands. On the way to the back stairs that led to the building's second floor, they pulled ski masks over their faces.

In their combat blacksuits and rubber-soled boots, they moved like silent shadows up the stairs. Al-Hauk had given them a phone number that had been traced to one of the rooms on the second floor. According to him, three terrorists were staying there.

Standing in front of the door of room 219, Lyons held out his gloved fist and silently counted down by snapping out his fingers. On the count of three, he lashed out with his steel-toed combat boot, splintering the wood around the lock and smashing the door open.

On each side of him, Schwarz and Blancanales pitched their stun grenades into the room. Disoriented by the explosions, the three men clustered around the TV set chose to dive for their weapons rather than surrender. It was a fatal choice, and a hail of 9 mm slugs tore into them.

"Clear," Blancanales called out from the kitchen.

"We're clear in the back rooms," Schwarz reported.

Without a second look, Lyons turned and headed for the front door.

"Ninety seconds elapsed time," Schwarz stated as he slid into the driver's seat of the pickup and reached for the ignition key. "Not bad."

"We're not out of here yet," Lyons reminded him. "Roll it!"

"We're gone."

Sirens were wailing as Schwarz pulled out of the parking lot and turned onto the street. Driving carefully to avoid attracting attention, he made the first left-hand turn onto a side street. Two blocks later he turned again and got back on the main street that would take them across town to the next target.

"THEY JUST HIT the first group," Kurtzman reported to Price. "Three down and no damage to our side."

"Send that on to Hal."

"I already did."

In light of the California bombings, the President had wanted these people taken out of action immediately, and Able Team could do it quickly and efficiently. But to make sure that Able Team didn't get into a situation where they needed to use their get-out-of-jail-free cards, Kurtzman had sent Brognola a list of their target locations. That way, the big Fed could use his Justice Department connections to make sure that federal and local law-enforcement agencies stayed out of the combat zone. Bodies tended to pile up when Able Team was working, and no one wanted the wrong bodies to get counted in the tally.

"When's their next hit?" Price asked.

"Less than an hour."

ABLE TEAM'S SECOND TARGET for the evening was a small house in a quiet, middle-class residential area. Lyons didn't know what a terrorist cell was doing hiding in a nice area like this, but he knew they were there, Blancanales had confirmed it himself.

Since this was a freestanding house with a backyard, Blancanales moved out to take up a position covering the rear this time while Lyons and Schwarz took the front. Blancanales had just stepped out from behind a hedge and was moving to a position to cover the rear door when a spotlight mounted on a pole by the patio suddenly snapped on. Motion detector!

Dropping to the ground, he triggered a single shot from his silenced Uzi. The weapon's discharge was silent, but the sound of the glass shattering and the bullet piercing the metal reflector echoed like a three-car collision in the quiet neighborhood.

In front of the house, Lyons and Schwarz dropped and froze when they heard the noise. "Pol?" Lyons whispered into his throat mike.

"Sorry about that," Blancanales answered. "There was a motion-sensor spotlight. I had to take it out."

Lyons clicked his mike twice to signal that he understood, but before he could move out again, a light snapped on inside the house and they saw a single shadow moving behind the curtains. A hand pulled the edge of the curtain aside and peered out into the darkness. Even though they knew there was no chance of their being spotted, Lyons and Schwarz both held their breaths, their weapons ready.

When the light was switched off again, the Able Team warriors got to their feet and moved to the door. They had lost the element of surprise this time and would have to go in with guns blazing. On the count of three, Lyons booted the door and they were in.

The man who had parted the curtains was stretched out on the couch. He rose to a sitting position and was bringing a pistol to bear when Lyons put him back down with a short burst. When Schwarz rushed past him for the rear rooms, a figure stumbled out into the hall with an AK in his hands. Schwarz triggered his silenced subgun, and the man uttered a strangled cry as he fell to his knees. Another short burst put him down on his face.

In the backyard, Blancanales spotted a dark figure roll through a partially open window at the far corner of the house, and he raked him with a burst from his silenced Uzi. The man crumpled against the wall. A few seconds later Lyons opened the back door and waved him inside.

They were doing a quick check for documents when Schwarz called out from the rear bedroom, "Back here."

Lyons stuck his head around the edge of the door and saw a young woman cowering in the corner of the room. She had pulled the bedclothes around her and was obviously out of her mind with fear.

From her long dark hair, dark skin and features, Lyons figured her to be of Middle Eastern extraction, and she looked to be in her early twenties. It wasn't uncommon for terrorists to bring their own women with them to keep security tight by not having to bring in outsiders for bed partners.

"Do you speak English?" he asked.

The woman nodded and pressed herself even tighter into the corner.

"Good. We won't hurt you, but I want you to stay where you are for at least an hour. Do you understand?"

The woman nodded again and cast her eyes to the floor. Lyons signaled to move out, and they left without another word.

"Damn." Blancanales ripped off his ski mask when they were back in the truck and driving away. "I missed the girl completely when I reconned that place. I should have spotted her."

"Who do you think she was?" Schwarz asked.

"Beats me. Somebody's girlfriend maybe."

"She's sure as hell running with the wrong crowd."

"Was, Gadgets," Blancanales said. "Use the past tense. Her crowd's gone now."

"She'd better start associating with a better class of people," Schwarz stated. "A young woman can never be too careful of her companions."

"You should start an advice column for the young and stupid."

"THERE WAS A WOMAN at the target site this time." Kurtzman wheeled around to face Price.

"Was she killed?"

"No, they left her behind with the bodies. She was a noncombatant."

Price was glad that the woman had been spared. Enough people had died as it was, and even if she was a part of the terrorist cell, it didn't hurt to leave her alive to be interrogated by the FBI.

"They have two more targets scheduled for tonight," he said, glancing at the clock in the corner of his monitor. "But I don't know if they're going to have time to hit both of them."

"I'll wait to tell Hal," Price replied.

"Good call."

THE THIRD TARGET WAS a second-story apartment in a modern Southern California–style building. "Why can't these guys ever take ground-floor apartments?" Schwarz grumbled. "I'm getting tired of climbing back stairs in the dark."

"They take second-floor rooms so they only have to watch the door and not the back windows."

"I know that."

"I know you know, but you asked, so I answered."

This was a repeat of the first motel-room hit: kick down the door, toss in the stun grenades and go in prepared to return fire. This time, however, there was a man awake inside the room. Though awake, the grenades had blinded him, and the AK he raised wasn't on target when he fired. The burst tore into the wall by Lyons's head, covering him with a cloud of drywall dust.

Blancanales loosed half a magazine into the terrorist as Schwarz ran past him to take out the occupants of the double bed on the other side of the room, both of whom had pulled pistols. They didn't have a chance to fire before Schwarz drilled them with chest shots.

"Let's go, guys," Blancanales said. "Someone had to have heard those shots."

Outside, the false dawn was lighting the eastern sky. It was time for Able Team to get off the streets. The fourth target would have to wait.

CHAPTER TWELVE

Yakov Katzenelenbogen poured himself a cup of coffee from the pot in the Computer Room and winced as he brought it to his mouth and took a sip. As soon as Price could clear him some space for an office, the first thing he was going to do was to get himself a decent coffee machine so he didn't have to drink Kurtzman's swill.

Even this early in the morning, Aaron Kurtzman was at his post, looking even more like his nickname than usual, and Katz knew that he had been up most of the night. Even though he had Hunt Wethers and Akira Tokaido to spell him on these long nights, if there was something serious going down, Kurtzman could be counted on to be at his keyboard. He claimed that he didn't need too much sleep because he only had to rest half of his body.

"How does the terrorist-incident board look this morning?" Katz asked.

"Nothing new last night," Kurtzman replied, wheeling his chair around. "So maybe we're through it."

Katz stared at the map showing the three terrorist attacks and the locations Able Team had hit during the night to try to preempt any more. "Able did a good job tracking them down," he said, "but I don't think that we're seen the last of it yet."

"Why's that?"

"Because we don't know what prompted this latest wave of attacks."

"What do you mean?" Kurtzman asked.

"This wasn't at all like the Trade Center bombing. That was the brain child of a madman who thought he could bring down the United States by striking at our physical infrastructure. Remember their list of targets included the UN headquarters building and the Lincoln Tunnel, as well as the World Trade Center. This latest round of mindless violence, as the press loves to call it, looks like it's being aimed at people, not structures. Rather like the Oklahoma City Federal Building hit."

"But there were people in the Trade Center, hundreds of them."

"Granted, but they weren't the primary target." He shrugged. "Sure, if they killed any of them, so much the better, but they were trying to bring the building itself down. To them, the tower was a symbol of America's economic strength, and destroying it was supposed to make Wall Street crash."

"Fat chance of that."

"You're right," Katz agreed. "But you have to remember how these people think. Since most of them come from nations that are barely out of the Middle Ages, they have no idea how a modern free market economy works. If they really want to make Wall Street crash, they'll have a better chance if they blow up a power station and knock out the computers. The U.S. economy is more than just concrete and glass."

"So, if they aren't trying for a stock-market crash or something else of a symbolic nature, what do you think they're doing?"

"I think that whoever's behind this is trying to keep us busy here at home. Think of how many cops and federal agents we have beating the bushes for terrorists right now. Some states have even called out the National Guard to secure critical facilities."

"But if that's all they're doing, they're sure expending a lot of their assets to do it. By the time this is all over, there will hardly be a foreign-born Muslim in the United States who hasn't been hauled in for interrogation."

"True enough," Katz agreed. "But while that's going on, no one's focusing in on the real problem."

"Which is?"

Katz grinned. "Damned if I know."

"But you're supposed to be the tactical expert around here," Kurtzman reminded him.

"And you're supposed to be the computer wizard," the Israeli countered. "When you can give me everything you can possibly get on these guys, I'll do my analysis thing and tell you what they're up to."

"That's the problem," Kurtzman said. "We're having a hard time connecting the dots. So far, we have bodies from three or four different countries, at least by their passports, but they can easily be passports of convenience. According to U.S. immigration records, they came into the country from different places at different times and, except for the fact that they were killed together, they seem to have nothing in common. Except, of course, that they're all some kind of Islamic fanatics."

"As far as we know."

"And we can assume that they're being financed by Iran, Iraq or maybe Libya."

"Never assume, my friend," Katz cautioned, waving a finger in warning.

"Who else, then?"

"That's what you have to find out."

"You're a hell of a lot of help."

"How did Able Team do last night?" Katz asked, changing the subject.

"Not bad." Kurtzman's fingers tapped out a menu change and called up the stats. "They hit three out of the four sites and racked up a nine-body count."

"What happened to the fourth target?"

"They ran out of time."

"The fourth group might panic, go to ground and disappear."

"We can always hope."

"Never hope," Katz said seriously. "Plan. Get the information I need, and I'll go to work with it. As it is now, I'm at an impasse." He shook his head. "I just don't know enough about those people."

Kurtzman looked weary and closed his eyes for a moment.

"But first," Katz said, "roll yourself out of here, take a shower, shave, have a good breakfast and then start looking. You're too tired to do anything right now."

As BLANCANALES had predicted, by midday the California terrorist wave of two days earlier was old news. Leading the headlines were the stories about the nine Middle Eastern immigrants who had been found dead in houses and motel rooms in Oakland, California. The fact that most of the bodies turned out to be illegals and that two of them had warrants out for their arrests on various charges was hidden on the back pages. There was also little mention made of the caches of weapons and explosives that had been found on the premises along with the bodies.

The headlines all screamed about hate crimes aimed at minorities, as if terrorist attacks were motivated by anything other than sheer hatred.

The Stony Man team knew better than to take seriously anything published about terrorism in a newspaper. The cries for a federal investigation into the California killings were being heeded, but not for the reason any newspaper editor wanted. Hal Brognola had every federal agency in the nation working to try to learn who these people were and why they were in the United States. More importantly they would be looking for connections to other such groups.

ON HIS THIRD MORNING at Dreamland, Jack Grimaldi woke at 5:00 a.m. to the sound of someone knocking on the door of his BOQ room.

"Up and at 'em, Flying Jack," Pete Hoffsteader called out. "There's an airplane out there waiting for us."

Grimaldi went to unlock the door and found that the pilot had a large foam cup of coffee in his hand. "Hope you take it black, 'cause that's what I brought."

"Come on in," Grimaldi said, reaching for the coffee.

The pilot dropped into the easy chair to wait for Grimaldi to dress. "I just got word that we're due to get this show on the road for real tomorrow."

Grimaldi was surprised because he had been scheduled to put in five days at Dreamland.

"And," Hoffsteader continued, "that means that we have to do the familiarization flight today. I don't want to take a complete newbie on a Mach 3 cross-country hop without checking him out first."

"Suits me," Grimaldi said, grinning as he reached for his flight suit. "I'm ready for it."

"I think you're ready for it, too, or I wouldn't be doing this." Hoffsteader's voice was serious. "It's one thing to fly a Blackbird in the VR simulator, but it's entirely another to strap yourself into the real deal. Some guys work out real well in the simulator but can't handle the actual aircraft. I know that you've got a lot of stick-and-rudder time, but believe me, a Blackbird isn't like anything you've ever flown in."

"Well," Grimaldi said, standing, "let's go see if I have the right stuff, as they say."

CHAPTER THIRTEEN

For a man who hated the West as much as Major Karim Nazar did, the Iranian had to admit that the CNN television network was a gift from God. Only a merciful God could turn an instrument of capitalistic greed and imperialistic oppression like CNN into a gift for his people. Because of CNN, Nazar was informed about the destruction of the Islamic action groups in California as soon as anyone else in the world.

He had no way of knowing what had gone wrong, but for so many of the freedom fighters to have been killed to quickly, it had to have been a total security breakdown. Beyond the bare facts, the CNN reports weren't giving him any information he could use, and they claimed that the police were baffled by the deaths, as well.

Nazar seriously doubted that. He knew that what passed for a society in the United States was chaotic and violent; one didn't have to watch CNN to realize that. But street violence couldn't account for what had happened to the groups, because they had been well armed. Also for three of the cells to have been hit on the same night ruled out an unfortunate coincidence.

He was convinced that the police knew exactly what had happened to the Islamic action groups and had probably been involved in the attacks, as well. The freedom fighters had been Muslims, and as everyone knew, Muslims were being hunted down in the cities of America. The real question was how much the police would be able to learn about the group's orders and objectives. He counted on the martyrs to hold to their code of silence if they were captured. But he also knew what could be gotten from a man under interrogation, so he had to move quickly if he wanted to put his diversionary plan back on track.

Even though the groups in California had been wiped out, they weren't the only martyrs ready to give their lives for the revolution. Nazar would immediately request that the council activate Islamic action groups in other parts of the United States and send them to their targets. He had wanted the California cells to go into action first because every American paid attention to what went on in California.

The security council had approved his first request quickly enough, and he was confident that they would do the same this time. He knew, however, that two of the older mullahs who sat on the council always urged caution when it came to taking action against the Great Satan. Since the first action groups had failed, he would have to argue strongly to get more of them activated.

The main obstacle he would have to overcome would be to convince the council to do what he asked without telling them why it was so necessary. Kessler's enhanced-warhead project was known to only a select few, and many of the council didn't know of its existence. He would have to depend on those who did know to persuade the others.

WITH THE BLACKBIRD'S deployment moved up a day, Phoenix Force had to move out a day early, as well. That was more than okay with T. J. Hawkins; he was ready to get the show on the road. For the past couple of days, all he had done was check over the mission equipment, then go over it again. Being thorough was one thing; busywork was something else. He had been in the Army long enough to know the difference.

He had also spent a little extra time with the Farm's armorer choosing the hardware he would take on the mission. While most members of the team had armed themselves with Heckler & Koch assault rifles, he had chosen to take an M-203 over-and-under M-16 assault rifle and 40 mm grenade launcher combo as his main piece. He had used it in the Army and knew it well.

Hawkins had been glad to find that Kissinger had had one of the earlier M-16s in stock. It featured the old-style full-auto/semiauto selector switch instead of the new 3-round-burst selector. He was a good enough shot that he didn't need the idiot switch on his rifle that sent three rounds downrange when one well-aimed shot would do.

Plus, as with a Ranger recon team, Phoenix Force moved out with only what they could carry on their backs. Calling for an ammo resupply in the middle of a firefight wasn't bloody likely, as McCarter was fond of saying.

While Hawkins felt that he was being accepted by most of the Phoenix Force commandos, he still didn't know where he stood with the team leader. He liked McCarter but he felt that the Briton was holding back around him. He didn't know if that reserve was the usual routine of not wanting to know the new guy too well until you saw if he was going to stay around, or whether it was just because McCarter was British and naturally reserved.

He suspected that it was the former rather than the later, though. He would have to earn his spurs with McCarter, but that didn't bother him. Like any good fighting man, he was confident that he could handle himself no matter what.

HAWKINS FELT right at home when he stepped off the Blackhawk chopper Brognola had provided to transport Phoenix Force and felt the humid heat hit him in the face. They had landed at Fort Stewart, Georgia, home to the 24th Infantry Division, as well as a

Ranger battalion, and he had staged out of there several times during his Army career.

Even though the post was so familiar, he felt a little strange knowing that he was no longer a part of the Big Green Machine and didn't really have a home there anymore. Leaving the Army had been a major change in his life and he was still adjusting to it. The Army had always been his home. Even after the death of his father, his mother had moved the family to a neighborhood right outside Fort Hood, Texas, so it had been almost like living on post.

Waiting on the chopper pad to meet Phoenix Force was an infantry captain and a squad of armed infantrymen arrayed in full battle dress. "If you'll follow me, gentlemen," he said, "I have orders to escort you to your plane."

"What's with the guns?" McCarter nodded toward the grunts.

"Beats the hell out of me, sir," the officer replied. "All I know is that I was told to have them on hand, so here they are."

The camouflaged C-5A Galaxy transport they were taken to was parked away from other aircraft, with a pair of gun jeeps and another infantry squad securing it. The Stony Man team immediately boarded and discovered that they were sharing the ride with several uniformed Air Force personnel. Most of them were wearing Habu patches on their flight line jackets, so they had to be the Blackbird's ground crew.

No sooner had they stowed their bags when a male airman flight attendant came into the cabin and told them to buckle their seat belts for takeoff.

"I usually like my flight attendants to have better legs," James commented as he buckled up.

"The ones I date don't shave every morning, either," Manning quipped.

THE GALAXY TRANSPORT carrying Phoenix Force turned onto the downwind leg of the landing pattern at Ufazek, Russia, her multiple-wheel landing gear locked down and her massive flaps fully extended. In the passenger deck of the massive cargo plane, Hawkins sat turned in his seat with his face pressed against the window as the C-5A touched down. He hated to gawk, but he had never seen Russia before.

As soon as the huge aircraft came to a stop, a Russian GAZ jeep with a large, hand-lettered sign on the back saying Follow Me in English, pulled out onto the tarmac in front of it. The pilot pulled in behind the GAZ and followed the vehicle to a parking spot in front of a large hangar. As soon as the pilot shut down the turbines, the crew chief opened the forward door and Bolan and Katzenelenbogen climbed down the ladder.

A Russian officer wearing the shoulder boards of an air force colonel stepped up to Bolan. "I am Colonel Viktor Popov," he said in English as his hand snapped up to a salute. "Welcome to Ufazek air base."

"I'm Colonel Rance Pollock," Bolan said, returning the Russian's salute. "We're glad to be here."

Katz stuck out his left hand and greeted the colonel in his own language. "I'm Amir Goldstein and I'll be the liaison officer for our people."

"Ah," the colonel said, smiling. "I'm glad that at least one of you speaks Russian. That will help make sure that nothing goes wrong."

When McCarter stepped down from the C-5A, he looked at his surroundings. Ufazek air base was situated in the middle of nothing—really nothing. These were the famous Russian steppes, a flat plain that stretched as far as the eye could see in any direction.

He turned back to the rest of the team. "I've seen some empty spaces before, but I don't think that I've ever seen any place quite this desolate."

Hawkins also took a long look around. "Back home this is what we'd call miles and miles of miles and miles. The plains of north Texas are positively crowded compared to this."

"I wonder what these guys do to keep from going completely bat shit around here?" James mused. "It's not like they can go to town after work for a couple of cold ones."

"Who says they do?" Hawkins countered as he watched the Russian ground crew approach the C-5A. "Those guys don't look too tightly wrapped to me."

McCarter looked over and smiled. "Don't worry about them. They're just your usual Ivan air force types. Sartorial splendor isn't one of their strong suits."

Hawkins grinned at the Briton's pun. "On top of that, they look like they're going to a hog cuttin'."

Now it was McCarter's turn to have a blank look on his face. The only time he cut a pig was when he had a piece of it on his plate. If this new man didn't start speaking the queen's English, he was going to have to hire an interpreter.

"Let's start getting this gear off-loaded so we can set up our operation."

WHILE PHOENIX FORCE set up its operations center, the second and third C-5As carrying the Air Force support team and the equipment needed to feed and care for the Blackbird landed at the Russian base. The last aircraft to touch down was a KC-135Q aerial tanker with a full load of JP-7 Blackbird fuel on board. She would off-load that fuel into the collapsible bladders the Air Force ground crew had brought along and go back for another load just in case.

The Air Force ground-support crew knew its business and quickly set up its equipment in the empty hangar. Phoenix Force did what it could, mostly heavy lifting, and the work went quickly. Within two hours they were operational.

"We're ready to receive the Blackbird," Katzenelenbogen told Bolan. "The air-traffic-control people are set up, and we've shown the Russians how to find it with their radar."

"Send it to the Farm."

CHAPTER FOURTEEN

Jack Grimaldi didn't need Pete Hoffsteader to wake him with carryout coffee this morning. He was out of bed before the alarm went off. There was no way he was going to be late for a day like this. In just a few hours he would be halfway around the world hurtling through the sky at almost three thousand miles per hour.

He had just finished dressing when the Blackbird pilot showed up at his door. "I see you got a head start on the day this time."

"Can't be late for this."

"Since you're ready, let's do it."

Grimaldi wasn't surprised to find that their first stop was the pilot's mess hall. Regardless of the mythology, hot-rock airplane drivers had to eat, too. Going into a low-blood-sugar attack at Mach 3 was a great way to ruin your day, to say nothing of messing up a billion-dollar airplane.

After a high-calorie, low-bulk breakfast washed down with orange juice and coffee, the two men went to get suited up. Even though the SR had pressurized cockpits, they still had to wear the special full-pressure flight suits. Once he was suited up, Grimaldi went on a walk-around oxygen pack to purge the nitrogen from his bloodstream. At eighty thousand feet, nitrogen turned into a gas and formed fatal bubbles in the blood. Breathing pure oxygen for an hour before a flight got rid of it.

When Grimaldi followed Hoffsteader out to the waiting SR-71, he wasn't only wearing the pressure suit and helmet, but he was also carrying a portable air conditioner to keep the suit cool until he was plugged into the aircraft's system.

He felt his heart speed up when he saw the Blackbird. This was it. In a little over an hour after takeoff, he would have crossed the United States and would be over the Atlantic en route to a remote airfield in the middle of Russia. He had flown some wild missions before, but nothing had ever topped this.

The ground-support crew was all over the SR, seeing to the last-minute details that went with the launching of this aircraft. Only the space shuttle required this kind of treatment. A single loose connection, a leaky hydraulic line or some other small fault that could be overlooked on another aircraft couldn't be allowed here.

Grimaldi climbed the access ladder into the rear cockpit and strapped himself in. As soon as he connected his pressure suit to the aircraft's internal air conditioner, he handed the walk-around unit to the ground crewman assisting him.

In the front cockpit Hoffsteader went through his prestart checklist and got ready to fire up the twin J-58 engines. The yellow start cart was already hooked up to the portside jet engine. As with everything else on the SR, it wasn't a turn-the-switch-and-light-the-fire kind of airplane. The two converted Buick high-output V-8 automobile engines in the back of the start cart were howling at full throttle as they brought the turbine blades up to speed for the engine start.

When the compressor blades were spinning fast enough, the fuel feeds were turned on, and the on-board start pump squirted a chemical igniter into the burner cans. The mighty J-58 lit off with a roar and the smell of burning kerosene. As soon as the number-one engine was running, the start cart spun up the number two and it was lit off. When both engines were running smoothly, Hoffsteader lowered the two canopies and locked them in place.

After going through another short poststart-pretaxi checklist, he called back to Grimaldi on the intercom. "You ready back there?"

"Do it, flyboy," Grimaldi replied.

The roar of the mighty J-58s rose to a screaming thunder as Hoffsteader advanced the throttles. "Countdown for takeoff," he called out as the SR started to roll.

AFTER A THUNDERING takeoff, Hoffsteader turned the nose of the sleek black spy plane to the east and stayed subsonic as he climbed to twenty-five thousand feet. There, hanging in the sky in front of them, was a Boeing KC-135Q aerial tanker with her boom extended. The early refueling would ensure that the Blackbird had her tanks completely full before starting her Mach 3 trip across the United States.

The KC-135Q was a special version of the old KC aerial tanker that had been in service with SAC for decades. While the rest of the Air Force had converted to using the newer McDonnell KC-10 tanker, the Blackbirds still needed the old Q Ships, as they were called, because they had the special tanking on board to carry the JP-7 fuel the SRs burned. It also had the special hookup boom needed to refuel them. The KC pilot had the four engines of his old bird cranked up all the way to fly as fast as he could with the fuel load he was carrying. Hoffsteader had the SR's twin J-58s throttled almost all the way back to fly at that slow speed.

The hookup to the refueling boom went without a hitch, and the KC tanker started to transfer JP-7 fuel to the Blackbird. As the fuel was transferred, the KC grew lighter and the pilot had to ease his throttles back to keep the tanker flying at a steady speed. Since it was a "cold" refueling, it went quickly. As soon as the boom was disconnected and retracted, the KC pilot banked out of the way so Hoffsteader could turn up the wick.

Smoothly advancing his throttles, the pilot let the massive J-58 engines come up to maximum RPM before punching in the afterburners. Grimaldi found himself being pressed into the back of his seat as the acceleration built and Hoffsteader pointed the spy plane's sharp nose into the sky.

Once the SR was at eighty thousand feet and clipping along at a little better than Mach 3, Hoffsteader came out of afterburner and backed off the throttles. At that speed and altitude, more than half of the engine's thrust came from the ramjet effect, and the resultant fuel savings gave the aircraft its great range.

Even though Hoffsteader was doing the piloting, Grimaldi was busy in the backseat doing what Blackbird SROs called running the black line. Even a minor error in navigation for just a few seconds would put them several hundred miles off course. The navigation map in the backseat showed their calculated flight path as a black line, and it had to be followed precisely.

Once the flight path was set, Hoffsteader called back, "The speed record from L.A. to London is three hours and forty-seven minutes, wheels up to wheels down. We won't be breaking that record this time because we're going to take it easy flying across the pond."

Grimaldi glanced to his instruments and saw that the SR was cruising at a steady Mach 2.9. That was taking it easy for a Blackbird.

When they passed through the terminator separating night from day on the earth below, Hoffsteader told Grimaldi to look up out of his small side windows. At eighty thousand feet, the stars were brighter than he had ever seen them before against a deep indigo sky. This was as close as he was ever going to get to space, and it was magnificent.

The eight-hundred-plus-degree orange-red glow of the wing's leading edge at Mach 3 made a nice contrast to the deep blue of space.

THE ARRIVAL of the SR-71 at Ufazek air base was carried out in great secrecy. After a second in-flight refueling over Germany, the Blackbird had made a Mach 3 dash over Central and Eastern Europe before slowing to a little over Mach 2 for the final leg over Russia during the night.

The Air Force sergeant who was acting as the Blackbird's air-traffic controller was on the radio in the Russian control tower when the SR was picked up on radar while it was still two hundred miles away. "Niner Seven One," he said, "this is Ufazek Control. I have you at forty-six thousand on a course of zero niner four. Turn to zero niner eight and begin your descent. The runway lights are on, and you will be landing from west to east.''

"Niner Seven One, roger," Hoffsteader sent back. "I'm beginning my descent now."

As with everything else about the SR-71, a landing was profiled and had to be flown by the numbers. Since the fuel was used to cool the engines at Mach 3 flight, if he descended too quickly, there wouldn't be enough cooling effect to keep the engine from seizing. If he came down too slowly, he risked running out of fuel.

"Ufazek Control, this is Niner Seven One," Hoffsteader transmitted when he was subsonic and down to twelve thousand feet. "I have visual on your runway."

"Niner Seven One, roger. You are clear to land."

Though the night was clear, the SR couldn't be seen until its sleek black shape was almost ready to touch down. Nose high, Hoffsteader put his main gear on the tarmac within a hundred feet of the end of the runway and rotated his nose wheel down immediately. The landing-gear brakes on the SR were marginal at best, and as soon as the nose gear touched the runway, the pilot popped the drag chute in the tail compartment to slow the plane.

When he finished his rollout, a Russian tractor with the special SR nose-gear towing device was on hand to hook up to the spy plane and get it out of sight inside the hangar as soon as possible.

INSIDE THE HANGAR Bolan and Katz were waiting as the canopies of the Blackbird opened and the ground crew wheeled up the access ladder.

"That's the only way to fly, man." Grimaldi was beaming as he stepped down from the rear cockpit. "A little over seven hours from Nevada to the middle of Russia."

"This is Major Pete Hoffsteader," Grimaldi said, making the introductions when the pilot joined him. "He's my chauffeur for this trip.

"Peter, this is Colonel Rance Pollock. He's in charge of the overall operation."

Since he was inside a building, Hoffsteader didn't salute. "Nice to meet you, Colonel," he said as he shook hands.

When Katz stepped up with his left hand out, Grimaldi said, "Amir Goldstein will coordinate everything we need with our hosts here. He speaks the language."

"Pleased to meet you, sir," Hoffsteader said.

"Just call me Amir."

"Gentlemen," Grimaldi said, "if you will excuse us, we need to find the latrine. It was a long flight."

WHILE THE BLACKBIRD was being serviced and readied for the mission, Pete Hoffsteader and Jack Grimaldi were the guests of honor at a special briefing being held solely for their benefit. Even though Iran was considered a Third World nation, petrodollars had provided it with a first-rate air force, and most of its aircraft were Russian made.

"I am air force Major Valeri Alikov," the Russian briefing officer said. "Several years ago I was a MiG-25 pilot—a Foxbat, as you call it. Now, I will tell you everything you need to know so you will not be afraid of the MiGs the Iranians are flying."

The Russian held up a large-scale model of a wicked-looking, twin-engine jet fighter. "What you are facing is called by us MiG-25PD. You call it the Foxbat E. This is an old aircraft to us now, and I am glad that it is gone. It was a pig to fly. It has no range. If you fly it too fast, the engines will explode. It does not have a weapons-systems officer on board, so the pilot has to fly and shoot at the same time. Worst of all, it cannot dogfight, as I think you say, with other fighters. In short, it is a big pig, but it carries missiles and they are not pigs."

The Russian pilot paused for a moment. "I also want to tell you that I think the idiot who sold those MiGs to the Iranians is also a big pig. Only a complete fool would ever let an airplane like that get into the hands of religious fanatics."

Hoffsteader and Grimaldi both grinned. It was nice to see a Russian who had a rational view of the world outside of Russia. If there had been more of them twenty years earlier, the world would be a safer place today. But with Russian weapons having been sold all over the world to anyone with enough money to buy them, it was difficult to get into a fight nowadays and not find some of them in the hands of the bad guys.

"The Iranian Foxbats," the Russian continued, "are powered by two Tumansky R-31-300 with over fourteen thousand kilos thrust. They can reach sixty-five thousand feet altitude and fly at Mach 2.8 for short times. At the altitude you will be flying your Blackbird, the MiGs will not be able to reach you. But since they can fly almost as fast, what I think they will try to do is to get in front of you and then shoot their missiles up at you.

"The missiles we sold with the MiGs are what we call R-23. NATO knows them as the AA-7 Apex. They have Mach 3.5 speed and a range of fifty kilometers. Their warhead is only twenty-five kilos, but that is enough if it hits you. They are semiactive radar guided, and the MiGs have look-down-shoot-down radar, as you call it."

He paused for a moment. "I do not know what kind of ECM protection your aircraft has against missiles like this. But if there is anything you can do to break the lock from the Foxbat's radar, the missiles will go off course. Your best thing will be to stay high, fly as fast as you can and try to stay away from them."

He smiled at the American aviators. "Do you have any questions?"

Both Hoffsteader and Grimaldi had minor questions about the flight characteristics of the Foxbat, which the Russian answered. When the briefing was over, he stepped up to each man, saluted, shook their hands and wished them luck. That was the least he could do.

CHAPTER FIFTEEN

"They have finished servicing the Blackbird," Aaron Kurtzman announced when Hal Brognola and Barbara Price walked into the Computer Room. "She's ready to launch whenever you give them the word."

One of the traditions about the Blackbird was that the missions were always called launches, as if they were spacecraft not airplanes. But considering that they flew higher than anything except the X-15 rocket plane and the space shuttle, it was appropriate.

"I have the final go-ahead from the President," Brognola said. "So tell them that they are free to go as soon as they have a window."

Kurtzman immediately called up the classified Keyhole-orbit schedule to see when the spy satellites were due to pass over Shabaz, Iran. Accessing the computers in the super secret NRO in Washington was no mean feat, but Kurtzman routinely broke their security codes as an exercise. Brognola had learned that complaining about him doing it and offering him the access codes openly didn't make any difference. He got off on breaking computer-security systems.

"The earliest good launch time is tomorrow morning," he said after studying the lists. "That will put their run over the target exactly in between the next two Keyhole pass-overs. If the Iranians are going to be doing anything down there that can be spotted from the air, they'll be doing it when they think the recon birds aren't watching."

Brognola looked up at the bank of clocks on the wall that showed the world's time zones. "And that's going to be after midnight here."

"I have to fly back to Washington," he said, glancing at his watch. "There's a National Security Council meeting on the terrorist attacks I need to sit in on. But I'll be back down here when they fly the mission. If they come up with anything, I want to be able to call the President about it immediately."

"If they do spot anything," Kurtzman said, "I'll have it here almost instantly. The real-time link with the retrans satellite is on-line. They've been sending me test patterns all day, and everything is working fine."

"If it continues working," Brognola said, "it'll be the only thing about this damned mission that has."

Price didn't know what was eating him. For a mission this complicated, she thought that it had gone rather well so far. If it kept up this way, they should be able to get the data and have everything wrapped up within twenty-four hours. What happened after that would be up to the White House.

Until then, though, she could switch operational gears and get an update from Carl Lyons. After finishing up in Oakland, the men of Able Team had relocated to south Florida and were working on the lead that there were other Islamic action groups in the area ready to go.

Going on what Tariq Al-Hauk had said about overhearing his leader talk to a man in Florida, they had obtained a list of the long-distance phone numbers that had been called from the target locations they had hit in Oakland. It would take a couple of days for them to run all the numbers down, but Price was confident that they would turn up something useful. They always did.

AT THAT PARTICULAR moment, Carl Lyons didn't share Barbara Price's confidence. They had just checked out the seventh phone number on their list and had found it to be another third-rate motel in Little Havana in the heart of Miami. Since they were in the Spanish speaking part of town, Rosario Blancanales was handling the inquiries. But he wasn't having any luck, either.

He shook his head when he got back to their car. "Same story," he said. "Three guys, probably Arabs, rented the room for a week, then left without leaving a forwarding address. The descriptions could be those of almost anyone in the Middle East. No distinguishing characteristics at all, except that one of them had green eyes.''

''Damn,'' Lyons growled. ''How many more numbers are on that list?''

''We have nine left,'' Schwarz said. ''And then we're back to square one.''

''Square zero, you mean. If you haven't noticed, this is a big town.''

''Maybe we can put an ad in the paper,'' Schwarz suggested. ''You know—'will the people who talked to the terrorists in Oakland, California, please call this number for an update on their condition.' That sort of thing.''

The look Lyons gave him would have peeled paint off a battleship, but Schwarz ignored it. Sometimes Ironman took life too seriously.

''Where's the next place?''

''About three or four blocks north.''

WITH KURTZMAN concentrating on the Ufazek mission, Lyons talked to Hunt Wethers when he reported in with the results of their canvass. ''It was a complete bust,'' he stated. ''Every number was a motel, and the occupants were long gone. It looks like they were changing motels every week as a precaution. It seems we're out of luck unless you have developed something new.''

"Give me the addresses of those phone numbers you ran down," Wethers ordered as he called up a map of the greater Miami area.

As he entered the addresses, their locations started popping up on the map as red diamonds. By the time he was done, the diamonds made a rough circle some two and a half miles in diameter. "If you haven't noticed," Wethers said, "your numbers are all in the same neighborhood."

"Yeah, Little Havana."

"Yes, but on, the map they're in a circle as if the suspects didn't want to be far away from someone or someplace. If you can find that person, place or thing, you may be able to pick up on them."

There was silence on the other end as Lyons checked out his own map.

"Can you run the phone directory from your end for me and cross-reference it to the map?" Lyons asked.

"What do you want?"

"Anyone or anything you can find in that area with an Arabic name or a connection with the Middle East—residences, business, restaurants, bakeries, mosques—give me the entire list."

"Can do. I'll fax it to you as soon as I'm done."

THE LIST WETHERS FAXED an hour later was long. Miami was always thought of as being a major center of Hispanic population, but the city had also attracted a large Middle Eastern population, as well. Something about the climate appealed to them.

Many of the locations on the list were shown as private residences. Most of the businesses were restaurants, mom-and-pop grocery stores or small neighborhood bakeries. There was one mosque, listed as having a Sunni rather than a Shiite congregation, that would have to be checked out. Just because they were Sunni didn't mean that they were automatically innocent.

The only large business in the target area was listed as a nursery and garden-supply outlet, the Garden of Eden.

"Are we going to hit the mosque first?" Blancanales asked.

Schwarz answered while Lyons was still thinking. "No. We do this Garden of Eden place first."

"Why's that?"

"The terrorist bombs used in both the Trade Center and Oklahoma bombings were ammonium nitrate and diesel. Since ammonium nitrate is a commercial fertilizer, why not check a place that should have it in stock all the time?"

A slow smile grew on Lyons's face. "I knew there was a reason I kept you around, Gadgets. Occasionally you come up with a good idea instead of being a pain in the ass. Let's take a drive by and look at this place.''

THE GARDEN OF EDEN nursery and garden supply looked like a typical establishment of the genre. The long, low building had the usual plants in pots out front, interspersed with concrete lawn decorations. Flamingos seemed to be very popular. A cyclone fence with rolled razor wire on top surrounded the enclosure behind the building, which held nursery stock from palm trees to potted plants.

"That's a nice fence they have," Schwarz commented as they drove past with the flow of traffic.

"Down here," Blancanales explained, "cyclone fencing is considered the height of fashion. If you have something and you want to keep it, you put a fence around it. If you really want to keep it, you do a cyclone fence with barbed wire on top."

"Let's go buy a plant," Lyons said.

"Not the three of us," Blancanales replied. "Just Gadgets and I. You go get a cup of coffee somewhere, and we'll pick you up later."

"What's the matter," Lyons snapped, "you think I look like a cop?"

Blancanales shrugged. "You said it, not me."

There was a Burger King restaurant on the corner of the other side of the street, and Schwarz pulled their rented Pontiac into the parking lot. "Why don't you have a burger or something while you wait? We won't be long."

Lyons opened the door and stepped out without a word.

"Touchy, isn't he?" Schwarz said as he backed out of the lot.

No salesman rushed out to greet them when Schwarz and Blancanales pulled into the almost-empty parking lot in front of the Garden of Eden. "Let me handle this," Schwarz said as he stepped out of the car. "I know my plants pretty well."

"Better than you know fashion, I hope."

They walked past the main building and into the forest of nursery stock before they saw anyone on the grounds. At the back of the lot was a large storage building with two vans parked in front of it. Men were off-loading sacks from the vans and stacking them in the building.

They were heading for a closer look when a man dressed in work clothes stepped out from behind a row of azaleas and blocked their route. "Can I help you?" he asked in accented English.

"You certainly can," Schwarz said. "I'm looking for some succulents for my new apartment. Or maybe a bonsai."

He turned to Blancanales. "What do you think, Ramone? Do you like succulents or bonsai best?"

Before Blancanales could answer, Schwarz had turned back to the gardener. "He lives there, too, you know, and I think that it's very important to start a relationship with the right kind of plants. You can't believe the fights I've had with some of my room-mates over—"

"They are inside," the gardener said, pointing to the main buildings.

The men off-loading the vans had stopped and were watching the confrontation with more than a casual interest.

"You have the bonsais in there?" Schwarz laughed. "Oh, you must have thought that I wanted a baby bonsai, something to put on a nightstand. On no—" he shook his head "—I'm looking for something larger. You know, something big enough to make a statement in a bedroom."

"All of the bonsai are in the building," the gardener insisted.

"Well, you obviously can't help me, can you? Come, Ramone, we're going."

"I really do wish you'd ditch the gay act when you're around me, Gadgets," Blancanales said when they got back into the car. "I don't like the way people look at me when you're doing that."

Schwarz shrugged. "It works. That guy had no idea that I was counting the security lights in the rear of their compound while I was talking to him."

"Did you catch the motion detectors?"

"Sure did, and I was close enough to see that they're plug-ins not hard-wired."

CHAPTER SIXTEEN

Every Russian airman on the base was on hand to watch the SR-71 take off early the next morning. After a final check of all of the spy plane's systems, Pete Hoffsteader and Jack Grimaldi walked out of the hangar in their pressure suits. The Russians went wild when they spotted them, cheering, stamping their feet and clapping their hands. Both men took theatrical bows, which drew even more thundering applause.

Fifteen minutes later, when Hoffsteader fired up his twin J-58 engines and they ignited with a whoosh, the Russians applauded wildly again.

Phoenix Force was also interested in seeing the legendary aircraft fly.

"These guys are easily amused," Hawkins said as he watched the Russians.

"You'd be, too, if you were stationed here," Gary Manning explained. "Plus, since they don't have Disneyland or Steven Spielberg films, they don't get to see too much of this sort of high-tech stuff."

"Someone ought to build these guys a theme park."

David McCarter overheard the comment and laughed. "They used to have one called Lenin Land, but it went broke."

"As soon as they have any money worth taking," Manning said, "somebody will give them what they want. What's that about the customer always being right?"

"I think the one about a sucker being born every minute is probably more on the mark."

Once the massive J-58 turbojets were up to operating temperature, Hoffsteader released the brakes and advanced his throttles all the way. A few yards down the runway, he lit off the afterburners, and the Blackbird leaped forward with long tongues of flame shooting out of the exhausts. The SR raced down the runway, her exhausts roaring as she rapidly picked up speed. A fresh cheer broke out when her nose gear rotated and she lifted off a second later.

In a few short minutes the Blackbird wasn't even a speck in the clear blue sky. It had vanished as if it had never been there, and the Russians reluctantly left their viewing places to return to the dull routine of their work.

The Americans went to Katzenelenbogen's ops center in the hangar to monitor the radios with him. They knew that their fate was tied into what the Blackbird picked up on her high-speed pass over eastern Iran, and they wanted to be the first to know what was going on down there.

In the backseat of the SR, Grimaldi quickly established communications with the ops center back at the air base. ''Ufazek Ops, this is Niner Seven One,'' he transmitted. ''How do you hear me? Over.''

''Niner Seven One, this is Ufazek Ops,'' Katz answered. ''We hear you Lima Charlie. Over.''

''This is Seven One, I have you the same. Out.''

Next he radioed to the Russian Il-76 Mainstay AWACS plane that had been sent ahead and was orbiting on station at thirty-two thousand feet. From there, the Mainstay could cover the Blackbird with her radars while she made her run over the target area and could give Hoffsteader and Grimaldi early warning if the Iranians decided to send up their interceptors to challenge them.

''Mother Hen, this is Niner Seven One. ''How do you hear me? Over.''

''This is Mother Hen,'' the Russian accented voice replied. ''I hear you good and we are tracking you. The sky is clear. I say again, the sky is clear.''

''This is Seven One,'' Grimaldi transmitted. ''Roger clear skies. Out.''

Lastly Grimaldi established the real-time data link from the SR's cameras and sensors to the retrans satellite overhead, which would send the information they picked up directly to Stony Man Farm. If everything worked as well as advertised, the photos and sensor readouts would be in Kurtzman's Computer Room within seconds of their being taken. If the NRO recon-interpretation team that had been tasked to analyze the information was as good as it was supposed to be, the analysis would be done before the Blackbird even got back to her home away from home.

When the data link was established, he clicked in the intercom circuit to Hoffsteader in the front cockpit. "We're all go back here," he said. "I have everyone on the line, and they're all waiting for the goodies."

"Roger," Hoffsteader called back. "We'll be starting the turn in ten minutes and will be coming up on Mach 3 as soon as we straighten out."

To limit their exposure over unfriendly airspace, the SR's flight profile was planned to take her south over Turkmenistan, do a sweeping right-hand 180-degree turn and come back over the target site heading north. That way, when the Blackbird entered Iranian airspace, she would be flying at Mach 3 on the edge of Iranian airspace, hopefully out of range of any interception.

As soon as the turn was completed and the SR was aimed like an arrow at Shabaz, Grimaldi went through his checklists.

"I've got a glitch back here," Grimaldi reported. "As soon as I turned on the sensors, I got red lights showing on the SRO panel."

"Shit!" Hoffsteader muttered. "I've got them, too. Try the reset button."

Grimaldi reached out and hit the switch. "No joy. The light's still on."

"Try to recycle the system. Hit the reboot switch."

He tried that, but with no luck. "It's not working, either."

"Okay," the pilot said. "I'm going to have to abort. Notify Ufazek."

"Roger."

Hoffsteader was grim faced as he punched the coordinates of their planned escape route into the navigation computer. With the sensors out, there was no use in completing the mission. Their exit route would still take them over part of Iran, but it would limit their exposure time to enemy action.

"THEY'RE ABORTING the flight," Aaron Kurtzman said, passing the word to Barbara Price and Hal Brognola. "The sensors aren't transmitting the data. Hoffsteader has aborted, and they're returning to Ufazek."

"What the hell is wrong with those people?" Brognola snapped. "I thought that plane had been gone over with a fine-tooth comb before they took off."

"Malfunctions happen," Kurtzman answered, since the members of the Blackbird's crew weren't there to defend themselves.

Brognola knew that malfunctions happened, and the more complicated the system, the more things there were that could go wrong. Nonetheless, he also knew that this could throw the whole program out the window. All it would take would be for the Iranians to get wind of the Blackbird, and they would duck under cover until it went away.

Plus, if word got out on Capitol Hill that a manned American spy plane had been sent on a mission without prior congressional approval, it would probably cost the President his job. The cold war congressional edict against aerial spying without prior approval when not at war could be invoked, and a political storm would follow.

"When's the next launch window?" Brognola asked.

Kurtzman's fingers skipped across the keyboard. "Keyhole Five's due to make a pass late tomorrow. So—" he paused and called up another menu "—that puts it off until Thursday at the earliest. But we don't know what caused the abort. I wouldn't waste time planning another flight until we know what went wrong with this one."

''The President's not going to like this,'' Brognola growled, knowing that most of that presidential disapproval was going to be directed at him.

''What's not to like?'' Kurtzman replied. ''Let's get real here. They have only the one plane, and they're trying to service it out of a Russian air base with a shoestring ground crew with limited equipment and supplies. If the President had wanted a full-scale effort, he would have called out the whole damned Air Force. This is supposed to be a covert operation, Hal, and covert operations run into these little glitches every now and then.''

Brognola knew that Kurtzman was right on the money, but he hated to be reminded of the fact. ''He still isn't going to like it.''

''Tell him that we can pull the plug and bring everyone home anytime he wants.''

''Dammit, Aaron, I know that and so does he. All I'm saying is that he's going to be disappointed. That's all. I know that they're doing the best they can under the circumstances.''

''If the President has any doubts about that,'' Kurtzman said, his hackles up, ''I'll be glad to talk to him.''

Brognola didn't respond to that. When the Bear had his claws out, it was best to leave him alone. With his hand fishing into his pocket for his roll of antacid pills, he left the room.

"You'd better lighten up on Hal, Aaron," Price advised as soon as Brognola had left the room. "You know that he gets this way when things don't work the way they were planned, but he doesn't mean anything by it. It's just his way of letting off steam."

"It's not helping the situation any, though," Kurtzman insisted. "The ground crew has to find out what went wrong, and I need him standing by to okay a courier in case they need a repair part or something expedited to them."

"He'll be ready," she reassured him.

Major Karim Nazar was furious, and he didn't care who knew about it. He particularly didn't care that the air force colonel standing in front of his desk in the Shabaz Facility looked as if he was just about to urinate in his pants.

Nazar didn't much like any man who wasn't in the Internal Security Force, and that went double for Iranian air force officers. All of them had been tainted by the West and carried the stink of heresy. For years they had been trained by Western air forces, especially by the Americans, and they had been contaminated by the unclean contacts.

During the first few glorious years of the Islamic revolution, the ayatollah, blessed be his memory, had purged the Iranian armed forces of unclean elements, and that meant that most of the air force officers had died. But when it was realized that without enough pilots the air force couldn't guard the skies over the motherland, the purge had been reluctantly ended. That didn't mean that the surviving air force pilots had been somehow cleansed of their contamination. They were still suspect.

As far as Nazar was concerned, the purging of the air force ranks hadn't gone far enough, not when things like this were allowed to happen. An American spy plane had flown over Iran unchallenged by the air force this time, and that wouldn't be tolerated.

Colonel Ahmed Mizra's lame excuse that this intruder had been a special airplane that could fly too high and too fast to be intercepted didn't sit well with Nazar. He knew that the MiG-25 fighters of the Iranian air force were the world's fastest interceptors and that their missiles could shoot down anything with wings.

''I could easily have you put to death for this blunder, Colonel,'' Nazar said with no more emotion than he would have displayed while ordering lunch. ''Tehran is not happy that the spy plane was allowed to escape. Since you are in command of the air force base that is responsible for the defense of this area, it is your responsibility to ensure the safety of the state. To do anything less is treason.''

The colonel blanched. No ISF officer was to be taken lightly. But this man, the Devil's henchman, as he was called only behind his back, was a real threat. Not only did he kill the enemies of the state, but he eliminated their friends and families, as well. Colonel Mizra had a family he loved dearly, and the thought of his wife and children in the hands of this man was more than he could bear.

"If the Yankee spy plane comes back, Major," he said earnestly, "my pilots will shoot it down then. I can promise you that."

"If they do not," Nazar replied, "I can promise you that you will gaze on God's face by the end of the day. No one, and particularly not the minions of the Great Satan, can be allowed to fly unchallenged over our beloved country."

"I understand, Major. It will not happen again."

Nazar stared at the pilot for a long time. "Get out of my office."

The colonel saluted and quickly left.

As soon as the man was gone, Nazar picked up the phone and placed a call to ISF headquarters in Tehran. "This is Major Nazar at Shabaz," he told the duty officer on the other end of the line. "I want air force Colonel Ahmed Mizra's son picked up and held for questioning. I suspect him of treason."

There was more than one way to ensure that the state's security was guarded. The interrogation of Mizra's son would reveal treachery; the interrogations always did. The colonel would be notified of this, and it would ensure that he did everything in his power to see that no more aerial intruders escaped.

Next Nazar called the Iranian army major who was in command of the two companies of troops that were assigned as the site's security force and ordered him to report to his office. Though he had done nothing wrong, the infantry officer was wary when he reported to the major. So far, he had managed to keep Nazar satisfied, and he wanted it to stay that way.

"Yes, Major," he said as he saluted. Though they were both the same rank, army officers always saluted officers of the ISF.

"The Americans and the Russians have taken an interest in what we are doing here," Nazar began. "They are flying spy planes overhead, and our own air force has allowed it to happen. Because of that, I have to assume that their spy flight was successful, and we must be prepared for an attack. I do not think that they will send a large force, but they might try to make a commando raid on this facility.

"And," he said, his voice lowered, "if they do, it cannot be allowed to succeed. The future of our nation depends on the project, and it must not be hampered in any way."

The infantry officer stiffened. "My men are ready, Major," he said. "We are strong enough to beat back any commando attack they can send against us."

"Make sure they are informed of this threat," Nazar ordered. "And I want you to personally inspect them each night. Any man found sleeping at his post will be executed the next morning."

"As you command," the infantry officer replied. No other reply was possible.

CHAPTER SEVENTEEN

Hal Brognola wasn't the only one who was feeling the pressure of the failed Blackbird mission. The SR-71's crew chief, Air Force Senior Master Sergeant Joe Benihana, was acting like a man possessed. He had been in the Blackbird program since he had been an airman second class stationed at Okinawa during the Vietnam War. He probably knew the spy plane better than even the men who had engineered and built them, and whenever something went wrong with a Blackbird under his care, he took it as a personal affront. That went double when the problem had been caused by someone else.

"Those NASA bastards really screwed up this bird, sir," he reported to Yakov Katzenelenbogen less than an hour after the plane returned to Ufazek. "They fitted some nonstandard electronics in it that aren't Milspec, and they're causing a problem. I'm surprised that the damned thing didn't fall out of the sky on the way over here. If those half-trained tech weenies of theirs would get their heads out of their anal cavities once in a while and read the damned manuals, they would know that you can't just stuff any old airplane part into a Blackbird and—"

"Okay, chief," Katz said, interrupting the solid stream of invective before the man had a stroke. "Do you know what went wrong?"

"Damned right I do, sir. Those NASA bastards—"

"If I get you the parts, can you fix it?" Katz agreed with the crew chief about the NASA technicians, but this wasn't the time or the place to get into that. Right now he had to get that plane back into the air.

"Sure, sir, but I have to have Milspec stuff, not that damned civvie NASA junk."

"You get me a list of what you need, what you really need, to fix that plane, and I'll get it to you as fast as it can be flown there. Okay?"

"Fair enough, sir." The crew chief was starting to calm down a little. At least his face wasn't as flushed as it had been. "I'll have the list to you within the hour."

"There's a man who enjoys his work," Bolan remarked as the stocky Benihana stomped off to yell at his ground crew.

"Maybe a little too much."

"What do you think?"

Katz frowned. "I guess it's all up to Hal and Aaron now. If they can get us the parts to fix that plane, we can try it again. If it can't make the run, I have a nasty feeling that you and the guys will be taking a closer look at eastern Iran on foot.''

''We'll be doing that anyway,'' Bolan said. ''I think we can count on it.''

''I'm afraid you're right about that.''

Both men knew that even with the most advanced technology at their command, nothing worked as well as a man on the ground with a weapon in his hand. And in a nutshell that was what Phoenix Force was all about. All of the high-tech gadgets, and that included the Blackbird, existed only to support the men who laid their lives on the line and did the job.

When, and if, the day came that the job could be done by machines, they could all retire.

''THE MAINTENANCE CHIEF says that they lost a transmission module,'' Katz reported to Kurtzman over the scrambled satcom link to Stony Man Farm a little over an hour later.

''Can you replace it from your stock of spares?''

''No. It's part of the new NASA-installed satellite-link system. Since it's not original Milspec equipment, they didn't have any spares for it on hand before we left.''

''What's the part number?''

Katz read off the number. ''And,'' he added, ''we also need a couple more items while you're at the store. The chief says that when the module blew, it took out several other components with it.''

''I'll chase those parts down and get them to you as soon as I can,'' Kurtzman said after taking down the rest of the list.

''We'll be waiting.''

With the list in hand, it was child's play for Kurtzman to get into the DOD and NASA computers, rummage through the classified stock lists and locate the parts they needed to repair the plane. Once he had them located, he got on the phone and, using Stony Man's high-priority supply-requisition code, ordered them to be pulled from the shelves and flown to Andrews Air Force Base outside of Washington immediately.

Then he called up to Price. ''I've located the parts they need at Lockheed Palmdale and Edwards,'' he told her. ''They're being flown to Andrews on an F-15 Eagle right now, supersonic all the way. So I need you to get Hal on the horn and tell him that we need to have White House clearance for a fast jet courier from Andrews to Ufazek ASAP. If he hurries, they can have the parts by tomorrow.''

''Good work,'' Price said. ''I'll pass that on to him immediately.''

''And I'll let Katz know they're coming.''

With that problem taken care of, Price mentally shifted gears. "Is Lyons planning on hitting that Miami nursery site tonight?"

"Just a recon, he said," Kurtzman replied. "He wants to see what's in the warehouse on the back lot."

"Let me know as soon as they have something."

"Will do."

HERMANN SCHWARZ SLIPPED along the cyclone fence surrounding the back lot of the Garden of Eden like a shadow. Dressed in a blacksuit with combat cosmetics covering his hands and face, he melted into the deep shadows cast by the halogen security lights inside the lot. Even when he quickly traversed a lighted area, he was difficult to see.

His objective was the control box for the motion detectors that governed the lights that weren't burning. For every light that was on now, there were two more waiting for the motion detectors in the yard to command them to turn night into blinding day. He also expected them to be hooked up to an alarm system, as well, so if they wanted to see what was in the warehouse, the motion detectors had to be disabled.

Blancanales and Lyons paused at the corner of the fence while Schwarz prepared to disable the control box before making their move. As they waited, they kept an eye on the single light that was showing in the back room of the main building. For a simple nursery and garden-supply store, the Garden of Eden had a lot of security, too much for Lyons's tastes.

He had wanted to go straight for the guy on guard in the building, snatch him and wring him out instead of pussyfooting around and peering into buildings on the back lot. It wasn't that he didn't have an appreciation for the subtle approach; it was just that bombing out on the phone-number list had frustrated him and he wanted information in a hurry.

However, when he had proposed that more direct plan of action, both Schwarz and Blancanales ganged up on him and changed his mind.

"We don't want to give it away until we find out if these guys are actually connected to the action groups," Blancanales said. "With those guys switching motels the way they have, they're jittery enough already. If we screw up and spook them, we'll lose them for sure."

Lyons had to agree that there was merit in that. The last thing he wanted was to lose these guys. He wanted them out of action before they could put whatever plan they had into motion and kill someone. So here he was, hiding in the dark waiting to go over the fence.

It was, however, a short wait. Schwarz showed up in a few minutes. "I got it," he whispered.

"Let's go."

The three men quickly worked their way down the fence to the gate that opened onto the access road to the warehouse. Schwarz had already picked the lock, so they went in. The lock and hasp on the warehouse door took but a few seconds to defeat, and they slipped inside.

The interior of the building looked like a storage area for a garden-supply store. There were rows of clay pots, planting trays, bamboo stakes and all the other material of the trade. Other rows of bagged bark dust, peat moss and planting soil took up most of the space. In the back corner, though, there was something out of place. An old-fashioned cement mixer was hooked up to an electric motor, and the motor was operating.

"What in the hell are they doing here?" Blancanales asked when he saw the slowly turning mixer.

Schwarz walked over, looked inside the mixer and at the empty bags on the floor. "Making bombs."

Recently commercial fertilizers such as ammonium nitrate had been manufactured with a clay coating on the granules so they wouldn't soak up moisture while in storage. That made it better for legitimate users—it cut losses in the warehouse—but it rendered it more difficult to use for making explosives. The clay coating not only withstood moisture, but it also prevented the diesel oil from soaking in.

To overcome this, the Garden of Eden bomb makers had obtained a cement mixer and, after loading it with ammonium nitrate and diesel fuel, were tumbling the mixture as if they were making concrete.

Thus they would ensure that the diesel soaked into the coated granules of ammonium nitrate properly. The resulting thick mush was a perfect "slow" explosive for things like car bombs.

Blancanales noticed several twenty-gallon plastic buckets of the completed mixture lined up against the wall. "Damn!" He shook his head. "They've got enough of this stuff mixed to blow up half the city. You want me to call the cops on this, Ironman?" Blancanales turned back to Lyons.

"Wait!" Schwarz said before Lyons could answer. "I've got a great idea. I know how we can take care of this situation and not risk losing the guys we haven't been able to track down yet."

"If we haven't found them yet, Gadgets," Blancanales asked, "how can we lose them?"

"We know they're here in Miami, right?" he explained. "We just don't know where in Miami. I can get them to come here, and then we'll know where they are."

"What do you have in mind this time?" Lyons asked.

Schwarz quickly ran though his plan, and even Lyons smiled. "What do you need?"

"Can you go back to the car and get my toolbox out of the trunk?" Schwarz asked Blancanales. "I'll also need four blocks of C-4 with detonators and a roll of wire."

IT TOOK LONGER than Schwarz thought it would to rig the device, and it was almost three o'clock in the morning before he finally had everything. The motion sensor he had taken from one of the light poles was hidden in the rafters over the main door. A man entering the building would have to turn around and look up to see it. Thin, dark wires ran along the rafters to the other side of the building, then down to the floor where the cement mixer stood. The four quarter pound blocks of C-4 plastic explosive were placed around the end of the mixer and the firing wires were tucked out of sight.

"Okay," Schwarz said as he put the last of his tools back in the toolbox and closed the lid. "Back out of here, and I'll arm the system."

After he joined his partners outside the warehouse, the three men made their way across the street to the city park that faced the back of the Garden of Eden lot. It was a perfect place to watch when the action went down.

"Okay," Schwarz said, grinning as soon as they were in their observation point. "Let's see how quickly they respond to a break-in."

Taking a small two-way radio from his side pocket, he turned it on and whispered into it. "Boo!"

Instantly the alarm in the warehouse sounded, and within thirty seconds, a man ran out of the main building with a pistol in his hand. He ran straight through the rows of nursery stock for the warehouse in the back of the yard. When he saw the twisted hasp on the door, he reached into his back pocket for a cellular phone. The Able Team commandos could see him waving his free hand in the air as he shouted into the phone.

"I think it's going down," Schwarz stated.

"It'd better," Lyons growled.

Ten minutes later, two inexpensive cars drove toward the yard, and Blancanales jotted down their plate numbers. When they reached the gate, the security man quickly let them through. After this went down, the drivers wouldn't be in any condition to interrogate, but they might have left something behind at their residences, and the plates would tie the cars to the addresses.

The security man was waving his hands again as five men got out of the cars with weapons in their hands, as well.

"Show time," Schwarz said as he activated the motion sensor.

The six men stood in front of the warehouse door and argued about the twisted hasp and lock that Schwarz had artfully arranged to make it look as though someone had tried brute force to break in and had failed.

"Come on!" Lyons growled. "Will you go through the damned door?"

As if he had heard him, the security man opened the door and walked in with the other five close on his heels. Two feet inside the door, the motion detector picked up the movement and set off the sixty-second timer. At the end of that short minute, a relay tripped and the night was briefly turned into day.

Even though Able Team had removed most of the explosive mixture from the warehouse, two hundred pounds or so had been left in the mixer and that was more than enough to do the job. Ammonium nitrate and fuel oil was what demo men called a slow explosive—slow in that its shock wave traveled at only seven thousand feet per second instead of the twenty-five for something like C-4. That made it a good "pushing" explosive for rough demo work.

When this two hundred pounds of the mixture went off, it "pushed" the Garden of Eden's warehouse over most of a two-block area. The six men who had been in the warehouse were also pushed. But since they were made of weaker material than the concrete blocks of the warehouse walls, they ended up in smaller pieces than the blocks. The night sky rained chunks of concrete and body parts.

The Able Team commandos raised themselves from the ground and looked across the darkened park at the Garden of Eden's back lot. The warehouse had vanished, and in its place was a smoking hole in the ground. There was little to burn, so there was no fire, but the dust hanging in the air looked like smoke in the glow of the few street lamps that hadn't been knocked out by the blast and flying debris.

"That takes care of that." Schwarz had a very satisfied look on his face.

In the distance they could hear sirens wailing as city emergency vehicles raced toward the nursery. "That's our swan song," Blancanales said. "We had better make ourselves scarce unless we want to try to explain this."

"What's to explain?" Schwarz asked, reluctant to take his eyes off his handiwork. "Those guys were mixing explosives, and as everyone knows, that's a dangerous business. They should have been a little more careful."

"Can it!" Lyons commanded. "We're out of here."

CHAPTER EIGHTEEN

Once the parts for the Blackbird had been secured and were on their way to Russia, Barbara Price had time to check with Able Team in Miami. Brognola hadn't been happy when he'd received news of the explosive booby trap they had sprung at the warehouse. He had been mollified, however, when it turned out that no civilians had been hurt by the blast. In fact, beyond a few broken windows, there had been no damage done to anything outside of the nursery and, of course, to the men who had answered the alarm.

While there was little left of the bodies to identify, when the FBI found the plastic buckets of ammonium-nitrate-and-diesel-fuel mixture Able Team had carefully moved outside of the blast radius, they got the message. The event was officially tagged as an accidental explosion caused by careless, would-be terrorists who had made a mistake while concocting their volatile mixture.

As soon as they left the park that night, Schwarz drove straight back to the motel. The first thing he did when he got there was to run the plate numbers of the two cars that had been parked near the rear gate through Florida's Department of Motor Vehicles. The first plate's registration address turned out to be one of the motels the action group had stayed at. Since they had already spoken to the manager, they passed on talking to him again.

The second car, however, turned out to be registered to a Hakim Amur, a Lebanese immigrant and the owner of the Garden of Eden.

Since they had been up most of the night, they all took a short nap before checking out Amur's address. They didn't expect the owner himself to be there—they recognized him from his driver's-license photo as being one of the men who had walked into the warehouse. The only way to talk to him would be if someone came up with a way to communicate with the DNA of blood samples or body parts, and small body parts at that.

That didn't mean that searching his house wouldn't prove helpful. There was always the possibility that he had left something incriminating behind that would help them wrap this thing up once and for all. Chasing blind after motel phone numbers was no way to track down terrorists.

The three awakened right after daybreak and dressed in casual street clothes for their visit to the late Mr. Amur's address. Their ensembles included bulky windbreakers that concealed a multitude of hardware. Just because Hakim Amur had been turned into fragments, it didn't mean that all of his associates were dead, as well. And since they had no idea how many terrorists were in the Miami action group, they went with a full load of hardware.

Blancanales had his CAR-15 Stubble, Schwarz his Heckler & Koch MP-5 and Lyons was packing his Colt Python, as well as his Atchisson Assault 12-gauge shotgun.

The address turned out to be a nice, but not too fancy, older two-story house on the corner, surrounded with a brick wall. "That's quite a place for an immigrant shopkeeper," Blancanales commented as they cruised past on their initial recon.

"He must have been selling a lot of ammonium nitrate fertilizer along with his posies," Schwarz replied.

"Either that, or he had a pipeline into the petrodollar fund," Blancanales said. One of the fine ironies of the age of terrorism was that much of the money Western industrial nations spent on Middle Eastern oil came back to them in the form of terrorist bombs.

"There's always that."

Since the Garden of Eden had been wired for security, Schwarz took a good look at the perimeter of Amur's house as they drove past and spotted more motion detectors covering both the house and the grounds.

"He's got motion detectors," Schwarz said, "but it looks like they're wired into an external control box. I can fix them in a flash."

Parking on the opposite side of the street at the end of the block, Lyons and Blancanales waited while Schwarz got out to work his magic. While Schwarz was disabling the alarm system, Blancanales kept a sharp eye on the house through the rearview mirror.

"I've got a watcher on the second floor," he said. "Middle Eastern male, midtwenties. But I can't see a weapon."

"That doesn't mean that it's not there," Lyons cautioned.

A few minutes later Schwarz walked back to the car with a grin on his face. "It's done," he said. "We can pop over the wall any place we want and won't set anything off."

"I don't know about that," Lyons said, watching the steady stream of traffic on both sides of the corner. "How about the main gate?"

The ornamental wrought-iron gate was the natural entrance point for a daylight job at this house. People driving by might think it a bit strange to see three men with guns going over the wall in a quiet residential district. Miami wasn't Los Angles, yet.

"There's a guy on the second floor watching it."

"We saw him, too."

"Why don't we use the cop-car routine, then?" Sahwarz said. "Just pop the light on top and drive on in."

"Maybe they don't like cops."

"How about the fire-department scam, then?"

Considering the blast at the nursery, a visit from the fire department wouldn't be suspicious. It took but a minute for them to drive around the corner, get the magnetic, generic fire-department insignia and stick it on the car's front doors. A dummy red light stuck on top of the car completed the disguise.

Once they were ready, Blancanales drove up to the gate and pushed the intercom button. A man with a strong accent answered, "What do you want?"

Bingo, Schwarz thought, a Middle Eastern accent. It wasn't over yet.

"We're from the fire department," Blancanales said as nonthreateningly as he could. "And we'd like to talk to Mr. Hakim Amur, please."

"He isn't here right now."

"Could we talk to his wife, then? Is she there?"

"No," the voice said. "There is no one here to talk to."

"Who are you?" Blancanales asked.

"Go away," the man insisted. "There is no one here who can talk to you today."

"So much for the quiet approach," Schwarz said.

"Go for it," Lyons snapped as he brought his shotgun from under the seat.

Schwarz put the Pontiac in reverse as if he were going to back out onto the street. As soon as he had a few feet between him and the gate, he snapped the shift lever into low and floored the accelerator.

Tires howling, the big V-8 under the hood launched the four-door sedan like a rocket. The five-mile-per-hour-impact plastic bumper didn't have a chance against the wrought-iron gate. But neither did the gate have a chance against the two-ton projectile that was backing up the bumper.

"Subtle," Schwarz muttered as he cleared his silenced H&K subgun for action. "Real subtle."

The watcher in the second-floor window didn't believe his eyes when he saw the Pontiac crashing through the gate. He was still trying to figure out what to do when the big sedan slammed to a halt at the steps leading up to the front door.

As soon as the wheels quit turning, the three men were out of the car, their pieces ready in their hands. Blancanales broke to the right, heading for the rear of the house as Lyons and Schwarz took the front door. As always, the Ironman's technique for opening doors worked again. The door lock would never be the same, but they wouldn't have to worry about that.

The watcher was halfway down the stairs when the door flew open and, as Lyons had surmised, he was packing. The AK-47 in his hands was just coming up when Lyons tracked him with the Atchisson and fired.

The buckshot blast caught him in the chest and slammed him against the staircase. When he slid to a sitting position on the stairs, the blood smears on the wall showed that Lyons had made a perfect shot. All nine buckshot pellets had connected.

Even before the blast echoed away, there was the staccato chatter of Blancanales's CAR-15 outside the back door. Apparently there was more than just the one of them in the house. The watcher had friends.

Not knowing the layout of the house, Lyons signaled Schwarz to take the stairs while he worked his way toward Blancanales. Schwarz didn't particularly like walking up stairs. They channeled you into a small killing zone at the top, and he had no intention of getting killed today.

Keeping to the wall side of the stairs, he stayed low, almost crawling, as he climbed the steps. Two steps down from the top, he lay flat and, leading with the muzzle of the H&K, inched his way up. As he had suspected, the gunman hiding behind the edge of the door at the end of the hall had the stairs covered. But his eyes were focused at man height not at carpet level, where Schwarz was crouching.

Rather than stupidly stand up and give the guy a target, Schwarz simply triggered a short burst from where he was. The 9 mm slugs chewed through the door and spit the gunman out into the hall. A second burst raked him across the chest to finish the job.

Lyons was starting into the kitchen when he caught a flash of movement from the corner of his eye. Rather than turn to see what it was, he threw himself to the tiled floor, twisting as he fell to bring his shotgun into line.

The 9 mm rounds from the gunman's pistol sang over his head and were answered by a single blast from the Atchisson. At this close range, the buckshot pattern had no chance to spread out. The nine pellets hit within an eight-inch circle and eviscerated the gunman.

Picking himself up off the floor, Lyons didn't even bother to check if the man was dead. It was difficult to live with your guts hanging out that way.

"I got one back here," Blancanales stated when Lyons slowly opened the back door and looked out.

"We got three inside, so I guess that's it."

"We'd better get a move on, then," Blancanales said. "The cops will be here before too long."

Schwarz had finished clearing the house. "The den's over there," he told his teammates, pointing to a door off the main entrance. "And someone's been busy in there."

A computer sat on the desk, and it was turned on. Boxes of papers were laid out on the floor, and the wastepaper basket next to the desk was overflowing, as if someone had been going through the papers when he had been rudely interrupted by Able Team's arrival.

"Do we grab all this stuff or let the FBI have it?" Schwarz asked.

Lyons glanced at the papers and trash can. "Let the Feds handle it," he said. "I'll have Barbara alert them that it's here. They can waste their time going through it all instead of our having to mess with it."

"Good plan," Blancanales said. "Now maybe we can relax and enjoy this tropical paradise for a day or two before we have to go kill someone else."

"Yeah," Schwarz agreed, brightening up. "Why don't we go to Disneyland? It's close by, isn't it?"

Lyons and Blancanales both stopped cold and turned to look at him. "Gadgets," Lyons said, slowly shaking his head, "you've got to get a life, son."

Schwarz shrugged. "It was just a suggestion."

THE ARRIVAL of the U.S. Air Force F-15 Eagle carrying the repair parts for the Blackbird wasn't quite the event that the arrival of the spy plane had been. So many American aircraft had flown in and out of the base over the past few days that seeing the star-and-bar insignia of the U.S. Air Force was hardly even novel anymore.

That didn't mean that these new American visitors were ignored. Always ready to prove their famous hospitality to their post-cold war comrades in arms, the Russians welcomed the Eagle pilots with orange soda, vodka and one of their famous lard-frosting cakes. The activity kept the two Americans out of the hangar where Senior Master Sergeant Joe Benihana and his crew were trying to get the SR-71 readied for flight again as soon as possible. For what was supposed to be a clandestine mission, half of the U.S. Air Force was in on it.

The crew chief was flogging his people as hard as he could while still taking the time to ensure that they didn't make a mistake. Benihana wasn't beyond getting his hands dirty, either. In fact, Katz found the sergeant hip deep in the guts of the SR's port-side electronics bay when he went to see how the work was progressing.

"You'll be able to fly this bird in the morning," Benihana promised when he pulled his head out. "And I can assure you that the damned thing will work properly this time. If those NASA bastards had bothered to check the—"

Katz had what he wanted to know and left the crew chief in midrant. He was afraid that if the sergeant ever got his hands on a NASA employee, any NASA employee, blood would be shed.

CHAPTER NINETEEN

"They're airborne," Kurtzman announced.

Brognola grunted acknowledgment around the end of the unlit cigar stuck between his teeth. Removing the cigar, he reached into his coat pocket, pulled out a roll of antacid tablets and stuck two of them in his mouth.

This time Kurtzman called up a computer-generated map to follow the Blackbird's flight. A blinking red triangle represented the progress of the SR across central Asia at Mach 3.

Brognola watched the red triangle move across the map. "If you're tracking the plane by a beacon, why can't they pick it up, too?" he asked Kurtzman.

"It's on a tight beam to the retrans satellite," Kurtzman said. "If they were above the Blackbird, they might be able to pick it up, but there's no way they can get up there."

"You say that the Blackbird is a stealth aircraft?" Brognola asked, remembering the briefing he had been given when this plan had first been proposed.

"Almost. It's what they call a 'stealthed' aircraft. It can be picked up by a large ground-based radar, but since it has the radar signature of a much smaller plane, it's difficult to lock on to with airborne targeting radar.''

Brognola knew the record of the F-117 Stealth fighters during the Gulf War. They had flown completely undetected into the heart of Baghdad through some of the heaviest antiaircraft defenses in history to deliver their two-thousand pound smart bombs and returned unscratched. He was confident that the SR would be able to do the same.

The cigar went back into his mouth as he watched the red triangle on the computer map. In a couple of hours this would be over.

BY NOW Jack Grimaldi had had enough time in the backseat of the Blackbird that it was becoming old hat to him. The blinding acceleration, the zoom climb to altitude and the deep blue of what little sky he could see from the two side windows of his cockpit. Even so, he could hardly call the flight routine.

Their flight plan again took them out over the Caspian Sea to the south and east of Iran.

''Feet dry,'' Hoffsteader called out, using the Navy term for when an aircraft flew over land after flying over water. In this case, the land below was Turkmenistan, where they would begin their eighty-mile-wide turn to the west that would put them on a direct heading for Shabaz and the secrets the Iranians were hiding there.

Again Grimaldi readied the cameras and sensors, but this time he didn't have any red lights showing on the control panel. "We're go back here," he told Hoffsteader. "Everything's on-line and rolling."

"Roger."

They were in the middle of their eighty-mile turn onto the recon leg of the flight plan when Grimaldi heard the voice of the Russian AWACS radioman in his earphones. "Niner Seven One, this is Mother Hen. Over."

"Seven One, go," he replied.

"This is Mother Hen. We have picked up four Iranian fighters taking off from Qum air base. Over."

"Roger," Grimaldi answered as he called up the map on his nav screen that showed the Iranian military installations and airfields along their flight path. "What's their vector? Over."

"They are climbing fast," the Russian replied. "And it looks like they are going to try to intercept you. We think they are Foxbats. Over." The Russian air controllers were having a lot of fun referring to their aircraft by their NATO code names to make it easier for their visitors.

Grimaldi wasn't surprised at that piece of bad news. If the Iranians were going to contest their flight, the Foxbats were the only fighters in their arsenal that had even a hope of reaching them. But he still didn't think that even they would be good enough to get the job done.

"Roger on the Foxbats," he transmitted. "Keep me informed of their vector and altitude. Out."

Grimaldi switched to the intercom circuit. "They've sent the Foxbats after us," he told Hoffsteader.

"I heard," the pilot replied curtly. "Warm up the fire-control system."

"It's up and running," Grimaldi responded. "What's our ETA to the recon area?"

"I have it as 18.3." Hoffsteader read the numbers off of his mission-profile map.

"That's what I have."

"I'm turning up the wick a bit, so keep your eyes on the profile. We'll be coming up on it a little faster."

"Roger," Grimaldi replied as he watched the Mach meter climb to Mach 3.3. Hoffsteader was flying all out, and he hoped it would be good enough.

WITH STONY MAN PATCHED into the ops center at Ufazek, Kurtzman got the news about the interceptors as soon as Katz did. "Katz says that the Russian AWACS is reporting that the Iranians have sent the Foxbats after them."

"Can they outrun them?" Brognola asked.

"Supposedly."

"What does that mean?" Brognola had assured the President that the Blackbird was the world's fastest aircraft and that it was in no danger from being intercepted by the Iranian air force. The last thing the Man needed right now was a repeat of the earlier B-1B fiasco.

"What it means," Kurtzman patiently explained, "is that the MiG-25s are also capable of Mach 3 for short runs. If the pilots have orders to trash their engines, they might be able to get into a position to make a head-on firing pass. They can't catch them in a tail chase, but if they are vectored into a position in front of them, they can make one firing pass with their missiles."

"Can they fly as high as the SR?"

"No," Kurtzman replied, "but their missiles can."

That wasn't what Brognola wanted to hear. His hand automatically went into his jacket pocket and peeled off two antacid tablets from the open roll. Walking over to the coffeepot, he reluctantly poured half a cup to wash them down. Even with the Blackbird traveling at Mach 3, it was going to be a longer day than he had thought.

COLONEL AHMED MIRZA had given his pilots orders to spare nothing to intercept the Yankee intruder. When he had told Major Nazar that there was a danger of the MiG's Tumansky R-31-300 turbines catching fire and exploding if they were run too fast for too long, he was ordered to do it anyway. Mirza hadn't needed to hear what would happen to the pilots if they didn't follow orders.

But even with the screaming turbines propelling the MiGs at almost Mach 3, the only thing that he had going for him was that the American spy plane had to make its run over a particular target area, and he knew where that target was. By swinging around to the north, he and his flight could get there before the American pilot and would be waiting when he made his run over Shabaz. Then it would be up to the four AA-7 Apex missiles he and each of his wingmen carried on their underwing pylons to put an end to the intruder.

Even though they were four to one, he wasn't sure that they would be victorious over the high-flying spy plane. He was certain, however, that if they weren't, he and his pilots would die before the day was out.

"NINER SEVEN ONE, this is Mother Hen. Over." The Russian's voice was loud in Grimaldi's earphones.

"Seven One," he answered. "Go ahead."

"The Foxbats have swung around to the north and are headed for your target area at top speed. It looks like they will get there before you do. Over."

"This is Seven One," Grimaldi answered. "Thanks for the warning. Out."

"I heard," Hoffsteader replied from the front seat.

"I want to go tactical now," Grimaldi requested, "and switch the recon package over to computer control so I can fight."

Even though the recon shots were the reason for the mission, there was nothing that said he couldn't let the computer handle that chore while he tried to keep them from being shot down.

"Roger." Hoffsteader's voice was tense. "Do it."

Once the computer had been tasked to take over the recon chores, Grimaldi switched on the Hughes AWG-9D fire-control system for the four AIM-54 Phoenix missiles housed in the Blackbird's belly. The Doppler-pulse radar came up immediately, and the screen lit up. Even at a range of almost a hundred and fifty miles, it picked up the four Foxbats instantly.

"I have them on radar," he reported tersely. "Four of them and they're closing fast."

"Roger."

Even though there were four Foxbats, the Iranians wouldn't necessarily have everything their own way. As the Russian pilot at Ufazek had pointed out, a Foxbat pilot had to fly and fight at the same. And as high as they were, the Russian-built interceptors would be difficult to fly. They would be mushing out, their wings not working all that well in the thin air. The Blackbird, though, with its blended fuselage and wing cross section, actually flew better at this altitude and took much of its lift from the fuselage shape.

Then there was the speed factor. Hoffsteader had the throttles jammed all the way forward, and the computer was working overtime to keep the two thundering J-58s working in tandem. Their closing speed with the MiGs would be some six thousand miles per hour, and the Foxbats would have time for only one pass. At that blinding speed, even the slightest mistake would throw an attempted intercept off.

Not that Grimaldi was about to let the Iranians get the first shot. He had four Phoenix missiles on board, and he intended to use each and every one of them. Unlike a more conventional fighter, the Blackbird's missiles were housed in internal bays rather than hanging on underwing pylons. The missile-bay doors would open to release the missiles only when the radar had a lock on a target.

The MiGs were still roughly fifteen thousand feet below them, but the Hughes fire-control system offered a look-down-shoot-down capability and could acquire and lock on to a target that wasn't flying at the same altitude. Although the fire-control system could acquire and track all four targets at once, Grimaldi took them on one at a time. He had used the Phoenix before, but it had been a while and this wasn't the time for him to make a mistake.

He locked on the closest MiG, selected the first missile in the port-side bay and pulled the trigger. "Fox One, Fox One," he called over the intercom to tell the pilot that he had fired.

Even though the Blackbird was traveling at better then Mach 3, the Phoenix pulled away from it as if it were standing still. Grimaldi let the targeting radar continue to paint the target to give the missile its guidance. Halfway to the target, the Phoenix switched over to its own radar tracking-and-guidance system. When that happened, the MiG-25 was as good as dead.

With the missile warning screaming in his earphones, the Iranian pilot tried to jerk his Foxbat around to get out of the way of the missile. But in the thin air, his heavy MiG didn't turn like a dogfighter. In fact, he hit a high-speed stall, and the Foxbat dropped a wing as it stalled out and tumbled through the sky.

The Phoenix missile didn't care if its target was under control or not. It simply didn't matter to its cold electronic brain. Once the missile's internal radar was locked on to its intended victim, nothing mattered. As soon as the Foxbat was within the blast range, the 132-pound warhead detonated.

The hardened steel rods embedded in the explosive material of the Phoenix's warhead sprayed out like a giant shotgun blast. The shrapnel shredded the MiG's forward fuselage, smashing the jet intakes and cockpit. With the engines shut down and the pilot dead at his controls, the Foxbat continued its plunge.

After the first missile had gone over to internal guidance, Grimaldi locked and fired on his second target. He watched his screen as the missile dropped away from the open bay and accelerated toward its target. He had opened fire at the Phoenix's maximum range. But at the speed they were closing with the MiGs, it was but a fraction of a second before they were in range of the Iranian missiles, as well. He saw the two lead Foxbats launch missiles at them.

The first of the AA-7 Apex missiles had been fired by Grimaldi's second target. Since he had fired first, however, his Phoenix connected before the Apex was even a quarter of the way to him. When the MiG exploded, the Apex lost its guidance and automatically detonated its warhead harmlessly several thousand feet below them.

The second Apex continued on its path, but it seemed to run out of steam, as well. It was still several thousand feet below them when it arched over and started back down. A few hundred feet later, its fail safe system detonated the warhead harmlessly.

The remaining two MiGs both fired a pair of missiles, but they were also unable to reach the high-flying Blackbird. In a flash Grimaldi realized that the MiGs couldn't fly high enough to reach them and that the missiles weren't powerful enough to bridge the gap.

One of the Foxbat's pilots came to the same conclusion and attempted to bank his plane for a better shot at the high-flying target. He forgot that he couldn't dogfight at sixty thousand feet and turned too sharply. The MiG's wings lost lift, and the fighter went into a flat spin. When the pilot tried to recover, he found that his control surfaces weren't working well, either. The heavy fighter flipped over onto its back and spun out of control.

Grimaldi locked him up anyway and sent a Phoenix after him.

Even with the dogfight going on, Hoffsteader continued to fly the recon profile. If they survived this, he wanted to have the goodies on board so he hopefully would never have to do this again. He was beginning to form a real dislike for Iran. By now the Blackbird was only eighty miles from the Shabaz Facility. In a few seconds she would be past it, and the mission would be accomplished.

Hoffsteader had his eyes fixed on the nav screen as they flashed over the target at three thousand miles per hour. "I'm going to break the egress profile," he called out. "We'll exit to the east instead of continuing north."

"Roger," Grimaldi said as he watched the last Foxbat still climbing to meet them.

CHAPTER TWENTY

Mizra glanced down at his tail-pipe-temperature gauges and saw that they were well past the redline. If he survived this fight, the engines in his MiG would have to be taken out and scrapped. But he knew better than to turn back now. He still had one missile left, and it would be far better for him if the engines exploded and he died in the crash than it would be for him to land safely and report that the American aircraft had gotten away while he still had a missile left unfired.

He was flying more carefully than his wingmen had, and his heavy fighter was under control but just barely. By carefully controlling his fighter with the slightest of movements, he had gotten higher than any of his wingmen. Their missiles, like the earlier ones he had fired, had failed because they hadn't been able to climb high enough or fast enough to reach their target. He should be high enough now to make a hit.

When he had a launch-lock tone in his earphones, he triggered his last Apex from the right inboard pylon. When he saw that the missile was running true, he knew it was time to get away. It was in the hands of

God now, but it never hurt to help the Merciful One. He dropped the nose of his plane and headed for thicker air and safety.

With the thicker air, though, came more humidity, and the last thing the overheated turbines in his Foxbat needed right now was water vapor, which would turn into superheated steam in the red-hot compressor blades.

When Mizra had dropped fifteen thousand feet, the air was thick enough that his control surfaces started responding normally. The air was also thick enough that it could carry moisture. With the turbines almost hot enough to melt the compressor blades, the humidity didn't cool them; it flashed into steam instead.

The colonel saw the exhaust-gas-temperature gauges peg past their redlines. His gloved hand reached out to retard the throttles when the port-side turbine seized. The resulting explosion ripped the engine bay apart and sent red-hot shrapnel slicing into the fuel tanks between the two turbines.

The Foxbat disappeared in a blossoming black-and-red fireball that appeared in the clear blue sky like a magician's trick. Colonel Ahmed Mizra didn't even have time to think that it was God's will.

JACK GRIMALDI WAS too busy trying to stay alive to notice that the last Foxbat had disappeared from his radar. As he watched the Apex missile the Iranian had fired approach on his fire-control screen, he knew there was little they could do about this one.

At the speed they were flying, they couldn't take evasive action. A violent maneuver at Mach 3 was almost as dangerous to the Blackbird as a missile hit. Even a thirty-five-degree bank was considered extreme.

"Can you break left?" he called.

"I'll try," the pilot replied.

Grimaldi waited until the last possible moment before calling out, "Break! Break!"

The right wing of the Blackbird came up, and the nose dropped a few degrees with the bank. There was a flash of light and the Blackbird suddenly shuddered and violently yawed to the right. Grimaldi was caught unprepared, and his helmet smashed into the side of the canopy, stunning him for an instant. When he could focus his eyes again, he saw that the plane was trying to fly sideways.

"I've got an unstart!" Hoffsteader yelled over the intercom. "I lost the shock wave in the right intake, and the engine's shut down."

A jet engine, even one as powerful as the J-58s of the SR-71, couldn't operate on air that was moving faster than the speed of sound. The massive shock cones in the front of the Blackbird's engine intakes were designed to move back and forth so they would always be in a position to create a reverse shock wave that would slow the incoming air from Mach 3 to subsonic speeds before it entered the first stage of the turbine compressor. When a J-58 lost its intake shock wave, it was like a compressor stall on a conventional jet fighter. The fire went out.

"I've got to put her down somewhere!"

"Can you make it to the Iranian border?"

Dying in the air was one thing; crash-landing in Iran and surviving to be captured was entirely another. Grimaldi didn't relish what would await them if that happened.

"I don't know," the pilot answered. "This damned thing isn't designed to fly with one engine out."

Grimaldi knew that was one of the classic aviation understatements of all time. An SR on only one engine was a crash trying to find a place to happen. The only thing that was keeping the aircraft from tumbling out of control this instant was that the Stability Augmentation System—the SAS—was engaged. This part of the computerized control system sensed and automatically compensated for the inherent instability of the Blackbird faster than any human pilot could.

While the SAS was keeping the plane from tumbling out of control and breaking up in the air, Hoffsteader kept trying to reposition the shock cone to catch the shock wave and restart the engine, but it wasn't working. For some reason the shock cone wasn't responding to his commands and was stuck in the wrong position for the speed they were flying.

"Do you want to punch out?" Hoffsteader asked. "I can keep her under control so you can eject."

"That's a big negative," Grimaldi said firmly. "As long as you can keep this thing flying, I'm staying in it."

"I've still got to bring her down."

"Go for it."

Even with the SAS engaged, Hoffsteader had his hands full trying to keep the big plane in the air while he attempted a descent profile. The problem was that at higher speeds, the on-board computer overrode the pilot's control of the throttle so that he didn't inadvertently cause an unstart condition by overcontrolling the plane. Since he already had an unstart condition on one engine, though, the computer was only making control of the plane more difficult for him instead of better. He needed to be able to use his remaining engine in ways that the computer didn't want him to.

Hoffsteader fought the Blackbird all the way down. The worst thing for Grimaldi was that there was absolutely nothing he could do to help Hoffsteader bring them down safely. There were no copilot's controls in the backseat of an SR, only a few critical instruments that gave him a glimpse of what was going on with the ship. He saw the altimeter winding down as if they were in free-fall, but he saw the Machmeter unwinding, as well. If Hoffsteader could keep the wings on the Blackbird until it slowed below supersonic, there was a chance of putting her down somewhere intact.

If not, there were always the bang seats, as Hoffsteader had suggested earlier. Over the long years that the SRs had been in service, several of them had gotten into trouble and the crews had been forced to eject. It was always dicey to have to pull the handle for an emergency bailout in any jet aircraft, but the Blackbirds had a good record for letting her crews get out intact.

Once the Blackbird's airspeed had dropped to Mach 1.3, the computer programming disengaged, and Hoffsteader had more control over the throttle of the remaining engine.

"Hang on!" he called out. "I've got a clear spot in front of me and I'm on final."

Since Grimaldi had no forward view, he had no idea where the pilot was trying to land. He already had his harness pulled as tightly as it would go without cutting him in two, but he tugged on the ends of the straps anyway as he watched the altimeter wind down.

Hoffsteader had gone through the desert-emergency-landing program in the VR trainer back at Dreamland and knew how it was supposed to work. The Iranian desert in front of him didn't look much different than the Nevada desert around Groom Lake.

Keeping the plane's long nose high, he gently eased the main landing gear onto the packed sand and cut the fuel to the remaining engine.

Knowing better than to try to apply the brakes, the pilot immediately released the drag chute. When the canopy popped out of the compartment on the tail of the SR and snapped open, it caused the nose to slam down hard on the sand.

Once the nose gear was on the ground, Hoffsteader let the Blackbird roll to a halt on her own. Using the brakes would only get sand in them, and the maintenance crew had enough work to do on her already.

When they finally came to a halt, Hoffsteader hit the emergency canopy release, and the two canopies snapped open on their hydraulic jacks. The skin of the ship was still too hot to touch from the Mach 3 run. Without the special boarding ladder on hand, it was a long jump down from the cockpits to the sand. But if they stayed in the cockpit without the air-conditioning running, they'd cook in five minutes. Even outside, if they didn't get out of their pressure suits, they would still cook, but it would take a little longer.

"We have to jump down," the pilot called back as he hit the emergency release on his seat harness.

Grimaldi had already figured that part out and actually beat Hoffsteader to the ground. "Now what do we do?" he asked once the pilot had joined him.

Hoffsteader pulled off his helmet. "I was hoping you'd be able to tell me," he said. "You're the spook. I'm just the airplane driver."

"My money is on trying to get in contact with Ufazek and let them know that we made it down alive. Striker won't let us sit here too long if there's any way he can get us out."

"What about the SR?" the pilot asked. "We can't just leave her here for the Iranians to capture."

"Damned if I know." Grimaldi shook his head. "Do you have a destruction pack on board?"

"Yes," Hoffsteader answered. "If I can remember how to make the damned thing work. I haven't even thought about it since I went through the initial orientation on it."

"You'd better try," Grimaldi said grimly. He didn't want to see the Blackbird destroyed any more that Hoffsteader did, but the alternative was unthinkable. "I don't think Washington is going to want to hear that we let the Iranians get their hands on it intact."

"As soon as she cools down a little bit, I'll get back inside and see what I can do."

"In the meantime," Grimaldi said as he reached for the survival radio in his flight suit's side pocket, "I'm going to phone home."

"THE BLACKBIRD IS DOWN in the Iranian desert," Aaron Kurtzman announced. "They weren't able to make it back across the border."

Hal Brognola looked down at the floor for a long moment without saying a word. There was nothing to be said when a mission went this bad. Not only had they failed to get the information, but they had also lost one of the world's most sensitive aircraft to an enemy, and the crew was in danger of capture. This was going to make the Francis Gary Powers incident look like a Boy Scout outing.

"But," Kurtzman continued as a series of notations scrolled past on his screen, "all is not lost. The sensor and video transmissions came through this time. We've got the goods on them."

Brognola felt a wave of relief wash over him. There was still a chance to salvage something from this incredible run of bad luck. "Is that aircraft fitted with a self-destruct package?" he asked.

"I believe it is."

"Find out ASAP," he said. "And if it is, order them to activate it immediately."

"What about Grimaldi and the pilot?" Price asked.

"I need to talk to the President first."

"THEY'RE DOWN SAFELY," Katzenelenbogen told Bolan after Grimaldi's call was relayed from the orbiting Russian AWACS, "and out of the plane."

"Where?"

Katz shook his head. "According to the AWACS, they're still roughly thirty miles inside Iran."

Bolan turned to the Russian colonel. "Viktor, what are your orders about a situation like this? Can you take us into Iran to get those men out and destroy that plane?"

The colonel thought for a moment. "That depends," he said slowly.

"On what?"

"I was told to extend every assistance to you that I could. But this may be outside my orders. However, if your government can guarantee me a small dacha in your state of California—you know, the places on the beach where the young girls run around with almost no clothes on—I think we can work something out."

"I'll try, Viktor, if you'll let me borrow one of your Mi-8s to take my men there so we can secure the area. I need to get my people out and make sure that plane's completely destroyed."

The Russian colonel was visibly shocked. "No. You cannot destroy your black airplane. It is much too beautiful."

"I also can't allow it to fall into their hands intact," Bolan stated flatly. "The sensors and cameras she has on board are more than top secret. Plus there's the fire-control system and the engines. We have to blow it up."

"Do you want to bring your Blackbird plane back here?" the Russian asked.

"What do you mean?"

"What does your Blackbird weigh?" the colonel asked.

Bolan turned to the crew chief.

"Sixty thousand pounds," Benihana answered immediately. "That's takeoff weight with a full fuel load. I don't know how much it will weigh now with most of the fuel gone. Probably more like fifty thousand."

"About twenty-three thousand kilos." Bolan made the metric conversion in his head.

"Wait," the colonel said as he gestured for one of the Russian pilots to come to him. The man saluted, and the colonel asked him a long question in rapid-fire Russian. The helicopter pilot thought for a moment before answering.

"He says," Popov translated for Benihana's benefit, "that he can pick up your Blackbird airplane with one of our Mi-26 helicopters. They can carry thirty thousand kilos."

"Does it have the range?"

"They have external fuel tanks and can be refueled in the air."

"But if you take it into Iran," Katz said, "it will be a sitting duck for their fighters."

"I will send a MiG fighter escort with it. After all, I cannot let the Iranians shoot down a Russian helicopter. Moscow would have my head for that."

"But you'll be risking an international incident if you send fighters into Iran."

The Russian shrugged expressively. "Your mission is as important to Moscow as it is to you, and I was told to help you in any way I could. Plus," he added with a smile, "what's a little international incident if I can get a dacha in California and a few pretty young girls to go with it?"

"I like the way you think, Viktor," Bolan stated.

"A man always has to think of his future."

CHAPTER TWENTY-ONE

•

Aaron Kurtzman wheeled his chair around to face Hal Brognola. "Striker wants to go into Iran after the Blackbird and bring it out."

"How in the hell does he think he's going to do that?"

"The Russians have a helicopter that they think can airlift it out intact," Kurtzman explained. "It's one of those Mi-26 heavy-lift machines they use to haul oil rigs around in Siberia."

"Can it take the load? That's a big plane."

"They think it can."

Brognola was caught on the horns of a dilemma. On the one hand the President was going to have a hemorrhage if he found out that he had ordered a border crossing into Iran without notifying him first. On the other he would have an even bigger hemorrhage if the Blackbird fell into the mullahs' hands.

He was screwed no matter what he did, so he might as well go for the gusto. He was tired of those damned people shooting down American planes.

"Tell him to go ahead."

"I already did."

"Someday you're going to do that once too often," Brognola growled, "and I'm going to retire you to a real farm."

WHEN DAVID MCCARTER ordered Phoenix Force to suit up, T. J. Hawkins grabbed his weapon and assault harness and sprinted for the door of the hangar. Outside on the tarmac, one of the green-and-brown-camouflaged Russian Mi-8 Hip helicopters was winding up and the rotor was turning. It felt like the good old days in the Rangers. The only difference was that the chopper waiting for him bore Russian red-star insignia instead of the star-and-bar of the United States.

Hawkins had been feeling useless since he had arrived at Ufazek, but this was something he knew how to do in his sleep. After cutting his combat teeth on an air assault into Grenada, he had moved on to chopper insertions in Panama, Kuwait and Somalia.

As he ran, Calvin James came up beside him and held out a Stinger antiaircraft missile launcher. "Take this!"

"Got it."

Scrambling inside the Hip, he buckled himself into one of the canvas-covered troop seats. The others scrambled in after him, and the Russian pilot lifted off before they even had time to belt themselves in.

Mack Bolan didn't have Brognola's approval for the recovery operation yet, but he had ordered the Russian pilot to take off anyway. Regardless of what the big Fed said about the Blackbird, they were going in after Grimaldi and Hoffsteader, so there was no reason to wait.

THE FLIGHT across the Caspian Sea was long. On the way, Bolan stayed in touch with Katz at Ufazek to remain updated on the status of the heavy-lift chopper. Colonel Popov didn't have an Mi-26 stationed at his air base, but he thought he could borrow one from his neighboring base and have it in the air before long.

"We're in Iran," McCarter called back from the cockpit. "Mother Hen says that there's no Iranian fighters in the air right now."

"Tell them to keep a close eye on them. If we know where the Blackbird is, you can bet your ass that they do, too."

A few miles inland from the Caspian Sea, the green of the coastal region turned into the bare, rocky sand of the high desert. Grimaldi had said that they had gone down in the desert, so they were coming up on him fast.

"There it is!" McCarter called out from the chopper's cockpit. "And I have two men on the ground."

Bolan looked out the door window of the Mi-8 and saw the matt black shape of the SR sitting on the sand. He couldn't see any major damage, but with an aircraft as sophisticated as the Blackbird, it wouldn't take much to disable her.

The plane had come down almost thirty miles inside of Iran, but at the Blackbird's top speed, that was only a few seconds' air time. This was just the latest piece of bad luck in what was beginning to look like a jinxed mission.

Bolan clicked in his throat mike. "Phoenix to Mother Hen. Over."

"Mother Hen, go ahead," the Russian AWACS radio operator answered.

"This is Phoenix. Can you patch me through to Ufazek? Over."

"Roger."

"Phoenix Control, go," Katz's voice came over Bolan's earplug.

"We have them spotted, and they seem to be okay. Over."

"Roger. The lift ship took off, and its ETA to your location is a little over two hours. Over."

"Roger, Phoenix out."

That was a long time to have to remain on the ground behind enemy lines, but it couldn't be helped. Not if they wanted to get the Blackbird back. He just hoped that the Iranians wouldn't be able to get their stuff together in time to make trouble for them.

GRIMALDI SPOTTED the approaching Mi-8 and yelled to Hoffsteader. "There's a chopper coming! See if you can raise it on the radio."

While the pilot reached for the survival radio, Grimaldi dug in the side pocket of his flight suit and drew the Beretta pistol he had borrowed from Phoenix Force's arsenal. If this wasn't the guys coming to get them, he didn't intend to go down without a fight.

"It's Striker," Hoffsteader reported.

Grimaldi put the safety back on the Beretta and relaxed. The cavalry had arrived.

Flaring out next to the Blackbird, the chopper quickly disgorged Bolan and the men of Phoenix Force. As soon as they were clear of the rotors, the Hip lifted off again and flew away to the north to find a remote place to set down and wait for Bolan's call to return to pick them up.

"Phoenix," the Russian AWACS radioed, "this is Mother Hen. I have three Iranian aircraft approaching your location. I advise that you take cover until I can get my chicks on station. Over."

"Roger, Mother Hen," Bolan replied tensely. "Keep me informed. Out."

"David!" Bolan called out. "The Russians have picked up bogeys headed our way, fast movers. Get everybody under cover fast."

Phoenix Force took what cover there was in an outcropping a couple of hundred yards from the

Blackbird and prepared to do what little they could to protect the helpless aircraft.

"Here they come." Grimaldi said, pointing to the southwest.

One of the three specks broke away from the other two and made a pass over the downed Blackbird. Grimaldi recognized it as a Sukhoi Su-7 Fitter wearing the red, white, and green rondelle markings of the Iranian air force, and its underwing pylons were loaded with UV-32 57 mm rocket pods.

As ground-attack rockets went, the Russian 57 mm S-5 missiles were lightweights compared to more-modern weapons. But all it would take was a single rocket hit to damage the Blackbird beyond any hope of repairing it outside of the United States. The Fitters had to be stopped at all costs.

When Hawkins saw the Fitter swing out wide in a climbing turn and head back in for a strafing run, he unslung the Stinger missile and quickly prepared it for launching.

During the Afghan-Soviet war of the 1980s, the CIA had supplied hundreds of AIM-92 Stinger missiles to the Afghan *mujahedeen* freedom fighters. In the rugged hills and valleys of Afghanistan, they had proved to rule the skies. The Stingers were so effective that Soviet close-air support of their ground forces became almost impossible, and without total control of the air, they'd had no hope of winning. The Stingers had done well against Fitters in the past and should do the trick again here.

Stepping into the open, Hawkins lifted the missile launcher to his shoulder. Locking the image of the diving Fitter in the launcher's optical sight, he pulled the trigger back to the stop to activate the tracking system. Inside the missile the gyros spun up to speed, the pressurized nitrogen dumped to cool the IR-seeker head and the UV receiver started looking for blank spots in the sky.

Unlike the earlier, simple heat-seeking missiles that merely locked on to the greatest heat source in the sky and followed it, the Stinger also had an additional ultraviolet-spectra guidance feature. This system prevented the missile from being decoyed by an aircraft dropping flares that were hotter than the plane's engine exhausts.

What this feature did was to search the sky along the line of sight of the IR-seeking head and determine if a large body was blocking the ultraviolet radiation of the sun, a body such as an aircraft. If there was, the system told the IR-seeking head to lock on and fire. If, however, there was no body blocking out a part of the sky, it told the missile guidance system to ignore that heat source and keep looking for another target.

In less than a second, Hawkins heard the launch-lock tone in his headset and he pulled the firing trigger past the stop. The launch charge ignited with a whoosh, boosting the missile out of the launcher. Twenty yards from the tube, the main rocket motor kicked in and accelerated the missile to more than Mach 2 in an instant.

When the Fitter pilot saw the dirty white launch plume of the missile, he tried to turn out of its path. He might have made it if he'd had the nerve to wait until the absolute last second before trying a sharp break. He panicked, slammed his swing wings forward and dived to try to make a low-level getaway.

The small triangular fins on the front of the missile swiveled to make a course correction to follow the diving Sukhoi as it started its evasive move. From the ground it looked as if the Sukhoi had dived like a hawk to eat the Stinger.

An instant later the Iranian fighter suffered a catastrophic case of indigestion. A blossom of flame appeared in the sky as the jet's fuel tanks exploded and detonated its underwing ordnance. The sky rained twisted Fitter pieces for several moments.

The other two Fitter pilots also recognized the Stinger's launch signature and decided to give Hawkins's position a wide berth. They were still trying to figure out what their next move was going to be when a flight of three Russian MiG-29 Fulcrums swooped down on them like hawks. Mother Hen's chicks had arrived.

The MiG-29s were one of the world's best dog-fighters, and they proceeded to make short work of the older and slower Fitters.

The first one went down immediately to a long burst of 30 mm high-explosive shells from the lead MiG's GSh-301 revolver cannon. The first shell exploded in the Fitter's aft engine compartment, and the rest walked up the length of the fuselage.

Any one of those rounds would have been enough to destroy the fighter, but the ones that tore open the Fitter's fuel tanks made the destruction spectacular. Vaporized fuel blew back into the open afterburner section and detonated, tearing the fighter in two.

Seeing his partner's fate, the remaining Iranian pilot tried for a low-level getaway. Jettisoning all of his remaining underwing ordnance in one dump, he swung his fighter's wings all the way back to the maximum sweep and slammed his throttle past the stop as he kicked in his afterburners. Against another opponent, the Iranian might have had half a chance. But his old Sukhoi wasn't quite up to modern dogfighting standards.

The Iranian pilot was on the deck and doing a little better than Mach 1.5 when the MiG flight leader spotted him on his fire-control radar and turned after him. From that point on, the Iranian pilot was dead.

With the MiG-29's look-down-shoot-down fire-control system, it was easy for the Russian pilot to pick the Fitter out of the ground clutter on the radar return, get a lock-on and fire a heat-seeking AA-2 Atoll missile at the fleeing Iranian fighter.

When the Russian's missile was low enough, it leveled out and flew up the Fitter's tail pipe. A billowing fireball formed low in the sky, and flaming wreckage slammed into the ground, where it exploded again.

The MiG flight leader did a slow victory roll over the smoking wreckage in the desert before pulling up into a steep climb like a homesick angel. Overhead his wingmen went into a wide orbit over the Blackbird in case the Iranians hadn't had enough.

"I never thought I'd be so happy to see MiG fighters overhead." Grimaldi shook his head.

"Times change," Bolan said.

"Don't they just."

"Phoenix, this is Mother Hen," the Russian AWACS radio operator called. "The sky is clear. I say again, the sky is clear. The heavy-lift helicopter is inbound and will be there in thirty minutes. Over."

"Phoenix, roger." Bolan replied. "Out."

"The Skycrane's coming," he told McCarter.

"Good," the Briton said, his eyes flicking to the three smoke plumes rising in the air from the downed Fitters. "I think we've about worn out our welcome here."

"I think you could say that." The Executioner also took in the crash sites. "It's too bad that we're not done with this place yet."

"Isn't it?"

WHEN THE GIANT RUSSIAN Mi-26 helicopter flew into sight, Hoffsteader put his helmet back on and slid up the visor.

"Where do you think you're going?" Grimaldi asked.

"I'm going to ride back in the SR when they lift her out," the pilot replied.

"Why?"

"That way I can use the rudders to help keep her lined up with the direction of flight. She's so heavy that if she starts oscillating on the sling, they'll have to dump her to keep from crashing themselves."

"But that'll put you at risk if they do have to drop it."

Hoffsteader shrugged. "Any time you climb in that aircraft, you put your life on the line. And from what's happened to me so far today, it'll be a piece of cake."

"Go ahead. I'll explain it to Striker and clear it with him."

"When you're done, how about explaining it to me? I must be out of my rabbit-assed mind to even think of doing something like this."

"If you're working with us, buddy," Grimaldi said, grinning, "I know you're out of your mind."

Hoffsteader gave Grimaldi a steady look. "Someday you're going have to tell me who you guys really are."

"Take my word for it." Grimaldi was suddenly very serious. "You don't want to know."

"I can almost believe that."

The Stony Man pilot didn't break a smile. "Believe it."

CHAPTER TWENTY-TWO

The huge Russian Mi-26 heavy-lift helicopter looked like a giant dragonfly on steroids as it touched down on the sand briefly to off-load the three-man recovery crew. Its bulging forward canopy, spindly landing gear and whirring rotor disk only reinforced that image.

"That is one butt-ugly helicopter," Hawkins remarked as he watched it take off again.

"It looks a lot like the old Skycranes they used in Vietnam," Grimaldi commented.

"Those were long out of service by the time I put on a green suit."

"You missed seeing something. I've seen them lift out an entire battery of 105s and their ammunition on one lift."

The Russian recovery experts knew their business. While the massive Mi-26 hovered out of the way, they scrambled over the top of the Blackbird and quickly affixed their lifting cables to the SR's hard points. When they signaled that they were ready, the heavy-lift chopper flew over and came to a hover directly above the spy plane. The winch operator in the Mi-26 sat in a aft-facing compartment and called minor adjustments to the chopper's pilots as he let down the winch lines to be hooked to the lifting cables.

As soon as everything was secure, Hoffsteader climbed back into the cockpit of the SR and strapped himself in. When he called over the radio that he was ready, the Mi-26's massive Lotaryev D-136 turbines changed pitch to howl at full RPM. Under the torque of over twenty thousand horsepower, the eight-bladed rotor spun faster and faster until the blades were almost a blur. Slowly the chopper rose straight into the air, lifting the Blackbird off the ground.

The winch operator played with his controls until the spy plane was riding straight and level. Once his oversize load was five hundred feet off the ground, the Mi-26 pilot nudged forward on his cyclic control, and the chopper started moving forward.

It was ironic to see the world's fastest airplane being carried beneath a helicopter. The SR-71 had set dozens of speed and altitude records, but this would go down in the books as the slowest flight ever made by a Blackbird.

As soon as the Russian heavy lift chopper and its unconventional load were out of sight, Mack Bolan brought the radio mike to his lips. It was time for them to get out of there before more Iranian aircraft or ground troops showed up.

Fifteen minutes later the green-and-brown-camouflaged Russian Mi-8 Hip troop carrier touched down on the sand in a flurry of dust. Running to it bent over to clear the rotor blades, Grimaldi and Phoenix Force scrambled on board. The Russian pilot then pulled pitch to his rotors and pointed his nose toward Ufazek and home.

McCarter buckled himself into the troop seat next to Hawkins in the chopper's cabin. ''That was a damned fine shot you made with the Stinger,'' he said. ''That Fitter had us cold.''

''No big deal,'' Hawkins answered modestly. ''That guy obviously had never come up against a Stinger before, because he didn't even try to fire flares or anything.''

''Nonetheless,'' McCarter said, clapping him on the shoulder, ''that was a damned fine shot.''

''Thanks.''

''I take it that's not the first time you ever used one of those things.''

''I've fired them at target drones before but never at the real thing.''

McCarter grinned. ''This was as real as it gets.''

''You got that right.''

''THEY'RE OUT OF IRAN,'' Aaron Kurtzman stated.

He and Barbara Price had been standing by in the Computer Room ever since the Blackbird had gone down. The President had been notified of the situation immediately and was also standing by to see how the crisis developed. If the Iranians captured the plane intact, an air strike would be ordered to destroy it.

"With the SR-71?" Brognola's voice betrayed his anxiety.

"Yes, everything's clear."

"Casualties?"

"Only a few Iranians and a couple of their fighters."

Both Brognola and Price relaxed visibly. "Get together all the information you have about this as soon as you can," he said. "I need to take it to the President and explain what happened over there."

"I can give you what I have right now, but I'll have to wait until the Blackbird gets back to the air base before I can report on any damage it might have."

"I'll take what you have now. I've got to report to the President as soon as possible."

"I'll alert your pilot."

MAJOR KARIM NAZAR didn't have anyone to take his rage out on this time. Colonel Mizra was dead, killed by the American intruders. Worse than that, however, was that even though the spy plane had been brought down, the Americans had recovered it before it could be captured or destroyed. Displaying a captured American spy plane in Tehran would have electrified the entire Muslim world. Everyone would have seen the proof of the Great Satan's transgressions against Iran. But that wasn't to be.

Nazar was more convinced than ever that the Americans were planning some kind of military action against the Shabaz Facility. For them to have made the risky effort they had to recover the plane meant that they were seriously concerned. The only question was what they would try to do next. His first thought was that they would use Stealth fighters or cruise missiles as they had used to destroy Saddam Hussein's Baghdad.

But if they did something like that, they risked open warfare with Iran, and the American President was still saying that he didn't want to worsen the situation between the two nations. Plus, now that the HAWK missile batteries had been installed, an aerial attack, even by cruise missiles, would fail. The HAWKs were more than capable of destroying the slow-flying missiles that had devastated Baghdad during the Gulf War. Nazar had enjoyed seeing Hussein's humiliation, even at the hands of unbelievers.

Then there was the protection that the dam provided. An air attack, even an unsuccessful one, would risk hitting the dam itself, and he didn't think that the Americans would be willing to damage the UN sanctioned project and its power generators.

Even so, it wouldn't be wise for him to underestimate them. Picking up the phone, he rang through to Wilhelm Kessler's office at the other end of the building. "There has been another incident," he said when the German answered. "We need to talk."

"I'll be right there."

"The Americans sent another spy plane over today," Nazar said when Kessler walked into his office.

The German bristled. He hoped that he wasn't going to start having trouble with these people as he'd had with the Libyans. He was too close to success to stop now. "I thought your air force had promised to stop them."

"They did," Nazar said, his voice tight. "The aircraft was damaged and forced down."

"Was the crew captured?"

Nazar shook his head. "No. Both they and the plane were rescued before we could move troops in to capture it."

There was little Kessler could say to that. He was smart enough to know that war always had an element of luck to it and it was a war that they were in now. Even so, this wasn't a good sign.

"What is the status on your project?" Nazar asked.

"I am almost ready to start molding the warhead casings," the German replied. "We have had to make even more adjustments to the molding machines to compensate for the density of the matrix material. I will be running some test castings tomorrow, and if they fit properly, we'll be able to start producing them within a week.''

"And then how long will it take to produce the five hundred we need and fit them to the missiles?''

"They can be finished within a month.''

Nazar's eyes gleamed. Within a month Iran would own the Middle East. The Islamic revolution would finally triumph over the forces of darkness, and God's will would be done. The Americans and the other forces of Satan would be helpless to stop the march of Islam this time. After the Middle East was consolidated under the rule of Tehran, they would be able to reach out even farther.

"It will be a great day, my friend.'' Nazar could call this unclean foreigner a friend because his work was making all of this possible.

"Is it still planned to use the first missile on Tel Aviv?'' Kessler asked.

"That is the plan,'' Nazar replied.

"I want to be there when the missile is fired.''

"I can see that you are.''

"But,'' Nazar said, returning to his major concern, "for you to be there on that great day, I have to ensure that day will come. That is what I must concentrate on now.''

"Do you think the Americans will try to stop me?''

"I think there is a good chance that they will, but I have taken added precautions. Short of going to war, which they will not dare to do, there is nothing they can do to hurt us here."

"I will hold you to that."

"Plus," Nazar said, "we have an operation underway that should divert attention from here."

"What is that?"

"The Islamic action groups in the United States have been activated. I think that before long, the Yankees will be so involved within their own borders that they will not have time to worry about what we are doing here."

"I hope that you are right."

BOLAN AND PHOENIX FORCE beat the heavily burdened Mi-26 back to the air base and were waiting when the heavy-lift chopper gently deposited its load in the tarmac in front of the hangar. A Russian tow tractor was waiting to hook up to the Blackbird's nose gear, and the damaged spy plane was quickly pulled into the hangar.

Before it had even rolled to a stop, Master Sergeant Benihana and the Air Force ground crew were all over it. Hoffsteader, Grimaldi and Katzenelenbogen watched as they examined the right engine. A minute later the crew chief called the pilot over.

"There it is," Hoffsteader said, pointing to the damaged shock cone on the right-hand engine. "That's why I had the flame out. Without the shock cone working properly to slow the incoming air, the engine won't run."

"If you could get the parts, do you think it could be fixed here?" Katzenelenbogen asked.

"You mean have the ground crew do it?"

Katz nodded. "With the help of the Russian mechanics, yes."

The pilot shrugged. "I don't see why not. The Russians work on their MiG-29s, and they're certainly state-of-the-art airplaines. With our guys instructing them, they shouldn't have any problems."

"Okay, have your people start taking that engine apart so you can get me a list of the parts you need."

THE WORD that the Blackbird had been safely returned to the base at Ufazek was well received at Stony Man Farm. "Katz says that they think they can repair the Blackbird so it can be flown home," Kurtzman reported to Price. "They're working up a list of the parts they need and will get it to us ASAP."

"That may be the least of our worries right now," Price replied. "Hal called and said he's bringing us a new mission for Phoenix Force."

"I take it that they've finished analyzing the data from the sensors and cameras."

"Apparently."

"And the President wants them to go in and take out the site."

"I'm afraid so." Price's voice was low. This mission had started out well, but it was beginning to look jinxed. Sending Phoenix Force against a target like that was wishful thinking at best. More than likely it, too, would become a disaster, and someone would get killed.

"That's not going to be easy," Kurtzman continued, thinking out loud. "After the Blackbird fiasco, they've lost the element of surprise and they'll be going up against a place that's going to be ready for them."

"I know. It won't be the first time, and I'm damned sure it won't be the last."

CHAPTER TWENTY-THREE

Hal Brognola's unmarked Bell helicopter flared out over the Farm's landing pad, and the pilot killed the turbine as soon as the skids touched down. As the rotor blades wound down to a halt, the big Fed stepped out of the aircraft to find Barbara Price waiting for him.

"We have confirmation of the threat," he said, answering the unasked question in her eyes. "The sensor readings are clear. They're making radioactive-cobalt weapons at Shabaz."

"And?" she prompted, knowing the answer even as she asked the question.

"The President wants Phoenix Force to take the place out. But," he added hastily, "they'll have help from the Russians on this, as well. Moscow is also very concerned and has offered every assistance short of open war."

The Stony Man staff was waiting when Brognola walked into the War Room and stepped up to the slide projector. Slipping a magazine of slides into place, he switched on the machine. An aerial view of the Shabaz dam area flashed on the big screen at the end of the room.

"This is the latest photo of Shabaz, Iran," he said. "And it was taken during the Blackbird's recon run. The sensor readouts and photo analysis both indicate that the Israeli Mossad's suspicions about this place are correct. The Iranians are definitely making radioactive cobalt there. Armed with this information, the Man has decided to take action before the project goes any further."

He locked eyes with Price. "He wants to know if Phoenix Force can launch a strike from the Russian air base."

"That depends," she replied, "on what kind of backup and support they can expect from the military."

"Nothing from the U.S. military beyond what they already have."

"The Man's catching political flak again?"

Brognola nodded. "The Iranians have raised a hue and cry over the Blackbird flights, particularly the last one when they lost the aircraft they sent to intercept it. But the President is playing dumb."

No one took that obvious opening and Brognola continued. "Therefore, we have to go covert all the way on this one, plausible deniability and the whole nine yards. However, like I said, the Man is making arrangements for the Russians to provide backup and transportation to the target. He shared the recon data with Moscow, and they're even more concerned than he is. After all, they're closer to Iran and are more likely to be targets for these weapons.''

''You're talking about a ground raid, aren't you?'' Price asked, her eyes flicking to the slide showing the impressive defenses around the isolated building.

''Actually I'm thinking more of an aerial assault. Striker will be given full access to the Russian choppers where he is, and they can be used to transport them to within striking range.''

''But you're still talking about walking in there and blowing the place up,'' she insisted.

''That is the plan, yes,'' he admitted.

''And if they can't break through?''

He paused before answering. ''If that's the case, there's going to be a terrible accident at the dam, similar to the one that took out Khaddafi's fertilizer factory, but aerial delivered this time. The President cannot risk this project continuing unmolested. One way or the other it will be stopped, you can be sure of that.''

''Then why not do that in the first place instead of risking our team?'' Price asked. ''Particularly if the Russians are in on this with us.''

''This is one time that I totally agree with you,'' he said candidly. ''And I argued for that option myself, but a consideration came up that I hadn't thought of.''

"And that is?"

"The problem is that we're dealing with metallic cobalt in powdered form this time. As you know, the isotopes are highly radioactive, and a couple of tons of cruise-missile-delivered high explosive will scatter it and contaminate a large area of Iran."

"That's their problem," Kurtzman said. "If they weren't screwing around with the stuff, there wouldn't be a problem, would there?"

"Again I agree with you," Brognola said. "The concern, though, is with the Qezel Owzan River rather than with Iran itself. The river flows into the Caspian Sea, and if it is contaminated, it'll create a major environmental catastrophe. The Caspian borders several nations, including Russia, and is a major food source for all of them. The President doesn't want to go down in history as the man who poisoned the Caspian Sea for the next thousand years."

With that kind of argument, there was little Price or Kurtzman could say.

"Okay," she said. "We send them in on foot."

"Get with Katz and Striker, work up a plan and I'll get the President to give the go-ahead."

"WE JUST GOT our marching orders," Yakov Katzenelenbogen reported to Mack Bolan.

The Executioner saw the look on his face and said, "Hal wants us to hit the site."

"Right. And he sent us a rational explanation of why they want us to do it."

Bolan raised one eyebrow. Explanations weren't one of Brognola's strong points. He was known as a bringer of bad news who didn't bother to dress it up. If he had taken the time to explain, the situation had to be more serious than usual.

"But," Katz added, "we'll be working with the Russians this time. They're going to provide the air support and a diversionary force for us, but we're to hit the primary target."

"Let's get the people together," the Executioner said, "and start hammering this thing out."

"You want me to bring Colonel Popov in on it at this stage?"

"Do that. If he's going to put his people on the line, he's earned the right to be in on the planning from start to finish."

"I agree."

"WHERE ARE WE GOING?" Grimaldi asked when he was told of the mission briefing.

"You're not," Bolan stated. "Brognola wants you to stay here with Katz and the Blackbird. I know you want to go with the lift ships, but we need you here."

"That's a long flight, in and out," Grimaldi reminded him. "It might be helpful to have me along if it gets sticky along the way."

"I know," Bolan agreed. He and Grimaldi had been through more than one aerial adventure, and the hotshot pilot was a good man to have along. "But Hal thinks you stay here. I think he's worried that the Russians will run off with the Blackbird."

"Hell, I should just sell it to them and we could all retire on the proceeds."

"Dream on."

THE PLAN THAT WAS worked up between the Stony Man staff, Bolan, Katzenelenbogen and the Russian colonel was complicated, but only because the situation itself was complicated. The latest Keyhole satellite photos showed that Shabaz had recently acquired a battery of three American-made HAWK missile launchers to add to the Russian-made SAM-6 defenses that were already in place.

The Homing All the Way Killers were older missiles, but they weren't to be shrugged off. Though the design dated from the fifties, they were still among the best ground-launched, medium-range antiaircraft weapons that had ever been made. Anything that the longer-ranging SAMs missed, the HAWKs were sure to hit. And each launcher carried three missiles.

A classic aerial assault on the site would result in the choppers being blown out of the sky like so many clay pigeons. The same went with a fighter-bomber attack. Unless Washington and Moscow were prepared to go all out and launch a Gulf War–style air strike with Wild Weasels and Stealth fighters leading the way, throwing pilots away made no sense.

The missile batteries, however, were vulnerable to a ground attack. A commando raid to take them out would serve two purposes: it would make a later aerial attack, were it seen necessary, much safer, plus it would draw the defenders' attention from the research facility, which was the primary objective of the raid.

Colonel Popov said that a platoon of Russian special forces, the Spetsnaz, had been tasked to take out the HAWK and SAM launchers. Moscow had also authorized the use of the helicopters to carry the raiders to Shabaz, but they hadn't cleared the use of MiG fighter cover inside the Iranian border.

Bolan and Katz didn't bother to ask why Moscow would allow the use of the choppers but had decided to withhold the MiGs. Russian politics was even more convoluted than American, and there probably wasn't a reason that made any sense. Nonetheless, with a little bit of luck they could pull it off with what they had to work with.

HAWKINS FOUND HIMSELF getting charged up as he prepared for the mission ahead of him. It didn't sound like the easiest thing he had ever tried to do, but it sure as hell beat baby-sitting an airplane. The perverse lure of combat was that it was exciting, and the adrenaline charged excitement washed away all fears. Now that he was getting ready to go into battle for the first time since Somalia, he realized how much he had missed it.

An outsider to the world of war had no idea how seductive combat was. There was something about risking your life, putting all of your tomorrows on the line for one glorious, exciting today that could never be explained to someone who hadn't done it. And even then, the only ones who really understood were those who had become one with the god of war.

Those few were the men who had learned to overcome their fears and would do their best no matter what the odds were against them. They didn't pray for the right outcome or look to luck to pull them through, and they never quit even when they were going down to defeat. These were the men who counted on their guts and their well-honed battle skills to achieve the outcome they wanted. Modestly, Hawkins put himself in that category, and he knew that he had earned that right.

While he still wasn't sure how well he was going to fit in with the seasoned Phoenix Force veterans, he knew that they were also true adrenaline junkies. The task they were facing was one of the most daunting he had ever encountered, but he had no fears. Even if it all blew up in their faces and they went down with guns blazing, he would still have no fears. Death in combat was not to be feared, not when you fought with brother warriors at your side.

Watching his teammates get ready for the mission was as familiar to him as the well-broken-in combat boots he was lacing on his feet. The things they did and said to each other, he had said and done himself a hundred times before. It was like going home for Christmas after a long absence and it felt real good.

For the first time since he had let Bolan and Katz talk him into this, he was dead certain that he had done the right thing.

ONCE MORE CNN managed to ruin Major Nazar's day. He had been so busy trying to keep track of the American-spy-plane situation that he almost missed the news from Miami, Florida. The story of the explosion at the garden-supply store was at the top of the hour, as was the investigation that had turned up several hundred pounds of ready-to-go fertilizer-and-diesel-oil explosive. The fact that it was reported that six men of Middle Eastern origin had died in the accidental blast made it clear that the Americans knew what was going on.

There was an additional report that the authorities were investigating ties between the Miami bombers and the recent terrorist attacks in California. Though the CNN report didn't say, it was obvious to Nazar that there had been a security lapse on the part of the Miami action groups. They had left something behind that made a connection to the Oakland groups and that was inexcusable. If he could, Nazar would have gladly executed the men who hadn't followed their standing orders to leave no paper trail.

Since they were already dead, though, he could do nothing. Worse than that, he knew that he wouldn't be able to go to the security council again and request that more action groups be activated. It had been a good plan, but it had been foiled from the beginning.

Now there was nothing to draw America's attention from what was happening at Shabaz, and he could expect some kind of attack. At least he had the HAWKs, and they could beat back anything short of a major aerial assault. Plus an armor battalion had been moved into the military base only thirty miles away and was on call in case he needed reinforcements. He was satisfied that he had enough forces at his command to beat back any commando attack. And once he had bullet-riddled American bodies to display in Tehran, the entire security council would be at his feet.

Not that he wanted any personal reward for the job he had done protecting the Shabaz project. He did what he did for the glory of the Islamic revolution. But if he were the chief of the Internal Security Force, the revolution would progress much faster and much smoother. With him in control and Kessler's cobalt weapons at his beck and call, Islam would triumph over the West.

CHAPTER TWENTY-FOUR

Colonel Viktor Popov tracked Bolan down early on the first morning of the mission prep at Ufazek. "I just got word that the Spetsnaz unit from Moscow will be here within the hour."

"That's good," Bolan replied. "I want to have the time to run through at least one practice with them before we go."

The Spetsnaz were the Russian equivalent of the U.S. Army Special Forces, with a touch of the Rangers and the SEALs thrown in. They were the elite of the Russian elite forces and had been formed to fight the *mujahedeen* during the Afghan war. Taking a page from the American Army's experience fighting irregular Vietcong forces in Vietnam, the Spetsnaz were experts in aerial assaults, ambushes, raids, sabotage and other small-unit actions.

For what Bolan and Katz had worked up for the Shabaz Facility, the Russian commandos were the perfect unit to join the Stony Man team on the mission.

THE STONY MAN TEAM had been wearing combat blacksuits at Ufazek to be instantly distinguishable from the Russians and the Blackbird ground crew. But now that they were going into Iran, they switched to American Army desert-camouflage battle-dress uniforms—BDUs—when they went out to meet the arriving Russians.

The Spetsnaz commandos stormed out of their Mi-8 helicopters, their weapons in hand, and fell into formation in front of Bolan and Katz. A young captain in the blue beret of the Spetsnaz stepped out smartly and took his place at the head of the formation.

"Captain Yuri Brunov, Second Special Operations Brigade," he reported as he brought his hand up in a sharp salute.

Colonel Popov took the salute and introduced Bolan as Colonel Rance Pollock. The Russian commando officer saluted again, and Bolan returned it.

"I understand that you have an interesting mission for us, Colonel," Brunov stated.

"I think your men will find it challenging enough."

"That is good enough for us, sir. We like a challenge."

HAWKINS WAS FAMILIAR with the Russian Spetsnaz. As an Army Ranger, he had studied them as probable enemies on a future battlefield. Now that they were working the same side of the street, he had to change mental gears. He had to admit that they were a sharp-looking bunch as they trooped into the briefing room to hear what they had been given to do.

McCarter introduced each member of Phoenix Force to the Russian officers and NCOs, using cover names, then launched into the briefing. The plan he laid out was complicated, but necessitated by the defenses around Shabaz. Using the latest satellite photos that had been faxed from Stony Man Farm, he pointed out the HAWK missile batteries that were to be the Russians' first targets.

"You have given us the lion's share," Brunov said. "And I am glad. I was afraid that we would have little to do. We came a long way to join you, and it would have been a pity not to have some fun while we are here."

McCarter smiled. "I can assure you, Captain, that you will have more than enough to do at Shabaz. In fact, the whole mission hangs on you. We won't be able to make our move until you and your men have been successful."

"We will be successful, sir. I can assure you of that. Most of my men were bloodied in the Afghan war, and the Iranians are children compared to the *mujiahedeen.*"

McCarter wasn't too sure about that, but he liked to see a man who was confident about his work.

WHILE THE BRIEFING for the Spetsnaz commandos was going on, Grimaldi was in another room going over the air-assault plan with the five Russian chopper pilots who would fly the mission. Three of them would pilot the Mi-8 Hip lift ships, two for the Spetsnaz and the third for Phoenix Force, and the other two were Mi-24 Hind F gunship pilots. Even though they were relying on speed, surprise and stealth to protect them, the two gunships were insurance that if something went wrong, there would be a way out.

Known as the Flying Battleship, the Mi-24 Hind had made its combat debut in the skies over the barren hills and valleys of Afghanistan. Though they were an older design, their heavy armor and even heavier armament made them a worthy opponent even against more-modern machines.

As an additional precaution, all of the Russian choppers going on the mission had been overpainted with Iranian air force markings. The phony markings wouldn't fool radar if they were picked up coming in low over the Caspian Sea. But they might make anyone who saw them pause before automatically blowing them out of the sky as they would do if they spotted the bold red stars of the Russian air force.

A PLAN AS COMPLICATED as the assault on Shabaz didn't come together overnight. That wasn't to say, however, that there wasn't as great a sense of urgency about the mission at Stony Man Farm as there was at Ufazek. Whatever the weapons the Iranians were making—and the Farm staff was still working with the Mossad and the CIA to try to pin that down exactly—they had to be neutralized while they were still at the Shabaz Facility. Once they were issued to the Iranian army units, it would take open warfare to track them down and destroy them.

Communications flew back and forth between Ufazek and Stony Man Farm, as well as between Moscow and Washington, as the details were hammered out. Information normally considered top secret was freely exchanged as even more residuals of the cold war paranoia were erased. If the world was to become a safer place in the future, Russia and the United States were the only two nations that could ensure that it did.

"I think it's finally a go," a weary Barbara Price told Aaron Kurtzman. It had been so long since she had last seen her bed, she could hardly remember what it looked like, much less felt like. Kurtzman didn't look much better than she did, but he was still charging ahead. Sometimes she thought that he was plugged in to some kind of mysterious energy source that emanated from his keyboard and was absorbed through his fingertips.

"You look like you could use a cup of coffee," he said cheerfully when he turned to face her.

She shuddered at the thought of assaulting her body with even more caffeine. "No," she said firmly. "I need to sleep. I need to lay my tired body down and let nature perform a miracle on it. You know, wash out all the fatigue toxins, flush the excess caffeine from the system, reoxygenate my brain cells, rest my eyes so they'll stop aching, give my feet a break, all that good stuff."

"Why don't you go take a nap, then, I'll let you know if anything happens."

"But they're about to move out, and I need to be here when Hal arrives."

"They've got a three-hour flight over the Caspian before they even reach Iran, and Hal will understand."

She rubbed her tired eyes. "I think I will try to sleep," she said. "But I want you to wake me when Hal gets here."

"Will do."

Everything was finally ready at Ufazek. The helicopters that would ferry the two strike forces had been serviced and double-checked. The fuel tanks were topped off, and the ammo bays of the Hinds couldn't hold another round. Every man of the strike forces, both the Phoenix Force warriors and the Russian Spetsnaz commandos, had gone over their equipment in detail. Their weapons were clean, their magazines loaded, all the radios had fresh batteries in them, as did the night-vision equipment. Their canteens were full to the top, and every man carried two days' worth of emergency rations.

Katzenelenbogen stood outside the hangar with Bolan as the men of Phoenix Force boarded the chopper that would fly them in. It felt strange for him not to be suited up and climbing aboard with them. "I don't like it, Mack," the gruff Israeli stated.

"What do you mean?" Bolan frowned. If Katz was having second thoughts about this operation, he'd better pay attention to them.

"Not going with them," he said, nodding toward the waiting helicopter.

Bolan understood exactly what the old Israeli warrior meant. After a life spent going to war in trouble spots all over the world, staying behind was difficult. But as they both knew, Katz was more valuable to Phoenix Force working where he was now.

"I have a feeling that we're going to need you more here this time. I know that the Russians have done everything they can to help us, but you know how that can change in an instant. If the situation turns bad against us, we'll be depending on you to keep us from hanging in the wind."

Katz knew that Bolan was right, particularly about the Russians not being completely dependable. Nonetheless, it still felt strange to watch his old comrades-in-arms fly off without him.

"I guess I'd better get this show on the road," Bolan said. "It's going to be a long flight."

"Take care, Mack."

"We'll be back."

"THEY'VE LIFTED OFF," Aaron Kurtzman announced.

Barbara Price looked much better after her nap and felt recharged to face what lay ahead. "What's their flight time to the LZ?"

"If they don't run into head winds over the Caspian Sea, they'll hit the landing zone at 1930 hours local, give or take a few."

Price glanced up at the bank of clocks on the wall. It was almost 1730 hours in Tehran now, so that meant two hours give or take. That would give her time to check in on the other things she had cooking before Brognola showed up and she had to concentrate totally on the Shabaz operation.

At the next cubicle, Hunt Wethers was ramroding the effort to locate the parts needed to fix the broken Blackbird.

She walked over to check in with him. "How're are you doing with it?"

"I just about have it wrapped up," Wethers answered. "The big hang-up has been finding a particular little drive motor that controls the movement of the intake shock cone. It's one of those things that has to be changed every so often, and there aren't all that many of them left from the original procurement.''

One of the reasons that the SR-71s had been taken out of service had been that very point. Every machine needed spare parts, and the government procurement system fell apart when it came to parts for older aircraft. Once the original contract for an item was finished, the company scrapped the tooling. So if more parts needed to be made, new tooling had to be done first, and the cost was astronomical. That had been a problem for years with almost everything the government ordered, but no one had ever bothered to change the system.

''But not to fear. I located one of them at Lockheed Palmdale in a stock of spares that's been in storage since Kadena closed out. As soon as it's been tested, it will be flown to Andrews to join the C-141 that's waiting to take the parts to Ufazek. They have a double aircrew, and they'll fly nonstop with aerial refueling.''

''Good work,'' Price said. ''That's one more thing I don't have to worry about.''

She also didn't have to worry any longer about the Able Team operation against the Islamic action groups in the United States. The FBI had turned up enough evidence at Amur's house in Miami that they had been able to take over the investigation and give Able a rest.

The only thing on her plate right now was the mission against Shabaz, and that was more than enough. Even though Katz had assured her that the Russians were in it all the way, she still had reservations. Although Stony Man had worked with the Russians on several operations since the fall of the old Soviet regime, they were still Russians and they had their own agenda. And that went double whenever the Middle East was involved.

The lure of Arab petrodollars was strong to a nation that desperately needed foreign currency to keep its economy afloat. Weapons, ammunition and high-tech-equipment sales were vital to Russia, and the Middle Eastern nations were their best customers. Hopefully the threat this time was big enough for Moscow to focus on the long-term gain rather than another quick sale.

One way or the other, she'd find out soon enough. The clock was running.

THE LONG FLIGHT over the Caspian Sea was made right on the wave tops and in complete radio silence. If something needed to be sent back to Katz, the Arabic-speaking Russian pilot of Phoenix Force's Hip helicopter would radio it in code to another Arabic-speaking Russian working in the Ufazek operations center.

On the flight the men of Phoenix Force and Bolan relaxed as best they could and most of them napped. Even though Hawkins had been in the Army long enough to know that a soldier should grab a catnap whenever he could, he couldn't sleep. Knowing that he had a long night's march ahead of him and that this was no time to be getting premission jitters, he laid back in the canvas troop seat and tried to rest anyway.

McCarter woke everyone when they crossed the beach into Iran. "Heads up, lads," he said. "We just entered the bad part of town."

Even over dry land, the Hip chopper stayed as close to the earth as it could. In the cockpit the Russian pilots followed a terrain-reading-radar navigation set as they made their way through the valleys, always keeping a ridge line between them and the radars at Shabaz.

The planned landing zone was eighteen miles from the objective, a good night's walk, but it was as close as the chopper could get without showing up on the dam's radar system. Had it not been for the unique configuration of the terrain at the landing zone, a valley flanked by a long ridge to the south, they couldn't have even gotten that close.

"It's clear," McCarter called out after scoping the area around the LZ with his night vision goggles.

Slipping into the shoulder straps of his ruck sack, Hawkins checked his weapon one last time and clicked it on Safe. Accidentally triggering a weapon while exiting a chopper was a stupid rookie stunt.

Flaring out over a clearing at the base of the ridge line, the Hip touched its wheels down. "Go! Go! Go!" McCarter shouted over the *wop-wop* of the rotors.

The men exited the Hip and ran a dozen yards to clear the rotor disk before going to ground. Behind them the Hip pulled pitch and lifted off.

CHAPTER TWENTY-FIVE

As soon as the Hip lifted off and flew north to its planned holding point, James looked around at the desolate landscape they found themselves in. Though the sun had set, there was still enough light to clearly see their surroundings.

"So much for a high-tech mission where we don't have to get down in the dirt," he said.

The area around the Shabaz dam was touted as an Iranian tropical garden, but they were starting their journey in a rocky, barren desert.

"'Into each life a little rain must fall,'" McCarter replied with a grin.

"There ain't been all that much rain here since before the Great Flood," Hawkins observed. "And it smells just like Iraq."

"Desiccated camel shit and dust?" James asked.

"Right on."

When the rest of the team took up security positions around the LZ, Gary Manning broke out the military-issue Global Positioning System navigation equipment to get a firm fix on their location. The GPS gear Stony Man had given them was the new Slugger

II system that had just been issued to the Army, and it was the most accurate infantry land-navigation system that had ever been developed.

GPS navigation worked by exchanging signals with the twenty-four Navstar satellites orbiting the earth at a height of 10,900 miles. When the GPS receiver made contact with three of the satellites, it used the satellites' precise locations in orbit at that particular split second to triangulate its exact location on the ground. The grid location that was shown on the readout was accurate to within five yards of wherever it happened to be on earth.

If the Slugger II system had a fault, it was that the GPS gear worked only as well as the map that was being used with it. But that wasn't a problem this time, because Stony Man had provided them the latest issues of the American military maps of the region. Ever since the Carter administration bungled the Iran hostage crisis, the DOD mapping center had been working overtime keeping the maps of Iran updated. Only a fool would think that the United States would never have to go to war with Iran.

"That Russian chopper pilot was good," Manning told Bolan. "We're within a hundred yards of where we wanted to be."

"Let's get moving, then."

Manning took the point with James as his slack and Hawkins on drag as the six men started for their objective roughly eighteen miles away.

"THERE IT IS," Wilhelm Kessler said proudly as he pointed to the hollow cylinder on the wheeled dolly. "The first production casting. We have fitted it to the dummy warhead, and it will work perfectly."

Major Nazar thought that the object looked rather unimpressive. It was little more than a length of large-diameter, thick-wall plastic pipe that had one of the open ends tapered for a third of its length. It had been painted with a thick coat of lead-based olive-color paint, which hid the light blue color of the plastic underneath.

Nazar wasn't deceived by the unobtrusive paint. He knew that it served to block the radiation from the cobalt dust that was impregnated in the plastic. Even with the coat of lead paint, the hollow plastic cylinder wasn't something that anyone would want to have sitting in his or her living room. Without the paint the plastic would have glowed in the dark.

It wasn't impressive, but Nazar knew what a technical accomplishment this first cylinder represented and what it meant for his motherland. These olive green casings would turn the standard thousand-pound HE warheads of the Scud missiles into one of the most deadly weapons in the world. They couldn't completely obliterate an entire city like the megaton nuclear weapons of the United States and Russia, but they would render a city uninhabitable for hundreds of years.

These cobalt bombs, even as crude as they were, put Iran in the forefront of world politics, because of all of the nuclear-armed nations, they were the only ones who actually had the courage and determination to actually use the weapons. And as surely as God had spoken to his Prophet, they would use them on the infidels.

The green banners of Islam would once more advance, and the decadent Western nations would fall before them like they had done in days of old.

"You have done a great thing here, Kessler," Nazar told the renegade German scientist. "And you will be well rewarded for it."

"The best reward I can have," Kessler answered, "is to be on hand when the first of the rockets is launched."

"You will be at my side, I promise you that."

THE LONG MARCH to the hills overlooking the Shabaz dam took most of the night. But the terrain was open, and with their night vision goggles, the Stony Man warriors made good time.

When they reached the back side of the hills, they went into a tactical formation. The recon-satellite shots hadn't shown the Iranians running any patrols in the hills, but there was no point in taking chances this close to the objective.

The false dawn found them on the crest of the hill looking down onto the dam. "We'll spend the day here," Bolan said as he scanned the complex through his field glasses.

"What if they run security patrols up here?" Hawkins asked.

McCarter smiled thinly. "Then they'd better not find us, right?"

Hawkins could only agree with that. Of all the small-unit operations he had ever been on, he had never been so completely on his own as he was here. This time there would be no one to call for help if it hit the fan. There were no U.S. Army gunships to fly in to aid him, no U.S. artillery firing in support and no ready-reaction force to reinforce them.

This was a small unit commando operation taken to its ultimate expression. There was nothing between him and death except the well-honed battle skills of the five men he was with. Even when the Russian Spetsnaz flew in later that night, it would still be the Stony Man team hitting the facility alone while the Russians hopefully drew the enemy's attention away from them. Six men against a company of infantry in prepared positions was not his idea of equitable odds. But it was a challenge to his fighting skills, and that was why he had signed on with Phoenix Force—he loved challenges.

While Bolan and McCarter kept watch, the other four men prepared fighting positions and took turns catching up on their sleep.

"THEY'VE ARRIVED at the dam," Katzenelenbogen stated.

"I still think it's too risky to have them wait all day in the open like that," Grimaldi said.

"It's got its risks," Katz admitted, "but it gives them a chance to completely scope out the target area and get used to the comings and goings of the garrison. Also they'll be able to move down into their attack position slowly as soon as night falls. That way, when the Russians hit the missile launchers, they'll already be in position to make their move."

"It still sounds risky to me," the pilot grumbled. "I like it better when it's a simple quick-in-and-quick-out job. The old slash-and-burn number."

"So do I. But those missiles make it impossible to pull off a standard aerial assault. They'd be blasted out of the sky before they were even within gunship range."

Grimaldi knew that was true, but he was of the old-chopper-pilot school, and old habits died hard. The good old days of going into a hot LZ under the covering fire of gunships to off-load troops was only possible when the enemy didn't have antiaircraft missiles.

"I'll go talk to the Spetsnaz pilots and make sure they're squared away."

"Do that," Katz said, glad to have Grimaldi occupied.

WITH ALL THE ATTENTION focused on the Shabaz mission, the replacement parts for the Blackbird arrived at Ufazek almost unnoticed. Senior Master Sergeant Joe Benihana jumped on them, however, as soon as the C-141 touched down. After borrowing a couple of Russians who spoke English to help his men, they quickly got the crates off-loaded from the plane and moved into the hangar.

As requested, he had been sent a complete intake-shock-cone unit instead of the individual parts that had been damaged. That would save him many hours of work, as he could simply swap the bad unit for its replacement rather than fit each part. And since the damaged shock-cone unit had already been removed from the starboard-side engine, the work was half-way done.

"Okay, boys and girls," Benihana bellowed. "All I want to see for the next several hours are assholes and elbows. You're about to set a world's record for installing an assembly, intake shock cone, J-58 Model K, one each. Now, get on it!"

Pete Hoffsteader and Jack Grimaldi joined the crew chief. "Sergeant," Hoffsteader said, "is there anything we can do to help?"

Benihana looked both of them up and down. "The best thing that you two gentlemen can do to help this process is to kindly get the hell out of my hangar. We have work to do here, and I don't need any distractions."

"You got it, chief," Hoffsteader said cheerfully. "We'll be in the radio room if you need us."

"Yes, sir."

"What's wrong with him?" Grimaldi asked as they retreated. "All we wanted to do was help."

Hoffsteader laughed. "He's just being a good crew chief. He's got a broken bird to fix, and he doesn't have the time to baby-sit two out-of-work airplane pilots."

Being reminded that he wasn't needed on this mission didn't make Grimaldi a happy man. For all the good he had done so far, he might as well have stayed in the States. "I guess I can always go clean the coffeepot or something useful."

"Don't sweat it," Hoffsteader said. "This thing isn't over yet."

THE SUN WAS GOING DOWN over Ufazek air base when the Russian Spetsnaz troops double-timed out to the two Mi-8 Hip helicopters waiting to carry them to

Shabaz. The two hulking Mi-24 Hind F gunships parked beside them looked like malevolent, mutant dragonflies squatting on the runway. Their stub wings were loaded with UV-32 57 mm rocket pods and laser-guided AT-6 Spiral antiarmor missiles. Under the stepped canopy of the nose was a six barrel 23 mm Gatling cannon capable of spitting out more than three thousand 23 mm armor-piercing and HE rounds per minute.

If the situation turned bad for the Russians and they had to call upon their aerial fire support, the two Hinds could devastate a large area of the dam site.

Colonel Popov, Hoffsteader, Grimaldi and Katzenelenbogen were on hand to see them off. The farewells had been brief, and with a final salute from the lead ship, Captain Brunov ordered the pilots to take off. They too had a three-hour flight before they could go into action and the young officer was anxious to get started.

"Do not worry," Popov told Katz. "They are good men and they will do their job or die trying."

"I just need them to do their job," Katz said. "Hopefully the Iranians will do all the dying."

HAWKINS WOKE instantly when Rafael nudged his foot. "It's your turn on guard," the Cuban said. "We start moving out as soon as it's completely dark."

Looking around, Hawkins saw that the sun was going down over the high plateau to the west. Sheltered by the hills around it, the dam was already in shadow, and the security lights had come on. The dam and the surrounding complex were well lit. Too well for his taste. He could clearly see the fighting positions, the sentries at their posts and the men working behind the lighted windows of the buildings.

The Russian diversion at the missile sites had better work as it had been planned. Walking in there cold was a good way for six men to die.

Taking his place on guard at the top of the ridge line, Hawkins dug into his rucksack and pulled out two ration packs, one for the breakfast he had missed and one for dinner. There was something about waiting to attack that always gave him an appetite. He didn't know who put together Phoenix Force's rations, but they sure as hell beat what the Army issued.

The light faded quickly as it always did in the desert, and after a last radio check with Katz, Bolan formed them up for the march down to their jump-off point. No one had anything to say as they gathered their gear. They had all been through it more times than they could count.

Hawkins had the slack position behind the point as the six men moved down toward the dam. Up on point, Calvin James took his time and carefully picked his way through the boulders and scrub brush, constantly alert for sensors, trip wires or anything else that might alert the Iranians that they were coming.

The last fifty yards they did on their bellies. There was a dip in the ground a hundred yards from the road, and they would wait for the Russians there.

CHAPTER TWENTY-SIX

The two Russian helicopters carrying the Spetsnaz commandos to their LZ had made the same kind of approach to Shabaz that the Stony Man team had made the evening before, flying flat out a few yards off the ground. They came in from the south of the dam, however, because the antiaircraft missile batteries were on that side of the lake.

As had been done with the previous team, the choppers dropped off the Russians short of their objective so they wouldn't risk being picked up on the radars. But because of the hills and ridge lines south of the dam, they were able to get in closer and faced only a ten-mile march to reach their targets.

The Spetsnaz troopers wore their special black-and-dark-gray night-camouflage suits, and every inch of their exposed skin had been darkened with combat cosmetics. The Kalashnikov AK-74s in their hands were also completely matt black from their silencer/flash hiders to their folding buttstocks. Even under the bright starlight of the clear night sky, the Spetsnaz commandos looked like moving shadows.

With their night-vision goggles in place to guide them, the Spetsnaz made good time to their objective. By running for fifteen minutes and then walking for five, they covered the ten miles in a little over an hour. When they saw the hilltop missile batteries outlined against the night sky in front of them, they silently broke into their six-man assault teams and continued on to their individual objectives.

From the dispersal point on, the assault teams moved slowly and cautiously. If they were detected on the way to their objectives and had to pull out, they wouldn't be able to call on the choppers to extract them because the missiles would blow them out of the sky. Until the launchers were taken out, the Russians were on their own.

The pointman of the Spetsnaz assault team approaching the first HAWK battery was known to his comrades as "the Nose." In Afghanistan it had been said that he could smell a *mujahedeen* from a hundred yards away through solid rock. He was closer to his objective than a hundred yards this time, and there was no rock between them, only sand. He had no trouble at all smelling the Iranians.

Carefully scanning the area in front of him with his night-vision goggles, the Russian located the sentry he had first smelled out. The Iranian was sitting with his back to him, leaning against a sandbagged position.

As the Russian watched him, the guard reached into his pocket, pulled out a cigarette and lit up.

The glow of the cigarette's tip glared brightly in the Russian's sensitive night vision goggles, but the Nose smiled in the darkness. He liked going up against amateurs. A sentry who smoked on guard duty was as good as dead.

After sending a click code on his radio to tell his comrades that he was making his move, he pulled the silenced PSS Vul pistol from his holster and flicked it off Safe. With his folding-stock AK-74 slung up over his back where he could get to it in an instant, the Nose crept forward on his belly as silently as a snake.

The sentry had to have sensed that death was coming for him. When the Nose was still twelve yards away, the Iranian turned around, his AK held ready across his chest, and peered out into the darkness. He looked but saw nothing. The red glow of his burning cigarette, even as faint as it was, had completely washed out his night vision.

The Nose knew there was little chance that the sentry would spot him, but he sighted the silenced pistol on the man's right eye anyway. If he lifted the AK, he would be dead before he could raise it to his shoulder.

The Iranian cursed himself for having the jitters, turned back around and, after laying down his AK, leaned back against the sandbags again.

The Russian shifted his aim slightly so that the three luminescent dots aligned on the target's head, steadied his hand and fired. The pistol's muzzle made a soft sound, and the 7.62 mm round took the sentry in the back of the neck at the base of the skull.

With his neural synapses instantly cut off by the bullet slashing through the spine, the Iranian collapsed against the sandbags. Before he could slump to the ground, the Russian commando got to his feet and dashed the last few steps to him. His hand shot out and grabbed the falling man, easing him noiselessly to the ground.

Crouching behind the sandbags, the Russian waited for a long moment to make sure that his kill had gone unheard. When there was no alarm, he reached down to his assault harness, took out his infrared flashlight and signaled to the rest of his assault team that the way was clear.

When the team leader caught up with him, the Nose silently pointed out the other positions he had spotted. The team leader nodded and whispered into his throat mike. While the team leader and the Nose secured their exit, the other four Russians split into two pairs and disappeared into the darkness to do what they did best. In the trade it was known as wet work.

All of the Spetsnaz had silencers on the muzzles of their AK-74s and, when fired on semiautomatic, they were almost completely silent. The faint sounds of the rounds leaving the muzzles was further muffled by the hum of the generators powering the radios and radars in the launch-control van.

One by one the pairs of commandos visited death on the other sentries, then upon their sleeping comrades. Within three minutes a dozen and a half corpses littered the hilltop. The last place to be neutralized was the launch-control-and-radar van.

With the generator humming loudly, there was no way that the duty crew inside could have heard anything that had gone on outside. The four shooters stood in front of the air-conditioned van's door while one of them knocked. When a voice inside answered, he opened the door and stepped back out of the line of fire. A brief fusillade of silenced rounds sent the three Iranians sprawling over their radar consoles and radio sets. Head shots guaranteed that they would stay there.

Now that the last of the launch-site crew had been eliminated, the four Russians went to work on the HAWK missiles and their launchers. Small but powerful radio-controlled shaped charges were placed on each of the missile's warhead sections. When they went off, they would cause the warhead itself to detonate and completely destroy the missile. A similar-shaped charge was placed against the gear housing of the launcher's traversing mechanism. There was no point in leaving anything behind that the Iranians might be able to use later.

While the Nose's assault team set the demolition charges on their HAWK battery, other assault teams did the same at the other two HAWK sites and the larger SAM missile launchers. When the signal to blow the charges was given, the entire hilltop would erupt.

When the last of the demo charges had been placed, the Spetsnaz assault teams joined up again and moved down the hill toward the dam complex for the second part of their mission.

WHILE THE RUSSIAN assault teams were sabotaging the missile launchers, the Stony Man team waited in the shadows at the base of the ridge to cross the top of the dam. It was dangerous for them to approach the research facility by that route, but the satellite photos showed that there were fewer fighting positions on the dam side of the facility compound's perimeter. To get there, though, they first had to take out the guard-house on their side of the dam.

The guardhouse sat at the side of the single-lane road that ran across the top of the dam and was directly in their path. Watching the dam during the day, they had seen that only two men were stationed at this guardhouse. From what they saw, their main duty was to check vehicles in and out before they drove across the dam.

There appeared to be no heavy weapons at the shack, but there was an alert siren on one of the light poles. That meant that the sentries had to be taken out silently and quickly before they could sound the alarm. James and Hawkins were tasked to do that job.

When the Spetsnaz teams had completed their demo work on the missile batteries and were in position for the next phase of the operation, Captain Brunov sent a signal to the Stony Man team to announce that they were in place and ready to begin their diversion. Bolan double-clicked his throat mike to acknowledge the message and signaled for Hawkins and James to do their thing.

The two Phoenix Force commandos silently moved forward, keeping to the deep shadows cast by the security lights. In the guard shack the two Iranians sat at a table apparently playing cards while they listened to music on a radio.

The final few yards of terrain directly around the shack were lighted by the pole with the siren on it, and it was as brightly lit as midday. Pulling the Beretta 93-R from his side holster, Hawkins quickly screwed the bulky silencer onto the threaded end of the muzzle. Flicking the selector switch to the 3-round-burst mode, he crawled forward on his belly.

He knew that James was covering him with his silenced H&K subgun, but he felt as if he were walking naked down Main Street in the middle of rush hour traffic. Someone had to notice the black shape crawling across the brightly lit sand. All it would take would be for one of the guards to step out to take a leak or a vehicle to drive up and he'd be dog meat.

With James whispering directions to him over his earplug, Hawkins crawled up to the partially opened door of the shack. He had decided against trying to shoot through the windows because he didn't want anyone to hear the breaking glass.

Looking around the bottom of the door, he saw that the first Iranian was sitting with his back to him and was partially blocking his shot at the second one. That meant that he would have to try a tricky little number and pray that it worked.

After switching the silenced Beretta back to semi-auto, he brought it up to the opening in the door and sighted in on the base of the first Iranian's skull. The single shot should make the man jerk backward in a death reflex and clear the shot at the second man.

With his thumb resting on the selector switch, Hawkins took his shot. The slight sound of the silenced round was lost in the noise coming from the radio, and as he had hoped, the Iranian's head snapped forward from the impact of the round, then jerked back in the death spasm.

With the pistol's selector snapped down to burst mode, as soon as the dying man's head cleared his shot, Hawkins stroked the Beretta's trigger, sending three 9 mm rounds into the horrified face and neck of the second man. He jerked backward and crashed to the floor as Hawkins wriggled into the room.

James joined him a second later and helped him lift the second man back into his chair, leaving him slumped over the table as if he were asleep.

When James sent the signal, the rest of the team moved forward. Rather than walk through the cones of light cast by the security lamps, the four men swung out to the upstream side of the dam and passed a darkened, deserted motor pool behind the guard shack. When they reached James and Hawkins, the two commandos fell in behind them.

The lake side of the dam wasn't as brightly lit as the other side, so they hugged the lake as they moved forward. There was an observation platform halfway across that was completely in shadow, and the Stony Man team stopped there to wait for the next phase to commence.

Bolan triple-clicked his mike and got a double click in response from the Russians. Bringing the mike to his mouth, he whispered one word. "Go!"

The hill closest to the facility's perimeter suddenly erupted in a flash and a thundering blast. The explosion had barely echoed away when a second blast erupted, followed closely by a third and a fourth.

The hilltops to the south of the dam were lit in an unearthly light. Then one HAWK missile's solid-fuel motors ignited, and the missile leapt from the launcher. With the guidance system not working, however, it immediately plunged into the ground and exploded, adding to the carnage.

MAJOR NAZAR WAS AWAKENED from a sound sleep by the thundering destruction of the first HAWK battery on the hills overlooking the dam. Before he could get out of bed, he heard the echoing rattle of small-arms fire and the man-made thunder of more demolition charges going off.

The Americans had arrived!

He jammed his feet into his combat boots and reached for his uniform jacket as he sprang out of bed. Snatching up his pistol belt and holster, he started down the hall for the radio room at the front of the building, buttoning his uniform jacket on the run.

"Quick!" he shouted to the sleepy radio operator. . "Call the tank battalion at Jezirel. Tell them that we are under attack!"

The radioman snatched up the microphone and was midway through the tank battalion's call sign when the lights in the building went out.

Without waiting for someone to try to restore the power, Nazar ducked around the corner to his office and groped blindly for the phone on his desk. Holding it to his ear, he was relieved when he heard the dial tone. They hadn't cut the phone lines yet. He quickly dialed the number of the military camp at Jezirel.

"Answer!" he snapped as it rang twice without being picked up.

On the fourth ring a sleepy voice answered.

"This is Major Karim Nazar at the Shabaz dam. We are under attack and need reinforcement now."

"Who is attacking you, Major?" the man on the other end said. "I do not understand."

"You idiot!" Nazar screamed. "We are being attacked by Americans! Get the camp commandant on the phone!"

He could hear the phone being put down and, while he waited, another massive explosion echoed from the hills. With the missile batteries out of action, the facility would be helpless before an aerial assault. He had to get the armor units in immediately to reinforce his infantry. Their self-propelled antiaircraft guns could provide some protection against helicopters.

"This is Colonel Hussein," a different voice said over the phone. "Who am I speaking to?"

"This is Major Karim Nazar of the Internal Security Force, and if you value your life, Colonel, you will send your tank battalion to the Shabaz dam immediately."

There was a slight pause on the other end of the line as if the colonel was thinking.

"I swear that I will personally flay you alive if you do not immediately follow my orders," Nazar snapped.

"As you command," the colonel automatically replied. Whoever this man was, if he was from the Internal Security Force, he had to be obeyed.

Now that the reinforcements were on the way, Nazar dashed out of the facility for the underground command bunker in the middle of the compound. If the missile batteries were being hit, he could expect the facility itself to be the next target.

CHAPTER TWENTY-SEVEN

Wilhelm Kessler also woke to the sounds of the explosions blasting the hilltop missile batteries. Cursing, the scientist hurried to the window to see what was happening. The hills overlooking the dam were aflame with billowing secondary explosions, and as he watched, the last SAM site went up in a thundering blast that shook the glass. He could see no helicopter gunships or jet fighters in the sky, but he knew that the Americans were bringing death and destruction to Shabaz as they had done to his research station in Libya.

This time, though, they wouldn't get away with destroying all of his hard work. Nazar's security force was strong enough to beat them back or at least to hold them until the reinforcements could arrive to crush them. But until then, the raiders could not be allowed to get into the production area. He had worked too long and too hard to create the technical innovations that made this weapons system possible. The cobalt-casting equipment had to be protected at all costs.

Snatching the 9 mm Makarov pistol from the desk in his room, he hurried down the corridor toward the molding-and-assembly area at the far end of the building. Bursting into the large room, he shouted for the half-dozen night-shift workers to take up their weapons. After the experience of the raid on the Libyan weapons lab, when he signed on to work at Shabaz, he had vowed that he wouldn't be defenseless this time. He had convinced Major Nazar to issue weapons to all of his technicians and had ordered them to keep the AK-74s at their workstations at all times.

Since most of these men had never fired a weapon of any kind before, they had all been given basic marksmanship training by Nazar's Iranian sergeants. They weren't trained soldiers by any means, but at least they would be able to defend themselves.

"What is happening, Dr. Kessler?" one of the French technicians asked, his voice shaking.

"We are under attack, you idiot!" Kessler screamed. "Are you deaf?"

The man backed off and, when he looked as if he were going to run for the door, Kessler raised his pistol and shot him in the back of the head. The technician was driven into a bench by the force of the 9 mm round and rolled off to slump on the floor, dead at Kessler's feet.

"Get to your weapons," he ordered the rest of the shocked technicians. "We are going to defend this area ourselves."

With glances at the pool of blood spreading under the Frenchman's head, they quickly obeyed. Wilhelm Kessler wasn't a man to argue with, not when he had a gun in his hand.

WHEN MAJOR NAZAR REACHED the command bunker, only the radioman and the duty NCO were there. "What is the situation out there?" he asked the radioman.

"I do not know, sir. The missile batteries do not answer my calls."

"Forget about them," Nazar snapped. "They are dead. What reports are you getting from the bunkers?"

Just then the infantry major in charge of the dam's security force ran into the bunker with his uniform jacket still unbuttoned.

"Why aren't you out there with your troops?" Nazar said, turning to face him. "We are being attacked!"

"But, Major—" the man started to say.

Nazar drew his Makarov pistol and racked back the slide to chamber a round. "Get out there with your men!"

The major's shoulders slumped. "As you command."

Nazar turned to the duty NCO. "You, too! Out!"

As soon as the two men were gone, Nazar locked the heavy armored steel door behind him. This was a command bunker, not a hiding place for cowards who were afraid to face the enemy. The only reason he was in there was that he had to command the security force defending the facility.

"Switch to the frequency for the tank battalion," Nazar ordered. "And get their commander on the radio."

As soon as the tanks arrived, he would have the raiders trapped. Until then, he would control the battle from the bunker.

ON THE HILLSIDE overlooking the dam, Captain Brunov and his Spetsnaz commandos were giving it everything they had. Following the diversion plan, they were pouring a steady stream of fire into the fighting positions and bunkers on the back side of the facility's perimeter.

For the raid they were armed with only their AK-74 assault rifles and a pair of RPG-7 antitank rocket launchers. For the job they were now facing, they could have used heavier weaponry, but they were making do with what they had. Already they had taken out two of the Iranian machine gun bunkers with only three of the 85 mm rockets.

To the Iranian defenders, it looked as if the Russians were trying to break through and attack the building itself. And as had been planned, they had the complete attention of Nazar's forces. None of the Iranians noticed the six men who dashed the rest of the way across the top of the dam and took up positions directly in front of the gate to the facility's perimeter.

HAWKINS WAS BACK in his element now. With the security lights killed, he had his night-vision goggles in place and was picking his targets through the ghostly green glow. The Iranians were in a blind panic, running from one fighting position to another as they moved to reinforce the bunkers on the other side of the compound.

Since all of the action was over there, no one was watching the back door. But that was about to change abruptly.

"Go!" Bolan spoke over the radio.

Hawkins had picked the firing port of the bunker in front of him as his first target. Lining up the rectangular opening in his M-203's sights, he triggered the grenade launcher. With its characteristic hollow thump, the grenade left the launcher and sailed through the aperture. An instant later a gout of flame shot out. A single man staggered out of the back and tried to run, but Hawkins cut him down with a short burst of 5.56 mm rounds.

Sliding the breech of the launcher open, he chambered another 40 mm shell and clicked it shut. His second target was a sandbagged machine-gun nest a hundred yards to his left. The Iranians had thoughtfully placed it at the corner of the rectangular perimeter, so it wasn't difficult to line up in the sights.

Again the over-and-under 40 mm launcher spoke. The HE grenade hit under the breech of the gun and detonated. The razor-sharp, prenotched wire frag in the warhead shredded the man behind the gun. His loader had shielded him from most of the blast, enough to make him decide to try to run for it.

Tracking the man through his rifle sights, Hawkins gave him a quick burst and saw the rounds slap dust from his jacket as they drilled through his torso. He staggered, spun and sprawled in the sand.

Now the Iranians knew they were there, but most of them had been ordered to the other side of the perimeter to reinforce the contact with the Russians. The few positions that were still manned had only one defender. With the machine guns knocked out, it took no time for the Stony Man warriors to clean up their side of the fence.

Once the fighting positions were silent, Manning and James jumped up from behind their cover and dashed for the door of the main building. A burst of

AK fire followed them, kicking up dust at their heels. James turned as he ran, his H&K spitting return fire.

Hawkins followed James's line of fire and saw the gunman hiding behind a sandbag berm. James didn't have a direct line of sight at him, but he did. A long burst of 5.56 mm rounds, drilled into his torso and dropped him where he stood.

Once Manning and James were at the main door to the building, the Canadian took a small charge from his rucksack and placed it against the lock. Setting the variable fuse for eight seconds, he hit the switch, flattened himself against the wall and counted down.

The detonation shattered the lock and slammed the heavy metal door back on its hinges. James had a frag grenade ready in his hand and tossed it in through the open door before flattening himself against the wall again.

The smoke of the detonation hadn't even cleared before Manning dumped half a magazine from his subgun through the door and followed it in. James was right on his heels, his night-vision goggles in place, but there were no targets in sight.

WITH JAMES AND MANNING securing the entrance to the facility, Bolan signaled for the rest of the team to join them. Hawkins held back to cover Bolan, Encizo and McCarter as they raced across the fifty yards of open ground to the safety of the building. When they reached it and turned to cover him, he made the run. So far, so good, he thought as he ducked inside the door.

"Calvin, T. J.," McCarter said over their comlink, "take the hall. Rafe, you cover our rear."

James and Hawkins took each side of the corridor leading to the assembly room. At the door James took a covering position while Hawkins took point.

Kessler was the first to open fire when he saw a dark figure appear in the open door. But, as with all amateurs who were shooting in the dark for the first time, his bullets went high. Hawkins dropped to the floor and rolled to the side, returning the long burst with a short one of his own.

Though Kessler had ducked back behind the huge mass of metal that made up the molding machine, the bullets ricocheted, and he felt a smashing blow to the top of his head and his left arm. His AK-74 fell from his hands as he crumpled to the floor.

"I've got you covered!" Hawkins heard James call out. "Go ahead and flush 'em, out!"

Hawkins started across the floor in a low crawl, his M-203 ready in his hands. When he caught a flash of movement to the right, he rolled to his left, bringing his weapon into play. But before he could shoot, James triggered a short burst that smashed into another piece of machinery. A cry of pain sounded and a man staggered from cover, crashing to the floor under a hail of bullets from Hawkins's M-16.

When another figure exposed his torso, James cut him down with a short burst.

When Hawkins called out that the room was clear, Manning, McCarter and Bolan joined them. While the other men took the demo charges from their rucksacks to affix to the machinery in the room, Manning went looking for the cobalt.

The demo plan called for them to destroy the heavy machinery in the facility. But since machinery could be easily replaced, rendering the stocks of cobalt unusable was their primary mission. And they were to destroy it in a way that would contaminate the building so it couldn't be put back into use again. At least not anytime within the next five hundred years or so.

"There it is," Manning said, pointing to the sealed chamber bearing radiation-warning triangles. "That's our target."

Manning knew better than to enter the chamber himself, so he rigged one series of charges to blow the door off its hinges and another one with a boost charge that would send it through the open door before it detonated.

"That's the last of them," Manning said as he switched on the detonator to the last charge. "Let's beat feet."

Bolan turned to McCarter. "Tell the Russians to give us two more minutes of heavy cover so we can get clear, then they can break contact."

"Roger."

The six men quickly made their way back to the main door and looked across the open ground to the inner side of the perimeter. The path was clear, so Manning and James covered them again as they sprinted across the sand to the bunker line. When the two men joined them, the Stony Man warriors headed directly for their escape route.

Halfway across the top of the dam, Bolan called a halt at the observation platform again. "We'll blow the charges from here. If something's wrong, I don't want to be all the way up on the ridge when we find out."

Ducking behind the concrete wall, Manning took out the demolition-control unit and raised the antenna. Hitting the Test button, he saw that all of the circuits were intact. "It's a go."

"Do it," Bolan said."

KESSLER SLOWLY REGAINED consciousness and realized that he was still alive. His head hurt, and he felt blood trickling down his arm and into his face, but he was alive. He could hear that the battle was still going on outside, but there was no firing in the assembly room.

Slowly getting to his feet, he saw the body of one of the Italian technicians sprawled faceup at the end of the molding machine. Another body lay crumpled in front of the rear door. Even over the normal odor of plastics and chemicals, the smell of gunpowder and fresh blood was strong.

The first of the production warhead casings was still on its dolly. But as he focused his eyes, he saw that something had been placed on it, something that had a blinking red light on one end.

Struggling to his feet, the German ignored his wounds and staggered over to the dolly. The object with the blinking red diode looked like some kind of demolition device. They were trying to blow up his project!

Pulling the demo charge free of the casing, he clutched it to his chest and shuffled for the nearest window. With his eyes fixed on his destination, he didn't notice the other charges with the blinking red diodes on the heavy machinery in the room. He was reaching out to break the glass so he could throw the charge outside when the blinking red light suddenly went black.

"No!"

The detonation blew the window and a large section of the wall outward. The bloody scraps of flesh and bone that were the remains of Wilhelm Kessler were scattered around the assembly area.

Almost simultaneously with the first blast, the demo charges on the machinery detonated, followed closely by the double explosion that ripped through the cobalt-containment room. In a flash a ghostly blue glow showed through the smoke and flame as the radiated cobalt dust was spread by the blast.

Being a heavy metal, the cobalt dust wasn't blown far, because it fell to the ground almost immediately. But, it was spread far enough to contaminate everything in the assembly area for the next several centuries.

CHAPTER TWENTY-EIGHT

On the hillside overlooking the dam, Captain Brunov and his Spetsnaz commandos had been giving it everything they had. When the Phoenix Force leader told him that he needed only two more minutes of covering fire so they could get free of the complex, he radioed the two RPG gunners and told them to fire off their remaining rockets. The barrage of 85 mm anti-tank rounds had slashed up and down the perimeter, blasting the bunkers and fighting positions.

The two minutes McCarter had requested were up now, but Brunov kept his men firing until a chunk of the back wall of the facility was blown out by an explosion. Following closely was a series of sharper blasts that shattered every window in the building. That was his signal to pull out.

"Group One, fall back," he ordered.

At his command a third of the Russians turned and raced for the top of the hill while the remainder covered them. Then, when the first group was firing from its new positions, the second group followed. When those men were in place, the last group simply turned and ran.

The withdrawal had taken but a few minutes, and now they were double-timing toward their extraction point on the back side of the hill. As they ran, Brunov radioed the choppers for their pickup.

"THAT'S IT," McCarter said as he watched the thick smoke pour from the shattered windows of the facility. "Now let's get our asses to the extraction point."

The explosions in the facility seemed to have shocked the Iranians. Even the ones facing the Russians stopped firing for a few stunned minutes. In the confusion the Stony Man warriors raced across the last half of the dam and disappeared into the darkness at the base of the ridge. Once they climbed it and dropped down over the back side, it was only another quarter mile downhill to the pickup point, and they'd be home free.

WHEN THE SPETSNAZ commandos reached their extraction point half a mile behind the hill, the Russians set up a defensive perimeter to await the lift ships that would take them back to Mother Russia. No one had been killed in the attack on the missile sites and the diversionary action, but six men had been wounded, one of them seriously. There were medical supplies on board the Hips, however, and as soon as they were in the air, the man would be treated.

Brunov was in contact with both the Hip troop transports and the two Hind gunship escorts as they came in low. The missiles might have been knocked out, but they didn't know what else was out there. The reports from the Hinds' gunners indicated that the area was clear and the extraction was a go.

With the two Hind gunships flying in a low, protective orbit, their gunners alert for any movement from the Iranians, the first Hip broke off and swooped for a landing. When the aircraft touched down, half of the commandos broke away from their defensive positions and clambered aboard. The chopper lifted off before the last man was even completely inside the door.

As the second Hip touched down, Brunov radioed a farewell to Bolan. "We are going now," the Russian officer said. "Good luck."

"Thanks for the help," Bolan answered. "We'll see you back at home base. Out."

THE SPETSNAZ HAD DONE a good job of cleaning up at the missile sites, but they had missed one man. The Iranian had been sleeping by himself at a little outpost overlooking the lake behind the dam and had been missed in the dark. When the demolition charges went off, he'd had enough sense to duck for cover and wait out the shower of debris.

Even though the dam had been well-protected by the missile batteries, Nazar had equipped his men with some of the shoulder-launched Russian Strella antiaircraft missiles. The Strella was a simple heat-seeking missile and wasn't as accurate or as unfailing as the more sophisticated American Stinger missiles. But for a shoulder-fired, low-altitude, antiaircraft weapon, it was adequate.

When the Iranian heard the first Hip touch down half a mile from his location, he remembered the Strellas and ran to the nearest guard post to find one. He was too late to take the first chopper under fire. But when the second Hip, carrying Brunov and the last of his commandos, lifted off, the Iranian lifted the launcher to his shoulder and sighted in on it. When he heard the launch tone telling him that the Strella's IR-seeking head had locked on to a heat source, he pulled the trigger.

The boost charge ignited with a whoosh, sending the missile on its way. A dozen yards out of the launcher, the main rocket motor cut in, and the Strella streaked into the night.

Since the Hip was flying away from him, the Strella flew directly into the jet exhaust of the chopper and detonated. An orange-red fireball lit the sky as the Russian chopper's fuel tanks exploded. Pieces of burning wreckage blazed through the sky like meteors as the Hip plunged to earth.

THE STONY MAN TEAM had crossed the dam and was halfway back up the ridge line to its extraction point when the Iranian Strella streaked up into the night sky. The Hip was high enough that when the missile zeroed in on it, the fireball was visible.

"Jesus," Hawkins said. "Wasn't that one of the Russian ships?"

James stared at the flaming debris raining to the ground. "I knew this had gone a little too well."

Bolan tried to call Brunov and, when there was no answer, he realized that the Spetsnaz commander had been in the Hip that had gone down. "Let's keep going," he said over the comlink. "There's nothing we can do for them."

When the team reached the top of the ridge, the men took up positions to cover their backtrail while Bolan contacted their ride home. He was calling their chopper when Katz broke in over the radio from Ufazek. "Striker," he said, "we've got a problem. There's been a change in the plan."

Bolan knew that for Katz to have called them in the middle of an extraction, the change, whatever it was, wouldn't be to his liking.

"The Russians are panicked about the loss of that chopper, and they're pulling the rest of their air support. You're going to have to get well clear of the area before they'll release them again. Find a cold extraction point, and they'll get you out."

Bolan didn't bother to curse their fair-weather allies. He had been through this too many times to waste the energy. He had to think. "There's a motor pool on the north side of the dam," he said calmly. "We'll go back down there and try to get a vehicle. If we can, we'll evade to the north."

"If you can get clear," Katz said, "the Russians promise that they'll come back to pick you up, but their hands are tied right now. Orders from Moscow. Popov was going to come for you anyway, but he was given a direct order to stand the choppers down until he got clearance."

"You tell Viktor to keep his people standing by," Bolan said. "We'll get clear one way or the other."

"Keep me informed."

"Will do."

"Phoenix," Bolan transmitted on the comlink, "this is Alpha. There's been a change of plans. The chopper has been cancelled, so we're going to go back down there and find a vehicle in that motor pool we passed on our way in. Everyone check in, over."

"Phoenix One, roger," McCarter replied. Like Bolan, he had been there before and would save the recriminations for later.

"Two" was all Encizo said.

"Phoenix Three, copy," Manning sent.

"Four, roger," James replied.

Hawkins had feared something like this when he saw the Hip go down. "Phoenix Five, roger."

HAL BROGNOLA JOINED Price and Kurtzman in the Computer Room, following a conversation with the President. "The White House has informed me that the Russians have pulled out of the operation," he said bluntly. "One of their choppers full of Spetsnaz was shot down and crashed. Everyone is believed dead."

"You mean that our men have been abandoned?" Price asked.

The participation by the Russians was the only thing that had made the long-distance raid even halfway feasible. Now the men would be stranded in the middle of enemy territory.

"They're not completely abandoned," Brognola replied. "The Russians say that when they reach a cold extraction point, they'll come back and pull them out. But they can't risk any more men or machines to Iranian fire. The loss of that chopper has them worried in Moscow."

"What did they expect?" Price asked. "People get killed in wars. Didn't they know that before they signed on for this?"

"They're concerned about the international repercussions now," he explained. "Dead bodies they can live with. The men all went in sterile with nothing to connect them with Russia. The chopper, though, was Russian air force and the wreckage can be traced. You have to remember that they get most of their foreign currency from Middle East trade and can't afford to be branded as an aggressor.''

"They promised that they would help us."

"And they will if Striker can get his men to a safe place to be picked up."

"That's not likely, now, it is? They're alone at the dam, and all the Iranians in the world are coming after them. How are they supposed to make their escape to a safe area?''

"Dammit, Barbara, I don't know! I'm as upset as you are. We'll just have to stay calm and ride this one out.'' On that note Brognola headed to the War Room to contact the White House again.

NOW THAT THE RUSSIANS were gone, the Iranians were milling around the destroyed facility and pulling their dead and wounded out of the perimeter fighting positions. No one was keeping an eye on the motor pool on the other side of the dam, and the Stony Man team was able to slip in completely unnoticed.

Most of the vehicles parked on the oil-soaked sand were Mercedes-Benz two- or five-ton trucks. Taking one of them across the open desert wasn't going to work. A sand-colored Toyota four-by-four half-ton pickup truck sat in a maintenance bay with its hood up, and McCarter went to check it out.

"Damn!" he said as he glanced under the hood. "They've got the carburetor off this one."

"There's an old Land Rover over here with a key in it," James called out from the bay next door as he slid behind the wheel. "I'll see if it'll start."

He pumped the throttle a couple of times before hitting the ignition switch. The starter engaged, but he could tell that the battery wasn't fully charged.

"Come on!" he muttered, pumping the gas. "Start, you bastard."

The engine coughed and died. Reaching out, he pulled out the manual choke and tried it again.

After coughing and spitting a couple of times, the engine's roar evened out. The battered muffler sounded loud, but there was no choice. "Get some gas cans and climb in."

Grabbing as many five-gallon gas cans as they could find, the men of Stony Man quickly stacked them in the back of the Land Rover and piled in after them. With the vehicle carrying the six of them, their gear and the extra gas, the aging vehicle would be at its maximum load. But they needed something that could negotiate any terrain, and that's what Land Rovers did best.

Hawkins was the last one to climb into the back of the rig. In his hands were half a dozen ignition keys. "No reason to make it easy for them to follow us," he said.

"I'll make it even more difficult," Encizo said, turning in his seat and taking a grenade from his assault harness. Pulling the pin, he lobbed it in the direction of the stack of fifty-five-gallon fuel drums at the end of the motor pool.

The detonation set off several of the barrels, and the motor pool was rocked by a thundering explosion. Pools of blazing gasoline quickly spread to the other barrels. Now the Iranians were sure to notice them.

"Let's go!" McCarter called out over the roar.

Manning had replaced James behind the wheel, and, hitting the clutch, he dropped the gearshift lever into first and engaged the four-wheel drive. "Hang on!"

Keeping up his RPMs so as not to stall the cold engine, he released the clutch, and the old Land Rover lurched forward. One of the gas cans started to fall out, but Hawkins grabbed it. Along with luck, gas was going to be the thing they would need most in the next few hours.

"You'd better get on it!" McCarter yelled over the roar of the broken muffler. "We've got tanks coming up the road along the lake!"

Manning floored the accelerator, and the Land Rover responded sluggishly but still picked up speed. Slipping his night-vision goggles over his eyes, he headed for the dirt road that cut around the bottom of the ridge. He had scoped it out while they were waiting on the top of the ridge and knew that it was headed the way they needed to go.

CHAPTER TWENTY-NINE

Major Nazar could barely contain his anger as he looked at the smoke pouring from the shattered windows of the research facility. The power had been restored, so he could see that the building wasn't badly damaged, just the one hole that had been blown in the back wall. But he knew there was no way that this facility could ever be put to use again for anything in his lifetime.

The radiation counter was clicking madly. The explosions that had destroyed the molding machinery had spread the deadly radiated cobalt throughout the building, contaminating it for a thousand years. It would cost a man his life to step inside it for even a moment. That hadn't stopped Nazar, however, from ordering two men to go inside and report back on the conditions they found there.

If he hadn't gone to the command bunker when the attack had hit, he would be dead in there with the foreign weapons technicians. Wilhelm Kessler, however, still hadn't been found, either dead or alive. Maybe the raiders had captured him and taken him with them.

"My men have inspected all of the bodies, sir," the young infantry lieutenant reported to Nazar. The major had been killed in battle the previous night, and the lieutenant was now the senior man of the security-force survivors. "But they still have not found Kessler."

"Forget about that filthy foreigner," Nazar snapped. "How many of your men are left?"

"I have forty-eight men still able to fight, sir."

"Get them in their vehicles and go after that truck the raiders stole from me."

The attackers, whoever they were, would be long gone by now, but the young officer knew better than to argue with Major Nazar. Men who did that took a long time to die. At least his late commander had died quickly in battle, and he fervently wished that fate for himself, a quick death.

"As you command, sir," he answered.

The young Iranian officer was back in five minutes. "All of the vehicles in the motor pool are damaged, sir," he reported. "The fire spread to all of them before it could be put out. I have my men trying to see if they can repair the ones with the least damage, but I do not know how soon they will be ready."

"Tell the officer in charge of the tank unit to report to me immediately," Nazar said.

"Yes, sir."

The armor battalion commander at Jezirel had only sent a mixed company of tanks, APCs and scout cars instead of his entire unit. Even so, they had arrived too late to have any effect on the battle. He would deal with that colonel later, after he caught up with the raiders, but for now his vehicles could carry Nazar and his infantry in the pursuit.

The tank officer tried to protest Nazar's new orders, saying that he didn't have authority from his commander. But the cold muzzle of Nazar's Makarov against the side of his head made him reconsider.

After a quick refueling from the barrels that had been blown clear of the fire, a column of five T-72 tanks, half a dozen BMP APCs and four BDRM-2 armored scout cars started down the dirt road into the hills to the northeast.

GARY MANNING WAS a good driver and he was trying his best, but the battered old Land Rover wasn't rewarding his efforts. To try to lighten the load, they had even thrown out the spare tire, jack and everything else that wasn't essential, but it wasn't working. Now he knew why the vehicle had been parked in a maintenance bay.

The engine was delivering only about half of the power it should have been putting out, and whatever was wrong with it seemed to be getting worse with every mile. It sounded terminal, and the only question was how long it would take before it self-destructed.

In the meantime, however, they were making only about twenty-five miles per hour, and they had well over a hundred miles to go before they reached safety.

"I want to stop and take a look at this engine," he shouted to McCarter.

Just then the engine backfired loudly, and the temperature gauge, which had been hovering on the high side, shot all the way over against the peg. Manning switched off the engine immediately. Like it or not, they were due for a maintenance stop.

Bolan and Encizo grabbed their weapons and ran for the slight rise in the ground they had just passed to watch their backtrail. McCarter stood up on the passenger seat with his field glasses, scanning the horizon.

Opening the hood, Manning saw that the radiator was steaming from several places. He knew better than to try to open the radiator cap when it was so hot. The water would boil out, and they'd really be stranded. "We're going to need some water," he said. "So check all the cans."

"Maybe these will help," James said as he handed Manning a battered canvas roll of hand tools. "I found them under the front seat."

With the basic set of wrenches, pliers and screwdrivers, Manning began to work on the hot engine.

James stood by in case he needed help, but Manning was doing fine on his own. A few minutes later he called out from under the hood. "I think I know what's wrong with it," he said. "The distributor's loose, so the timing's off."

"Can you fix it?" McCarter asked.

"No sweat."

While Manning worked under the hood, Hawkins refilled the gas tank from the five-gallon cans. Having been in the desert before, he was careful to check each can to make sure that it contained gas, not diesel or water, before he poured it in. The last thing they needed was a tank full of something the Land Rover couldn't burn. One of the cans did contain rusty water, and he handed it to James to refill the radiator.

"I think you'd better get this crate put back together and get us on the road," McCarter commented as he lowered the field glasses. "We have company coming, and it looks like armor."

Manning tightened the nut holding the distributor clamp. "Try it now," he told James.

The engine started on the second try and, after sputtering for a second, roared louder than before. "The timing was off and that's also what made it heat up so much. It should cool down a little now."

McCarter recalled Bolan and Encizo, and, crowding into the back of the Land Rover, Hawkins couldn't help but glance over his shoulder and hope that he didn't see a tank.

YAKOV KATZENELENBOGEN was keeping close tabs on Phoenix Force. They had almost a two-hour head start on their pursuers, but he knew it wasn't enough. And now that they had been forced to stop and work on the Land Rover's engine, they had lost most of that lead. Now that the sun was up, enemy choppers would take to the air and track them down in no time if they were still on the road. They needed to find some place to hole up.

Working with the images in the Stony Man computers, he and Kurtzman were examining the area they were traveling through to try to find the closest place they could find safety. The problem with a desert was that it didn't offer much in the line of cover and concealment. Hiding behind a sand dune wasn't going to cut it.

"Striker," Katz said, "there's a hilly region to the west a few miles off your route that's got some good outcroppings. If you can get in there, you'll have a decent chance of holding out until we can get something going to extract you."

"Roger," Bolan replied. "I got it on the map and we should be able to make it there."

When Katz replaced the radio microphone, he saw Colonel Popov standing behind him. "It is bad for them, no?" he asked.

Katz rubbed the back of his neck with his left hand. "Yes, Viktor, it is about as bad as it can get."

"I am so sorry." The Russian sounded sincere. "I did not think it would come to this. But—" he shrugged "—with the idiots they have in Moscow now, who can tell what they will do? What do you think your government will do?"

"I don't know," Katz answered honestly. "For the life of me, I just don't know."

"I understand my own government when they do things like this," Popov admitted. "They do dishonorable things because, while they are a new government, much of their thinking still follows the old Soviet pattern. They have not learned that a nation's honor is the most valuable thing it can have.

"Your government, though, is more experienced," the Russian said, shaking his head. "I do not understand why they are doing this. Those men did their job and they should be brought out of there at all costs. I always thought that your people were better than our people."

"You have good people in your country," Katz said. "We all know that. But most of the time our politicians aren't any better than yours are. National honor doesn't mean much to politicians who are always looking for personal advantage instead of the right thing to do.''

"It is a sad thing," Popov said. "It was better in the bad old days when we were still enemies."

Katz hated to admit it, but the Russian had a point.

MAJOR NAZAR HAD commandeered one of the BDRM-2 armored scout cars and had raced ahead of the slower-moving vehicles to track the fleeing raiders himself. The Land Rover's wheel tracks in the barren terrain were easy to follow. When he passed a spare tire and a pile of tools, he wondered if the Americans were having trouble with the vehicle they had stolen from him.

"Close up with me," he radioed back to the armored car closest to him.

With the two scout cars running side by side, Nazar reached the top of a rise in the ground and saw the dust plume of another vehicle a mile in front of them. Taking out his field glasses, he focused on the plume and saw that the men in the vehicle were wearing black uniforms. It had to be the Americans.

"Get a tank up here immediately!" Nazar called over the radio.

When a sand-colored T-72 tank clanked to a halt beside him and the commander leaned out of his hatch, Nazar pointed to the distant dust plume. "Take them under fire," he ordered.

MANNING WAS NURSING the Land Rover, playing with the manual choke to get the most out of the dying engine. Even correcting the timing hadn't worked, and he realized that the engine was simply worn-out. Land Rovers were built to last, but only when their engines didn't live on a steady diet of sand in the air intake. Apparently cleaning air filters wasn't a big thing in Iran.

"Over there!" McCarter shouted. "There's the outcropping Katz told us about!"

"Go for it!" Bolan said.

Manning set his course when the crack of the tank gun sounded loud from the rise behind them. Hawkins snapped around and saw the puff of smoke from the barrel forming in the air. He ducked instinctively even though he knew it was a futile gesture. As soon as that gunner had them zeroed, they'd be buzzard bait.

The tank-gun shell impacted well in front of them, but chunks of red-hot shrapnel sang over their heads. One chunk hit something in the front of the Land Rover with a thud, but Manning ignored it. Even though the tank shell had missed them by a dozen yards, he yelled, "Hang on!"

He cranked the wheel sharply, and the Land Rover abruptly changed directions. A few seconds later he turned again. Even though a tank gun's sighting system was designed to hit moving vehicles, he didn't want to make it any easier for them. One hit and they'd be history.

He floored the gas pedal, but the engine didn't respond. The temperature gauge was pegged again, and steam poured from under the hood. The radiator had to have taken a hit. The engine would seize tight before much longer, but there might be enough left in it to get them to the bottom of the hill.

With a final backfire, the Land Rover stopped dead on the sand as the engine abruptly quit. But the outcropping was only a couple of hundred yards in front of them.

"Go! Go! Go!" McCarter shouted as he jumped from the Land Rover.

Grabbing their gear, the Stony Man warriors sprinted for the hill after him.

SEEING THE ENEMY running for the hill, Nazar brought the radio microphone to his lips. "Tell the tanks to cease fire," he ordered.

Now that the Americans had stopped, he had them where they couldn't escape again and he wanted them alive at all costs. Parading them through the streets of Tehran would be a fitting end to this debacle. And it might even save his own life. He would have to answer for the destruction that had been visited on Shabaz, and bringing the Americans in chains before the council could help his case.

He remembered with great satisfaction seeing the bodies of the American pilots who had been killed in the failed rescue attempt during the so-called hostage crisis. The corpses had been displayed in Tehran, where crowds had gathered to spit upon them and to mock the Great Satan who had so disastrously and publicly failed. How much better it would be for him if he could parade live Americans in chains instead of merely their dead bodies.

But even if he couldn't capture them alive, their bodies would do almost as well.

"Circle that hill," he radioed to the commander of the tanks and scout cars. "Let none of them escape.

"Send your men after them," he ordered the infantry officer who was bringing his troops up in the APCs. "I want them taken alive."

"As you command," the lieutenant answered. He knew that he'd just been handed a death sentence, but he'd be killed just as quickly if he didn't do exactly as the major said.

CHAPTER THIRTY

Leaving the overheated Land Rover at the base of the hill, the men of Stony Man scrambled up into the rocks. Behind them they heard the rumble of tank and scout-car engines and the rattle of tracks drawing closer with every second. Halfway up they found a plateau with clear fields of fire to their front and sheer cliffs to guard their rear.

"This is it," McCarter called out. "Find a hole and get in it."

Since there were so few of them and so much area to cover, the men spread out with at least twenty yards between their fighting positions. That gave them a hundred-yard front, but still left them able to support one another if the enemy got too close.

Hawkins found himself a nice little pocket in the rocks formed by three big boulders. It was big enough to fight from yet small enough that it would take a direct hit to dig him out. This was looking a little too much like an Alamo scenario to him, but if he was going to die here, he wanted to make the bastards work for it.

Twenty yards to Hawkins's right, Rafael Encizo had found a similar rock foxhole. "Hawkins," the Cuban called out.

"Yo."

"You and I will work this together. Watch each other's fronts and give covering fire if we have to move."

"Got it."

So far, Hawkins had had little interaction with Encizo. There was something about the Cuban that didn't invite the kind of off-the-wall exchanges he had enjoyed with James and Manning. He could tell that Encizo was a serious man, and he didn't feel comfortable wisecracking around him. Now, though, he would have to back him up if it got heavy in his sector, and he knew that Encizo would do the same for him.

Now that he had a fire teammate, Hawkins went about arranging his fighting position. Using his bare hands, he dug sand out of the bottom of the hole to make it even deeper. Since the Iranians had heavy weapons, there was no point in stacking more loose rocks in front of him. A tank shell hitting them would create rock fragments, and being killed by a chunk of rock was still dead.

"Here they come!" McCarter shouted.

Hawkins looked out and saw a ragged line of infantry moving out from the vehicles. The men didn't look as if they had their hearts in their work, so he decided to give them a little reality check. They were at the maximum range for the M-203's grenade launcher, but he was confident that he could make the shot.

Using the top notch of the launcher's ladder sight, he got his sight picture, took a deep breath, let the air out slowly and fired. Good one, he thought as he watched it fly through the air.

Arcing out over the rocks, the grenade landed at the feet of the man who looked as if he was directing traffic down there, an officer or an NCO. The detonation blew him off his feet and scattered half a dozen of the men closest to him. Most of them got back up, but two of them stayed on the sand.

That wasn't bad for a two-hundred-yard shot, and Hawkins smiled in self-congratulation. The smile froze when he saw the turret on the closer armored car swivel around until the long barrel of the 57 mm cannon mounted in the turret was aimed directly at him.

One of the cardinal rules of combat was that you didn't draw unwanted attention to yourself unless it was absolutely necessary. He had violated that rule, and the bill was about to come due.

"Incoming!" he yelled as he dived for the bottom of his hole.

The 57 mm gun barked, and the round whistled over his head to detonate in the rocks behind him. The gunner adjusted his aim, and the second round hit between him and Encizo showering them both with rock fragments. Expecting the third round to land in his lap, he briefly thought about abandoning his hole, but the scout car didn't fire again.

When he looked out, he saw that the infantry had used the cover of the scout car's cannon fire to move up into the rocks, which was why the gunner had ceased fire. He was afraid that he would hit his own men.

Jacking a 40 mm round into the open breech of the launcher, Hawkins sighted in on the lead man and triggered the weapon. Before the grenade even had a chance to fly the hundred and fifty yards, he had switched the M-16 to semiauto and was snapping off aimed shots.

To his right and left, Encizo and James were doing the same. Since the best defense was a strong offense, they were making sure that the Iranians understood that they weren't out for a stroll in the sun. If they wanted the six Stony Man warriors, either dead or alive, they were going to have to pay the price to get them and the price would be high.

The Iranians continued their advance in the face of their enemy's well-aimed fire. The rocks gave them good cover, as well, but every time one of them broke cover to move up, he took a hit.

Hawkins almost felt as if he were back on the firing range as he carefully squeezed off his shots. Return fire was ragged, but there was still a lot of bullets flying through the air. An AK round sent a rock chip into his face, and he felt the blood come.

Spotting the shooter, he drilled him through the upper body with one shot, then gave him one more for good measure.

"THEY REACHED THE ROCKS," Katzenelenbogen reported to Kurtzman at the Farm, "and the Iranians have them surrounded. They are sending probing attacks, but Striker thinks they can hold until their ammunition runs out."

"How long will that be?" Brognola asked.

"That depends entirely on the Iranians," Katz stated. "If they throw a steady stream of troops against them it won't last very long. If the Iranians aren't willing to spend the manpower, they might be able to hold out for a couple of days."

"I'm working on getting them out of there," Brognola replied. "Tell them to hang on."

"So," Price asked after Katz broke the connection, "what's this rescue plan?"

"The President's working on it," the big Fed told her. "But he has a real problem right now. The Iranians are screaming in the UN about a raid by Russian and American air and ground forces on the UN sponsored dam at Shabaz. The President is denying that any U.S. troops took part in any such action, and Moscow is backing his play."

"That's all well and good," Price said. "The age-old cover-your-ass routine by telling lies in the UN. But is he doing anything positive to try to get them out of there before they're overrun?"

Brognola was a long time in answering. "He's not going to leave them there."

Price gave him a hard look. "You don't sound sure, Hal, and I don't like that."

"Barbara, the Man's in a very difficult situation on this right now."

"You might want to talk to Mack about being in a difficult situation," she said.

"I know that the President's talking to the Russians right now and trying to find a way to break this stalemate. He's even offering them trade guarantees if the Arab nations put an embargo on Russian goods. He's doing everything he can to try to get them back into the game."

"The clock's running," she said bluntly. "And since there's no overtime in these playoffs, he'd better get a move on it."

THE ROCKS IN FRONT of the Phoenix commandos' position were well littered with Iranian bodies. At least a dozen of them had paid the price for trying to dig their enemies out of their holes. They were pulling back now, and Stony Man team was letting them go. With the ammunition situation what it was, they would conserve it until the Iranians got in close enough that every round would be a killer.

In his rock foxhole, Hawkins counted his magazines and 40 mm grenades. He had only had five grenades left in the last bandolier, but he was doing okay on magazines for the M-16. He also had three full mags and a partial for the Beretta, so he was still in the game. When that ran out, he had his father's old Randall fighting knife, so it wasn't that he would be completely defenseless. After all, Jim Bowie had taken out quite a few of them at the Alamo with his knife before they got him.

"Yo, T. J.!" James called out from the hole to his left.

"Yeah?" Hawkins called back.

"You okay?"

"Damned straight," he replied. "I haven't had so much fun since the day my little brother went to take a shit and the hogs ate him."

James shook his head. "I think you've been in the sun too long, man."

Just then a round spanged off the rock in front of him. Even though late, he ducked anyway as he heard the report of the rifle below. Time to get back to work.

"Keep an eye on them," McCarter said over the radio. "They're hitting our flanks."

Carefully rising, Hawkins saw an Iranian hiding behind a rock a hundred yards away. When he saw the man aim at him again, he ducked and loaded a grenade into his M-203.

Readying himself, he popped up, got his sight picture and fired the grenade. The Iranian tried to get out of the way, but Hawkins was on him in a flash. Three quick shots dropped him back in time to take the force of the grenade's explosion.

Not seeing any more targets in his sector of fire, he noticed that a pair of Iranians was keeping Encizo busy while a third gunner climbed higher into the rocks to get a clear shot down at him. Taking careful aim, Hawkins waited until the climber showed himself again and squeezed the trigger.

The round took the Iranian in the shoulder. The man twisted, lost his footing and fell.

Encizo quickly took out the other two. "Thanks," he called out.

"No sweat."

A TOTALLY FRUSTRATED Jack Grimaldi walked the flight line at Ufazek air base. He had been in the ops center with Katz listening to the radio chatter and had to get away for a while before he broke something. The guys were holding their own, but he knew that they couldn't last for long. If something wasn't done fast, they would die in those rocks.

As he walked, his eyes took in every detail of the flight line, particularly the details of the area where the Mi-24 Hind gunships were parked. He was looking for an armed airplane he could steal, any armed airplane, but he wasn't having much luck. Every warplane with a weapons load had Russians standing guard on it.

With the guards on the Hinds, there was no way he was going to get into one without blasting his way in. And killing Russian airmen would be a poor way to repay them for all the hospitality they had shown the Americans. It wasn't their fault that their government had crapped out on a deal.

The same thing went for the MiG-29s on ramp alert, and they weren't even loaded with ground-attack ordnance. They were configured for aerial-interception duties, and air-to-air missiles weren't going to do much against Iranian tanks. And, of course, they were guarded, as well.

The only plane he could get his hands on without killing someone was the Blackbird, and it didn't carry ground-attack weapons, either.

On the taxiway, a MiG-29 Fulcrum was turning onto the end of the runway. As it revved its turbine to get ready to take off, Grimaldi automatically turned to watch it. He was a pilot, and pilots watched planes take off.

With flames shooting out of its twin exhausts, the Fulcrum pilot came off his brakes, and the jet fighter leapt forward. Halfway down the runway, it was in the air, gear tucked up, and was climbing almost vertically for altitude. The sound of the MiG-29 breaking the sound barrier as it climbed thundered over the base and shook Grimaldi where he stood.

Suddenly the Stony Man pilot stopped cold. To save his friends, he needed to deliver some kind of weapon that would take out tanks, but there was nothing that said that the weapon had to contain high explosives. He had just remembered that there were other ways to create a high-speed shock wave, which was the primary purpose of any explosive.

After getting his thoughts in order, Grimaldi went to locate Katzenelenbogen. One way or the other, he wasn't going to let his friends die in Iran.

"I'LL PASS THIS ON to the Farm for their consideration," Katzenelenbogen said after hearing Grimaldi out. "All they can do is tell us that it's a no-go."

"I'm not going to take no for an answer." The pilot's face was a study in determination. "Now that the Russians have bugged out on them, it's up to us to get our guys out of there, and this is the only thing I can think of to do it with."

"I said I'd talk to them about it," Katz repeated. He felt as strongly about the situation as Grimaldi did. But he also knew the nasty realities of clandestine operations, the cold, razor-sharp facts of life that applied any time politics became involved with a military operation. Regardless of their value to the nation, this might be the mission when the Stony Man team was kissed off because the political situation demanded it.

"Talk good," Grimaldi answered, his voice low. "And make damned sure that they listen to you."

"I will, Jack, you know that."

CHAPTER THIRTY-ONE

"Grimaldi has come up with a plan to help Striker."
Aaron Kurtzman had a very strange look on his face
when he turned around to face Hal Brognola.

"What's that?" Brognola asked.

"He wants to use the Blackbird to attack the Iranian armored force."

"That plane's armed with Phoenix missiles, not
Mavericks, and even I know that you can't use a
Phoenix against armor."

"He says that he wants to use the plane's sonic
boom as a weapon."

"What?"

"It might work," Kurtzman said carefully. "How
many times have you read in the paper about some Air
Force jet jockey breaking some old lady's window
when he cracked Mach unity too close to the ground?"

"Forget it. The President wants that plane returned ASAP. It got shot down once and almost exposed the operation. He's not going to approve
anything that puts it at risk again."

"Grimaldi's not going to like that."

"He has to toe the line like everyone else around this place."

Kurtzman turned back to his keyboard without a word. When Brognola was under this kind of pressure, it didn't help to press him. It didn't mean, however, that the matter had been decided. As always, there was more than one way to look at the word *no,* particularly at Stony Man Farm.

"HAL SAYS NO." Katz found Grimaldi in the front of the hangar by the Blackbird. The new intake shock cone was finally in place, and the crew chief was running the final tests on its critical control system. The plane would soon be operational again.

"Did he give you a reason?" Grimaldi's jaw was tight, his voice grim.

"He said that the White House won't clear it because they don't want to risk losing the plane again."

"So one Blackbird is worth trading six lives for, is that it?"

Katz knew what was pressuring the pilot, and he didn't take his comment personally. "I only know what the Bear passed on to me."

"I'm going anyway," Grimaldi stated flatly.

"Have you discussed this idea of yours with Hoffsteader yet?"

"No."

"I'd talk to him first if I were you," Katz recommended. "Remember he's the airplane pilot on this mission, and you're only riding shotgun. If you can't get him to go along with it, you can't get off the ground because you can't fly that thing by yourself."

"Okay," Grimaldi conceded. Katz did have a way of getting to the meat of the matter.

"And," Katz continued, "when you're done talking to him, come to see me."

Pete Hoffsteader was checking off the final items on the postrepair checklist when Grimaldi approached him. "How are your friends?" he asked when he saw the pilot.

"There's no change. They're still surrounded, cut off and there's not a hell of a lot they can do by themselves against tanks and armored cars."

"What is Washington saying?"

"Nothing yet," Grimaldi replied. "The President is still 'consulting' with Moscow on the situation. It seems that everyone's worried about the political fallout in the UN."

Grimaldi stepped closer to Hoffsteader and lowered his voice. "I've got a plan that I think might get them out, but I'll need your help." He nodded toward the SR-71. "And I'll need to borrow your plane."

"What is it?"

After Grimaldi outlined his plan, making sure to add that it didn't have official sanction, Hoffsteader looked out the open door of the hangar at the clear blue sky.

"You know," he said almost to himself, "I've had a good career in the Air Force for a long time now. I got to be a pilot like I had wanted to do since I was a kid. The Air Force has been real good to me, and most of the time, I think that I should be paying them rather than taking pay for doing what I do."

He turned back to the SR-71. "I mean look at that plane sitting there. Men would kill to even ride in that thing, much less fly it. And like I said, they even pay me to do it. And now, you want me to flush all of that down the toilet."

"It's not for me, Pete," Grimaldi said seriously. "You know that.

"If you get canned for it," Grimaldi continued, "I'll see that you get a flying job somewhere else, the CIA or DEA."

"I won't be flying anything but an iron bunk in a military prison when they get done with me."

Grimaldi wasn't surprised at Hoffsteader's reaction. After all, he was asking the man to put his whole life on the line for men he didn't even know. Even though he was a pilot, he knew that most pilots didn't have a bond with the men on the ground the way he did.

"Okay," he said. Short of putting a gun to the man's head, there was no way he could make it work. "Forget that I brought it up."

"But," Hoffsteader said, smiling slowly, "I do have to make a test flight to check out the new intake shock cone before we make the flight back to Groom Lake. And since we're running our own air-traffic-control center here, there's no one to tell me where to fly. If we happen to drift across the border at Mach 3 because we get distracted and aren't paying proper attention to the black line, that's not a crime."

"Are you sure?" Grimaldi asked. "I need to have a firm commitment on this."

The pilot shrugged. "Sure, why not? I haven't broken any international laws or violated presidential directives lately."

Grabbing Hoffsteader by the arm, Grimaldi started for Katz's radio room. "Tell Striker to hold on," he shouted. "We're on the way."

Katz smiled when the two pilots outlined their test-flight cover story. "I'll notify the Farm," he said. "But you'd better get going as soon as you can."

"Consider us gone."

While the pilots dressed in their pressure suits, Katz called Viktor Popov into the radio room and closed the door behind them.

AARON KURTZMAN TURNED to face Hal Brognola, who was occupying Hunt Wethers's cubicle for the duration. "Hoffsteader and Grimaldi are going to take the Blackbird up for a test flight to check the repair work they did on that engine," he reported. He didn't bother to add that the test flight would take the spy plane a hundred miles into northeastern Iran.

"When do they think they'll be able to start back?" Brognola asked.

"They didn't say. They have to see how the repair work holds up before they can schedule their return."

Brognola was tired. This had been a grueling grind for the past several days, and he was exhausted. The lack of sleep, irregular meals and too much of Kurtzman's coffee had taken their toll. There were too many balls in the air, and he was having trouble focusing on all of them.

"Okay," he said. "Tell them to let us know as soon as they've completed it and are ready to come home."

"What's Striker's situation?" Brognola changed topics. "Is he still surrounded?"

"Striker says that there's no new movement around their position, but that there's no sign that the Iranians are going to go away, either."

"Is he still planning to try to escape tonight?"

"That's the plan."

"How long till sunset over there?"

"About three hours."

Brognola got to his feet. "I'm going to get some sleep. Call me at sunset, Iranian time."

"Will do."

PRICE KNEW Kurtzman well enough to recognize when he was being evasive, and she knew that he had just lied to Brognola big time. She didn't necessarily have a problem with that, just as long as she knew why the lie had been told and what it was. If it was something that would save the team, she was all for it, no matter what the repercussions would be in Washington.

After giving Brognola enough time to leave the room, she turned to Kurtzman. "Are you going to tell me, Aaron, or do I have to guess?"

"What do you mean?"

"You know what I mean. You just sandbagged Hal, and I want to know why."

Kurtzman looked grim. One of the major drawbacks to working with Barbara Price as long as he had was that he couldn't hide anything from her even when he tried. But since she was the Farm's mission controller, she needed to know what was going down, so he would have had to tell her sooner or later.

"Okay," he said, "I lied but I really had to."

"And exactly why is that?"

"Because Jack Grimaldi talked Pete Hoffsteader into trying to use the Blackbird as a dive-bomber on the Iranians."

"You're joking!"

"I wish."

"But they don't have any ground-attack weapons."

"Oh, yes, they do. They have a weapon that's never been used in warfare before."

"And that is?"

"A sonic boom. They're going to try to use the SR's sonic boom to destroy the Iranians."

Price thought that she had heard it all over the years, but this one shocked her. "It that possible?"

"Theoretically," he answered cautiously. "The shock wave could be aimed, and since it's moving at the speed of sound, some seven hundred miles per hour at sea level, it can do a lot of damage."

"But how about our guys? Won't the shock wave pass over them, as well?"

"They'll have to take cover, but we think they'll survive it."

"You think."

"Dammit, Barbara, it's the only thing Katz and I have been able to come up with to try to save them. They're trapped and, even if they can break out, they're still going to be on foot while the enemy has vehicles. The Russians will come in and pick them up as soon as they can find a cold extraction zone, but it has to be cold. With an Iranian armor column on their ass, they can't accomplish that. Plus they're almost out of water and ammunition. We either do something to get them out of there today, or they're finished.''

Price knew that the plan was as farfetched as anything she had ever heard, and she knew that the repercussions would be severe. But those were her guys out there, and if there was anything she could do to help get them out, no matter how impossible it sounded, she would.

''Tell them to do it.''

''I already did.''

THERE WAS LITTLE FANFARE when the Blackbird prepared for flight this time. Even though the truth about the planned mission had been shared with no one except Colonel Popov, everyone knew that something extraordinary was going on. And since even seeing a Blackbird parked on the ground was extraordinary, this had to be serious.

To keep from tipping off the Iranians, the Russian AWACS wouldn't take to the air this time, and the mission would be flown in complete radio silence. The satellite transponder that had allowed Stony Man Farm to track the SR on the recon flights would also be turned off. This mission would be flown in complete secrecy, and when it was over, there would be no proof of any kind that it had actually taken place. A test flight would be entered in the plane's log book, and that should cover it.

This time there would also be no long flight south before turning around for a leisurely recon run. This would be a Mach 3 run all the way, a high-speed dash so that even if they were picked up on radar, there wouldn't be enough time to get anything in the air to stop them.

When Grimaldi and Hoffsteader walked out to get into the SR, the usual crowd formed to watch. But as if they were in on the plan, they stood in silent tribute. They knew these men were putting their lives on the line and honored it.

There was little radio chatter once the cockpits were closed except for the required responses to the preflight checklists. After the twin J-58s were fired up and they had taxied to the end of the runway, Hoffsteader ran through his last checklist.

When it was done, he clicked on his intercom. "You know that we're probably going to rip the wings off trying this stunt, don't you?"

"Yep," Grimaldi answered.

"I just wanted to make sure that you knew," Hoffsteader said. "I'm coming off the brakes now."

With twin flames blazing out of the afterburners, the SR-71 Blackbird shot down the runway.

CHAPTER THIRTY-TWO

Mack Bolan looked down on the Iranians encircling their makeshift rock fortress just outside of small arms range. At his side, David McCarter mentally counted the opposition for the tenth time, but the numbers didn't get any better no matter how many times he added them up.

"It's going to be a bitch making it out of here," McCarter stated.

Bolan nodded. He had been in the game far too long to try to fool himself, or anyone else, about the odds. "It's going to be dicey," he agreed. "But if we stay here, we'll be lucky to last out the night. We sure as hell won't make it until noon tomorrow."

"I did spot a scout car over on the far right flank that we might be able to grab on our way out," McCarter said.

"To do that, we'll need to leave someone behind to set up a diversion," Bolan argued.

"I know," the Briton said. "I figured that I'd ask Encizo to stay with me."

"No. One way or the other, we all go out together."

''We still have a couple of hours yet before we have to make that decision, and the situation might change before then.''

Both men knew that it was highly unlikely that the situation would change in their favor. But they were both professional optimists. It went with the territory.

In his hole, Hawkins expertly reassembled the newly cleaned 40 mm grenade launcher for his M-203. He had only three grenades left in his bandolier, and he wanted to make sure that he got the best out of each and every one of them that night. He knew that three 40 mm HE grenades more or less weren't going to make much of a difference to the final outcome, but he wanted to go down fighting.

''T. J.!'' James called out from the hole on his left.

''Yo.''

''How are you fixed for grenades?''

''Since I have the Thumper,'' he answered, ''you can have mine.''

''*Gracias.*''

''*De nada.*''

And it was nothing. Before long they would be completely out of ammunition no matter who used it up.

''STRIKER, THIS IS FLYBOY. Over.'' Grimaldi's voice broke in over the radio.

''Striker,'' Bolan answered. ''Go.''

"This is Flyboy. Look in the sky to the east, you should be able to see me. Over."

There was a glow in the sky to the east, but it wasn't the rising sun. The sun was going down in the west, and this glow was a deeper red, shaped like a slender arrowhead. Also it was high in the sky, at least twenty thousand feet, and moving at a very fast clip.

Bolan knew that it was the SR-71 flying at high Mach, her skin glowing from the friction of the atmosphere. He had no idea what Grimaldi thought they would be able to do to help them, but the ace pilot obviously had something up his sleeve.

"I've got you spotted. What's the plan?"

"Get your guys undercover and protect your ears and eyes. And I mean protect them good. We're going to make a low-level Mach 3 pass. It's going to be loud, and there's going to be a lot of sand blowing around at supersonic speed. I think that it's going to take care of your opposition for you."

"I don't have time for this, Jack," Bolan said.

"Dammit, Striker, I'm not putting you on. We're going to hit them with a supersonic shock wave, and we expect that it will even knock out their tanks. You've got to get under deep cover ASAP or it will take you out, too."

"What's your ETA?" Bolan asked.

"You've got under five minutes," Grimaldi said. "So you'd better haul ass."

"Take cover!" Bolan called out. "Grimaldi's coming!"

SINCE THE SR was flying better than three times the speed of sound, she was outrunning the thundering roar of her twin J-58 engines. Someone looking directly at her as she dived twoard the earth would have seen only the glow of her flying surfaces and the flame of her twin exhausts. Almost too quickly to register with the human eye, the Blackbird flashed over the Iranians and started climbing back into the sky.

In her wake the desert erupted. When the shock wave touched the ground, a solid wall of sand was blown up and out at better than seven hundred miles per hour. It was the mother of all sandstorms, and it was moving at the speed of sound. Nothing living could stand in its way and keep on living, and nothing built by man could withstand it. Even solid rock would never be the same after it had passed over.

Major Nazar caught a glimpse of movement out of the corner of his eye and turned to look over his shoulder. A sand-colored wall a half mile wide was moving across the desert at them, and it was moving faster than any sandstorm he had ever seen. It was a scene right out of hell, the devil wind that scoured the flesh off of a man's bones and filled his lungs with burning-hot sand. And it was coming straight for him.

He tried to yell for the men to take cover, but his voice was lost in the rising hiss of the sand. The shock wave was moving at supersonic speeds and made no noise itself. But the roaring hiss of the sand being blasted from the desert floor and flung into the air rose to an eerie scream.

Jumping from his command car in a blind panic, Nazar took off across the desert, running from the death that was about to overtake him. Even though he knew that it was hopeless, the primitive man inside his brain told him to run and he did.

With his legs pumping like a sprinter's and his head glancing over his shoulder, Nazar watched the screaming wall of sand hit the first of the vehicles, a Russian-built BPM armored personnel carrier. The twelve ton vehicle was bowled over like a toy car and sent crashing into the one parked next to it.

An instant later the leading edge of the shock wave sent Nazar flying through the air before it slammed him to the ground. He tried to crawl, but the force of the blast pinned him in place. The sand shredded his uniform, and he felt the flesh being flayed from his bones in strips. But the burning sand filling his throat and lungs kept him from screaming his agony.

It seemed like an eternity before the red fog of pain finally blanked his brain.

As SOON AS the manmade storm passed, the six Stony Man commandos dug their way out of their sand-filled fighting positions. They were covered with sand, and their weapons wouldn't fire again until they had been completely disassembled and cleaned. Their ears rang with the echoes of the sandstorm's roar. Their eyes stung and their throats were raw, but they were alive. The Iranians who had surrounded them weren't.

Overturned armored cars, APCs and trucks littered the desert as though it were a scrap yard. Some of them were half-buried in the sand, while others had been scoured clean of paint on the side that had faced the blast. Interspersed between the vehicles lay the bodies of the Iranian troops. Some were little more than bare skeletons lying twisted in the postures of agonized death. Others were unmoving lumps half-covered by sand. Nothing moved in this surreal tableau.

"Jesus and Mary," Encizo said softly, his hand moving to cross himself.

"I can almost feel sorry for those poor bastards." Hawkins shook his head as he surveyed the wreckage of the Iranian armored column.

"Save your pity," McCarter said coldly. "They wouldn't have had any for us."

"Are we going down there to mop up?"

"No." The Briton shook his head. "We're staying right where we are until that Russian chopper shows up."

When Hawkins looked over at him, McCarter went on. "This is a hard game we play, and it's not like the wars you fought in the American Army. By the time the Stony Man team is called in to do a job, the situation has gone too far to play the game by any rules except the rule that we win. We don't take prisoners—unless there are special circumstances—and we don't aid the enemy's wounded. We go in, do the job as best we can and then get the hell out."

"I don't have a problem with that," Hawkins said. "I just wanted to know the rules."

McCarter locked eyes with the younger man. "The rules are that there aren't any rules."

Hawkins nodded. That was something he could understand. In his years in the Army, he'd had no trouble following the rules until it came to actual combat. When the bullets started flying, it was crunch time, kill or be killed, and the rules were suspended.

As far as he was concerned, there were no rules in combat beyond that of doing whatever was necessary to live and to win. When your life was on the line, following the rules and losing wasn't an option in his way of thinking.

"I can live with that," he said.

"I thought you might." McCarter let the trace of a grin flit across his face as he stuck his hand out. "Welcome to Phoenix Force, T. J."

Hawkins had a sheepish grin on his face as he reached out to take his hand. "I'm glad to be here, I think."

McCarter laughed. "You'll do, lad, you'll do."

**A downed American superplane throws
Stony Man into a new war against an old enemy.**

STONY MAN™ 25
SKYLANCE

When the Air Force's pride and joy, America's advanced
top-secret reconnaissance plane, is shot down in western
New Guinea, Stony Man is dispatched to do the impossible:
recover the plane or destroy it. Caught in the cross fire of a
raging civil war, Bolan's army goes up against the shock
troops of a first-world industrialist fighting his private war
against America....

Available in November at your favorite retail outlet.

MILLION DOLLAR SWEEPSTAKES

The postal system branches out...from
first-class to *first-class* terror

THE Destroyer

#104 Angry White Mailmen

Created by
WARREN MURPHY
and RICHARD SAPIR

Hell is being hand-delivered in a rash of federal bombings
and random massacres by postal employees across the
nation. And CURE's Dr. Harold Smith sends Remo and
Chiun to root out the cause.

Look for it in October, wherever Gold Eagle books are sold.

**Don't miss out on the action in these titles featuring
THE EXECUTIONER®, and STONY MAN™!**

SuperBolan

#61445	SHOWDOWN	$4.99 U.S.	☐
		$5.50 CAN.	☐
#61446	PRECISION KILL	$4.99 U.S.	☐
		$5.50 CAN.	☐
#61447	JUNGLE LAW	$4.99 U.S.	☐
		$5.50 CAN.	☐
#61448	DEAD CENTER	$5.50 U.S.	☐
		$6.50 CAN.	☐

Stony Man™

#61904	TERMS OF SURVIVAL	$4.99 U.S.	☐
		$5.50 CAN.	☐
#61905	SATAN'S THRUST	$4.99 U.S.	☐
		$5.50 CAN.	☐
#61906	SUNFLASH	$5.50 U.S.	☐
		$6.50 CAN.	☐
#61907	THE PERISHING GAME	$5.50 U.S.	☐
		$6.50 CAN.	☐

(limited quantities available on certain titles)

TOTAL AMOUNT	$
POSTAGE & HANDLING	$
($1.00 for one book, 50¢ for each additional)	
APPLICABLE TAXES*	$_____
TOTAL PAYABLE	$_____
(check or money order—please do not send cash)	

To order, complete this form and send it, along with a check or money order for
the total above, payable to Gold Eagle Books, to: **In the U.S.:** 3010 Walden Avenue,
P.O. Box 9077, Buffalo, NY 14269-9077; **In Canada:** P.O. Box 636, Fort Erie, Ontario,
L2A 5X3.

Name:_____

Address:_____ City:_____

State/Prov.:_____ Zip/Postal Code: _____

*New York residents remit applicable sales taxes.
 Canadian residents remit applicable GST and provincial taxes.

GEBACK15A